<u>Praise for *After Midnight*:</u>

"Those who have gobbled up every vampire story since Meyer's *Twilight* will find this a satisfying, quick read."

—*VOYA*

"Coming off as *Twilight* crossed with *Romeo and Juliet*, this YA debut for Viehl has a lot of appeal and some genuinely surprising twists."

—*Realms of Fantasy*

dead of night

A
YOUNGBLOODS
NOVEL

dead of
night

Lynn Viehl

flux
™
Woodbury, Minnesota

First Edition
First Printing, 2012

Cover illustration by Steven McAfee
Cover images: Woman © iStockphoto.com/quavondo
               Man © iStockphoto.com/Factoria Singular
               Sky © iStockphoto.com/acilo
               Cat eyes © iStockphoto.com/alexnika

Flux, an imprint of Llewellyn Worldwide Ltd.

Library of Congress Cataloging-in-Publication Data
Viehl, Lynn.
  Dead of night/Lynn Viehl.—1st ed.
     p. cm.—(The Youngbloods; #2)
   ISBN 978-0-7387-2646-5
[1. Vampires—Fiction. 2. Books and reading—Fiction. 3. Brothers and sisters—Fiction. 4. High schools—Fiction. 5. Schools—Fiction. 6. Florida—Fiction.] I. Title.
  PZ7.V6668De 2012
  [Fic]—dc23

                                   2012002207

Flux
Llewellyn Worldwide Ltd.
2143 Wooddale Drive
Woodbury, MN 55125-2989
www.fluxnow.com

Printed in the United States of America

For my niece, Briana,
with much love
from your Enchilada.

One

Most people have two lives. One is the life we carry on in the open where everyone can see it. It's who we are to our family, friends, and even strangers. In this life we are part of the real world. It's our day-to-day life, our normal life.

We also have another life, one that we have on the inside, out of sight. It's like a reflection of normal life, only with everything we feel and think and dream of and want to do added to it. Sometimes people close to us sense that life, or we trust them enough to share bits of it with them, but mostly we live it alone. That's our inner life, our personal life.

When we have to hide who we are inside from everyone in our real life, then we start living a third life. A secret life. And no matter how careful we are, it's what happens in the secret life that can ruin all the others.

That cold December morning I began in my normal life: living on a horse farm in Lost Lake, Florida. I was doing chores inside while my two brothers, Patrick and Grayson, were working with our new horses. Gray and I had just started winter break from school, so we wouldn't have to go back until January. Trick, who was thirty and our legal guardian, had quit his job and moved us from Chicago to Lost Lake so we could settle down and he could have his dream of breeding horses.

My normal life was nothing special. To everyone in town I was Catlyn Youngblood, a fifteen-year-old girl who had just moved to town in August. I hadn't been at school long enough to make many friends, but I'd never been much of a social butterfly. I liked to ride my horse, Sali, read lots of books, and sometimes write bad poetry.

Most of that was even true.

After breakfast I finished my kitchen chores and started the laundry. It would have been nice to have a mom to handle the housework, but our parents had been killed in a car accident when I was little. By the time I folded the last load of towels and put them away, I checked the time. It was only 10:15 a.m., which made me wonder if my watch needed a new battery. But no, the wall clock in the kitchen also read quarter-past ten. Trick had promised to take me into town for my job interview, but the appointment wasn't until three.

That left me four hours and forty-five minutes to do

the rest of my chores, make lunch, decide what to wear and practice looking responsible and reliable so I'd get hired and earn some extra spending money.

Most of that was true, too.

"Cat?"

I thought of Shakespeare's twenty-ninth sonnet, my favorite poem of all time, and recited it in my mind as I walked back to the kitchen. *When in disgrace with fortune and in men's eyes, I all alone beweep my outcast state…*

Trick stood at the back door, and hay and dirt covered his black T-shirt and jeans. "I need the first aid kit."

I stopped thinking about troubling heaven with bootless cries, whatever they were. "What now?"

"Flash had another tizzy. Gray's hurt." He held up one dirty hand. "Not bad, but—"

I didn't wait to hear the rest, but grabbed from under the sink the big white plastic case with all our first aid supplies. "How bad is not bad?"

"Not that bad." He looked down at me as I pushed past him. "I can take care of it."

"Sure you can," I said, heading toward our barn. "You can also give him a nice infection."

He caught up with me, dusting his palms on the sides of his jeans before glancing at them and sighing. "All right, but I'll warn you now, there's some blood."

"When Flash throws a fit, there usually is." I saw our problem child palomino tied and hobbled in the front training pen. Gray's horse looked angelic with his creamy golden hide and silky white-blonde mane and tail. Which he most certainly was not. As soon as Flash saw me he swung around so I was looking at his rear.

"Yeah, yeah, I know," I muttered. "Talk to the hind-quarters."

Inside the barn Gray was sitting on a bale of hay. He looked pale, and held an old rag against his left temple. The blood staining it and the front of his shirt made my stomach clench.

"I'm okay," he muttered as I reached him.

I put down the kit and tugged the rag and his hand aside. The distinct shape of the ugly gash on his temple made me take a quick breath. "Flash did this?"

"He didn't mean it." My brother tried to put the rag back, but I tossed it out of his reach. "Come on, Cat."

In the past Flash had never hurt Gray. Now he was injuring him almost weekly. I didn't buy it. "This is, what, the fourth time he didn't mean it?" I demanded as I opened the kit. "Or the fifth?"

My brother put on his sulky face. "It's not that deep. Just give me some band-aids."

"Only if you put them over your mouth." I checked his ears for bleeding, but found none. "Any headache?"

His broad shoulders moved.

I made a victory sign with my hand in front of his nose. "How many fingers?"

"None. Claws? Two." He flinched as I yanked his too-long golden locks out of his face. "Hey."

"Look at me." I used a pen light from the kit to check his pupils, both of which dilated normally. "You keep up

4

this feud with Flash and I'm going to have to take another first aid course. The one for treating reckless brothers who don't know how to hold their horses."

Gray muttered some words he wasn't supposed to use under his breath.

"Nice language." I used some antiseptic to soak a gauze pad. "This is going to burn like blazes. You want a stick to bite down on, tough guy?"

"I told you, it's not—" His voice turned into a pained grunt as I began cleaning the hoof-shaped cut. "For crying out loud, will you take it easy with that stuff?"

"As often as that stupid horse has been clobbering you lately, I should keep the bathtub filled with peroxide and dip you twice a day." Now that I had wiped away most of the blood, I saw that the cut was mostly superficial, although my brother was probably going to end up with a spectacular bruise.

I applied some antibiotic ointment as I glanced at Trick. "The Red Cross instructor said even minor head wounds can be unpredictable. We should take him over to the E.R. to be checked out."

"I'm not spending the rest of the day sitting in a waiting area." Gray got to his feet. "Where's Flash?" He didn't wait for an answer but stalked out of the barn.

"Let him go, Catlyn," Trick said, catching my arm as I tried to follow. "He's embarrassed."

I turned on him. "He got kicked in the *head,* Patrick. He's lucky his brains aren't leaking out of his ears." Now

I saw a dark, wet patch under the dirt on his shirt and pointed to it. "What is that?"

Trick glanced down. "Gray's blood."

"It better be." I looked past him at the horses, all of whom had their heads over the stall doors to watch us (next to humans, horses were the nosiest creatures on earth). That's when I noticed the empty space between Sali and Jupiter. "Where's Rika?"

"By now"—my brother rubbed the back of his neck—"on the other side of the farm."

Paprika, a pregnant mare my brother had recently bought, had been causing trouble since coming to the farm. An elegant Arabian the exact color of her namesake spice, Trick had told us she seemed good-tempered. And she had been, until we'd led her out of the trailer. The minute she'd stepped off the ramp she'd started fighting her bridle. Even after Trick had hustled her into her new stall she'd fussed for hours.

My brother intended to return her and get his money back, which was when he discovered Rika's former owner had moved out of the state the day after he sold her to us.

Since we were stuck with Rika, we tried to make the best of it. Gray, who had trained our other horses, began trying to gentle her. His experience dealing with Flash's tantrums made him a lot more patient than me or Trick, and his quiet, calm handling usually soothed the most aggressive mule-heads. For some reason, however, the Arabian didn't like him.

Gray had tried everything: training her alone, letting

her run first, putting her on a lead rope, and sticking her in the smallest pen. Where, I suddenly realized, Flash was now in his timeout.

"Did Grim put Flash in with Rika?" I demanded. Grim was one of my nicknames for my brother, as was Grouch, Gross, and every other Gr-word that fit his surly personality.

"He tried to." My brother's expression turned wry. "For about ten seconds."

I couldn't believe it. Pairing a steady, well-trained horse with a troublemaker was one way to reinforce herd behavior; but Flash was about as calm as a hurricane. "Trick, when you want to put out a fire, you don't throw gasoline at it."

He glanced at the barn door. "Gray knows he screwed up," he said in a lower voice. "Now let it go."

"Yeah, sure." The frustration I felt was not so much about my brother's carelessness as the reason behind it. Ever since the Halloween dance Gray had been making a lot of dumb decisions, and some of that was my fault. I closed the first aid kit and went to grab my saddle, a coil of rope and a set of blinders.

Most pregnant mares became a little jumpy when they were ready to deliver; with her personality Rika would be ten times worse. "Could she be getting ready to foal?"

"Not yet, she's only thirty-two weeks." He dragged a hand through his hair. "You don't have to go after her."

"Of course I do." I opened Sali's stall and led her out.

"She's not going to let you or Gray get anywhere near her now."

Once I had my Sali saddled, I had to force myself to use the mounting crate. If I were by myself I would have just jumped up from the ground to her back, but like a hundred other things it wasn't something I could do in my so-called normal life.

Pretending to be good old clueless Catlyn was the only way I could keep living my normal life. That didn't mean I had to like it.

Sali's hide, the color of bittersweet chocolate, gleamed in the mellow sunlight. I kept her to a walk until we passed Gray, who was checking Flash's front legs. I looked into my middle brother's sky-blue eyes, but all I saw there was anger and resentment. "You'd better put him in his stall before I get back with her."

I tapped Sali's sides with my heels, and we took off. Normally I would keep her in her walking gait to start off a ride, but we had to catch Rika. Sali raced easily across the pasture at a smooth, gliding lope. I spotted some fresh clods of dirt and grass and guided her to follow them.

One hundred and forty acres around the old farmhouse belonged to us, so Sali and I had a lot of ground to cover. At first I worried the Arabian might have made for the woods bordering our land so she could hide; the density of the trees and the brush growing there would force me to go after her on foot, and I didn't feel like playing hide-and-go-seek. But the tracks she'd left made a beeline to the open back pastures, where only a handful of enormous, ancient black oaks still grew.

Sali lifted her head to sniff the air, and then turned as we both saw a reddish blur of movement along the back fence.

"All right, girl." I reined in Sali, reaching for my coil of rope and adjusting the slipknot. "This has to be quick but careful. You ready?"

Sali snorted a small cloud of white breath in the chilly air. She was always ready.

I leaned forward and hooked the reins over the horn to free both my hands. "Now."

Sali took off toward the fence, and once we were within sight of our runaway I released two coils of rope.

Rika's sides already bulged with the bulk of her unborn foal; now sweat and foam made dark diagonal streaks over it. As soon as she saw us she veered away from the fence; she was smart enough to avoid getting boxed in between Sali and the wire. But the burden of the foal slowed her, and she couldn't keep ahead of us. As soon as we got within ten yards I tossed the end loop of my lasso high over her head. As the loop came down I jerked my wrist, pulling it back so that it fell over her head. Immediately I hauled back the slack, tightening the slipknot.

Rika fought to free herself from the lasso, and jerked the line across the back of my wrist. I ignored the rope burn and her caterwauling as I came alongside her and hustled her over toward the fence.

"Okay, okay," I said in a soft, soothing voice as I swung

off my saddle and got in front of Rika's head. "You've had your fun, now it's time to think of the baby and settle down. Settle down," I repeated as she kicked out with her hind legs.

Sali whickered her annoyance with Rika as I kept a tight hold on the rope. I also kept talking as I inspected the Arabian. Her dark red sorrel hide made it hard to make out fresh wounds, but I found some scratches on her forelegs and her right flank, and a bald spot on her tail. I didn't see any signs of the edema at the bottom of her belly, and she didn't have any fluid streaks on her hindquarters that would mean she was delivering the foal too soon.

"I've got bad news, girl," I told her as I kept my hand on her back and made my way around to her nose again. "You're going to live."

Rika's head drooped, and her nose touched my shoulder briefly.

"Believe me, I feel the same way." I stroked her short nose before I looked into her eyes. I knew it was safer to put the blinders on her, but she looked so defeated I didn't have the heart to. "Listen, I know you don't like it here, and my brothers scare you, but there's no place else to go. So come back to the barn with me and Sali now, okay?"

Rika looked as if all the fight had gone out of her, but I knew better, and kept her tethered until I was mounted again. She fussed a bit more, nipping at Sali, who showed her dominance as lead mare by head-butting Rika until she quit.

"Here we go, ladies. Let's take it nice and slow."

I kept both horses at a walk all the way back to the barn. Rika didn't give me any trouble until we came within sight of the pen, but fortunately Gray had put Flash away. I led the Arabian to the back of the barn instead of the front, where I dismounted and led Rika into the treatment pen where we put the horses for vet checks and vaccinations. I couldn't give her too much water, which would have made her sick, but I put enough in the trough to keep her occupied while I put Sali away.

"You'll be next," I promised my mare, giving her an apple cookie and kissing the white blaze on her nose before I went to the supply cabinet.

It was too expensive to call the vet for every little thing, so we did a lot of simple doctoring ourselves. First I checked the rope burn on my wrist, which wasn't bad, and then grabbed the horse kit. After bathing the Arabian with a lukewarm spray, I rubbed her down and smeared some salve over her scratches. Once I finished I put a little of the special pregnancy formula feed in the fence bucket as a treat. Rika shuffled over, giving me one last suspicious look before dipping in her nose.

"You're welcome," I said, and turned to see my oldest brother leaning against the fence. "Not interested in helping?"

"You had everything under control." Trick came and examined my handiwork. "Looks like she tangled with some wire. I'll check her records and see when she had her last tetanus shot." He took the dirty towels and jar of salve from me. "Now *you* need a bath."

"Now I need to take of Sali," I corrected him.

"I did that while you were washing Rika." He smiled a little. "Thanks for catching her."

"Anytime. And I don't mean that." I glanced over my shoulder at the Arabian before I added, "Trick, there is something wrong with that horse. She's not just bad-tempered or wild. Something is setting her off."

"Arabians are usually wound pretty tight," he reminded me.

"No horse is that tight all the time." I followed him into the barn. "And I don't think it's personal. I think she'd be this way with anyone, anywhere. It's like she hates the world."

He thought about it for a minute. "I haven't found any scars on her that would indicate she was abused in the past."

"Maybe her old owner didn't beat her." I knew how stupid that sounded, but my brother knew a lot more about horses than I did. "Could he have locked her up, or starved her?"

"She's not underweight, she doesn't have any significant scars, and her muscle tone is fine." He rubbed the back of his neck. "I'll call Dr. Marks and see if he still has her old records. He may have treated her for a fall or a bad injury."

Severe stress could cause horses to misbehave, and getting hurt was extremely stressful. While the injury could heal in a few weeks or months, the memory of what caused it stayed with most horses. Some could never again be ridden or worked.

Rika had challenged me and Sali, but only after we had cornered her. She should have responded well to Sali's presence, as horses had herd mentality and for them two were always better than one. Something else had made Rika run, something that made me wonder just what had happened with Gray and Flash.

"You should ask the vet if he knows who trained her," I said. Some owners hired professionals who were harder on the horses than was necessary; the type who always referred to training as "breaking in." If Rika had been bullied during training, she might always associate it with fear.

My brother nodded. "I'll give him a call later."

The slant of the sunlight through the barn windows made me glance at my watch. "It's almost noon. I'll take a shower before I fix lunch. You can still drive me into town for my interview, right?"

"I said I would." Trick closed the supply cabinet door. "I don't like the idea of you working through the holidays, though, especially in town by yourself. If you need money for clothes or Christmas gifts, just ask."

"What I need is something to do besides clean the house, bake cookies and sing 'Frosty the Snowman' until winter break is over." Those weren't the reasons I was applying for a job in town, but they sounded convincing enough. "It's just part-time anyway, and whatever I earn will go right into my college account. Minus whatever I spend on you and Grim for Christmas," I tagged on.

No one would ever call my oldest brother clueless or stupid, so I endured another of his silent, measuring stares. I kept my expression normal.

Just when I thought I might not have pulled it off, he patted my shoulder. "All right, little sister. We'll see how it goes." He went to look at Rika.

I smiled at his back. *Oh no, you won't.*

Two

After fixing lunch for me and Trick (Gray didn't come in from the barn when I called him), I went upstairs to pick out what I was going to wear to my interview.

I didn't have a lot of choices; I was the only girl in the family, and living in the country all my life had never turned me into a fashionista. Most of the time I wore jeans, T-shirts and flannel shirts. Sometimes when it got hot in the summer I wore shorts and a tank top, but that was about it.

I'd have to break out my Justin case.

I took out the old garment bag and draped it across my bed to unzip it. Inside were seven outfits: three dresses, two blouse-and-skirt sets, one pants suit and Old Reliable. Girl clothes made me nervous. When I wore jeans and T-shirts, no one noticed how skinny my legs were. The stuff in the bag was just in case I needed a nice outfit (which is why I called it the Justin case).

I wanted to wear my dark purple pants suit, but it was made of silky material that didn't seem right for a job interview. I looked at the dresses, which were pretty but kind of young, and the blouses and skirts almost shrieked schoolgirl. I wanted to look mature; someone who could be depended on to work by herself.

Finally I took out Old Reliable. The black dress didn't have any frills or lace or girly stuff, and the fit and knee-length hem made me seem a little older. It wasn't like I had anything better, so I carried it into the bathroom.

Ever since applying for the job I'd been experimenting with my hair to come up with a better style than how I always wore it (loose, ponytail or braid). I hated using pins and barrettes, which hurt my scalp, but sometimes while I was reading I would twist up my hair and use a pair of black and mother-of-pearl chopsticks to hold it off my neck. I tried that and liked the way it looked.

I went to get my flat-soled black shoes, and nearly walked into Grayson.

"Hey." He shuffled backward and stuck his hands in his back pockets. "You look nice."

This from Gray, who barely spared me a grunt when he was in a good mood, and had been mostly mute around me since Halloween. I decided he should get a taste of the silent treatment, and walked around him.

Gray followed me to my bedroom, where he caught

the door before I could close it in his face. "Can I talk to you for a minute?"

I looked at him while I began silently counting to sixty.

"Trick said I should … " He stopped and braced an arm on the door frame. "I mean, I apologize. For this morning."

So it wasn't his idea. That made the apology so much more sincere. I shook my head and tried to close the door again.

He stopped it with one huge hand. "I'm also sorry I've been kind of a jerk lately."

Kind of? Understatement of the millennium. I started tapping my foot.

"It's not your fault. It's me. So I'm sorry. Okay?"

He still wouldn't look me in the eye, and I was tired of standing there. I turned my back on him and went to find my shoes.

"Cat, you don't have to go work in town," Gray said. "I'll move out to the barn."

Laughter bubbled up inside me, and I let it loose. I couldn't help it; the thought of Gray spending all of winter break sleeping in the hayloft was just too funny.

"I'm serious."

So he sounded. I slipped on my shoes and came out to see him standing by the window. Sometimes I stood there to look out and admire the birds that sometimes perched in the pine tree next to the house. Sometimes I did other things which I didn't think about when I was around my brothers. "You're not moving out of the house."

He glanced at me, his expression wary but hopeful. "I'm not?"

"You'll freeze out there, or our new problem child will bust out of her stall and trample you to death." I pointed at the wound on his temple. "I know it was Rika who kicked you in the head."

"How?"

"The dent in your skull is too narrow; Flash has a wider hoof. Besides, the only thing that palomino loves more than sulking is you." I picked up my purse to make sure I had my wallet and some lip balm. "I'm not getting a job so I can avoid you. You're off the hook."

He walked over to me. "Then why are you doing it?"

Trick must have put him up to this, I realized, to see if I'd tell Gray something different. When it came to interfering in my life, my brothers were like a championship tag team.

"You can't tell Trick," I warned. When he nodded, I sat down on the edge of my bed and put on my best woeful face. "There's this guy I want to see."

"Yeah?" He reached back and shut the door. "Who is he?"

"He's really amazing," I confessed. "Tall, dark, kind of big but not fat. He's a bit older than me, but I think once he gets to know me the age difference won't matter."

Gray's throat moved as he gulped. "How much older?"

"I don't know." I pretended to think. "It's really hard

to tell exactly how old he is. But that doesn't matter to me. He's dreamy. A real strong, silent type."

"Cat, listen," Gray said quickly. "Whoever this guy is, he sounds like bad news. You can't—"

"But he's not. Bad, I mean. I mean, yeah, he might come across that way, but he's not." I produced a heartfelt sigh. "He can't be bad. He'd get fired."

"Fired?" my brother echoed.

"From his job, silly. I mean, he is the guy in charge around here." I fluttered my eyelashes. "I love that about James."

"James?"

I nodded. "James Yamah."

"You have a crush on Yamah." He eyed me. "*Sheriff* Yamah."

"I know, he's married and an adult, but that's no big deal." I waved my hand to emphasize this. "By the time his divorce is final, I'll be old enough to get hitched. Then I'll finally have the life I always wanted. Taking care of Jim, vacuuming out his patrol car, dusting off his gun belt, polishing his mirrored sunglasses—"

His shoulders slumped. "Okay, I get the joke now."

Knowing he didn't, I smiled. "Good. When you tell Patrick that you apologized, you be sure and mention that I'm getting a job so I can have something to do over winter break. Something that does not include two nosy, overprotective brothers who never want to let me out of their sight."

He shuffled his feet. "We care about you."

I heard the anger and guilt behind the nice words, and had to bite my own tongue to keep from exploding with rage. I couldn't even think about why I was so angry; I didn't dare.

It had only been a month, and already this situation was driving me crazy. How was I going to live this normal life for two and a half more years, until I was an adult and could move out?

"I've got to go now or I'll be late for my interview." I tucked my purse under my arm and walked around Gray to the stairs. I could feel him watching me, but he didn't follow me down. He was probably waiting for me and Trick to leave so he could search my room for love notes that weren't there.

I found Trick sitting at the kitchen table and reading a pamphlet the vet had given him on immunizing breeding stock. He had also changed into clean clothes which were, like everything in his closet, black.

"Hey, we match." I pretended to pat my hair. "Almost."

"I could shave your head, too, if you'd like." He inspected me. "That dress makes you look very grown-up."

"Good, then maybe she'll be fooled and pay me adult wages." I glanced at the clock. "You ready to go?"

"Sure." Trick stuck the pamphlet in his back pocket and took down from the wall rack the keys to Gray's truck.

We made it all the way out to the driveway before he asked, "Did you and Gray bury the hatchet?"

"He volunteered to spend the winter in the barn." I shrugged. "I'm still considering the offer."

"You're tough." He opened the truck door for me.

The tight feeling in my chest didn't start until fifteen minutes later, as we left behind the farmland and crossed over into town. Downtown Lost Lake wasn't very big—a pitcher with a good arm could probably throw a curve ball from one end to the other—but the townspeople had packed plenty of shops along the two main roads. I'd be spending thirty hours a week here, working alone inventorying books while Mrs. Frost was up north visiting her grandkids.

If I get this job.

As we passed the town's cemetery, Trick had to veer around two men unloading an angel from the back of a delivery truck. I looked across the headstones at some other men who were digging around the biggest of the family tombs. "Did someone important die?"

"I don't think it's a funeral," he said. "I read in the paper that some vandals damaged one of the tombs. They're probably fixing it up."

"That's gruesome." My voice cracked on the last word. "Sorry, I'm a little nervous. When you were working for that computer company, did you ever hire anyone? I mean, do interviews with them?"

He nodded. "A few times. Why?"

"I think I need a practice run." I sat up a little straighter. "Okay, ask me some interview questions."

He thought for a moment. "How many programming languages do you know?"

I glared at him. "First pretend you're the little old lady owner of a bookstore café."

In a deliberate falsetto, he asked, "Who wrote *War and Peace*?"

"Tolstoy. That's too easy. And quit it with the silly voice."

He nodded. "Who was the author of *I Know Why the Caged Bird Sings*?"

"Dr. Maya Angelou." I crossed my arms over the butterflies filling my stomach. "Ask me something about me."

He pulled the truck into one of the slanted parking spaces along main street. "Have you lied about anything on your application?"

I felt bewildered. "Why would I lie?"

"You'd be surprised." He put the truck in park and shut off the engine. "What do you consider your greatest personal strength?"

I'm a great liar. Not that I could say that to Mrs. Frost or Trick. "I'm a hard worker, and I don't need to be supervised." Which made two strengths, not one. "Which is the better answer?"

"Either one." He turned toward me. "Now what's your greatest personal weakness?"

"I don't have any job experience." That didn't sound so great, and then I knew what to add. "Yet."

"I think you're ready."

I looked down the block at the powder-blue and white front façade of Mrs. Frost's shop. The hand-painted sign hanging from a bracket by the door made me want to giggle—or maybe it was hysteria setting in. I got out and joined my brother on the sidewalk, and fought back the impulse to call the whole thing off so he could take me back home.

I felt so jumpy I could have hopped all the way home. "I'm glad the shop will be closed for the holidays. If it were staying open, she'd probably make me say, 'Welcome to Nibbles and Books' to everyone who came in the door."

"She still might have you answer the phone that way, if anyone calls." He looked past me. "Whenever I went for a job interview, I always pretended like I was meeting a good friend, and just hanging out and talking with them."

I couldn't imagine Trick hanging out with anyone, but then his life had been very different before he'd gotten custody of me and Gray. "Does that work?"

"Did for me." He gave me a one-armed hug. "I've got to go run an errand at the town hall. Meet me there when you're through."

I squared my shoulders and walked down to the bookstore café. From outside I could see most of the little tables in the front were occupied, and more customers were browsing the shelves in the back. I took a deep breath, opened the door and went inside.

The inside of the shop smelled of gingerbread, coffee and books, an odd but nice combination that made me feel a little more cheerful. Although there were at least twenty people in the shop, it was fairly quiet, and those who were talking kept their voices low, as if they were in a library or church.

Behind the long counter two ladies were busy making sandwiches and pouring drinks, which a third woman loaded onto a tray to carry to the tables. As the waitress saw me, she unloaded her tray and came over. "Table for one, Miss?"

"Ah, no, thank you. I have an appointment with Mrs. Frost." I'd picked up and dropped off my job application at the café counter, so I hadn't yet met the shop's owner.

She waved toward the back. "Her office is behind Women's Fiction. Just knock first in case she's on the phone."

I thanked her again before I headed back to the office. After I knocked, an impatient voice responded with, "Come in, come in."

The bookstore's office had to be the most untidy, cluttered space I'd ever seen. Stacks of boxes and books lined the walls and occupied every flat surface; dozens of posters about bestsellers and photographs of authors papered the walls.

A lady I assumed was Mrs. Frost sat behind the desk, a ledger open in front of her. As neat as her office was untidy, she wore her silver hair pulled back with combs. The navy-blue dress she wore was even plainer than mine, but her understated makeup and dainty pearl earrings added an aura of elegance.

"You're my three o'clock, which means I'm running later than I expected," she said without looking up from the check form she was filling out. "I'm Martha Frost, and you're Catherine?"

"It's Catlyn, ma'am. Catlyn Youngblood." I watched her shift two boxes from the chair next to her desk. "If you're busy I can come back later."

"That's kind of you to offer, but if I don't make a decision today, I'm going to miss my plane to Baltimore." She gestured at the chair, and as I sat down she skimmed through a stack of applications.

I hadn't considered that so many other people would be applying for the same position. As bad as the economy was, a lot of people were probably looking for work. My heart sank a little as I realized I'd have to be the least-qualified applicant.

"Here we are." Mrs. Frost put on a pair of reading glasses. "You're fifteen years old, you live in the farming community, and you're a sophomore at Tanglewood. Straight-A student, very good." She turned the page over. "You live with your brothers?"

"Yes." There was never any easy way to say it, so I kept it short. "Our folks were killed in a car accident. My oldest brother Patrick is my legal guardian."

She asked me a few more questions before she set aside the application. "As I mentioned in the ad, the job entails working thirty hours a week around the holidays. I need someone to inventory the shop's stock as well as catalog a collection of rare books I've just acquired. The work has to be done during the evening, as I've rented the shop to a college testing assistance service that will be holding their tutoring classes here during the day. Have you heard of Julian Hargraves?"

"Just what I read about him in the paper," I admitted. "He was really old when he died."

"One hundred and seven, bless him," she said. "Julian collected rare books about all sorts of occult topics. He was not a friendly man, but on a few occasions when I delivered a special order to his home, he asked me to stay for tea. Just before he died, he instructed his estate manager to sell his entire collection to me for thirty dollars."

I wasn't sure I'd heard her right. "You mean, thirty dollars a book?"

"Thirty dollars for the entire library." She saw my expression. "It's completely ridiculous, of course. Julian had books that individually were worth thousands of dollars; I know because I sold them to him." Mrs. Frost smiled. "But enough about Julian. Why are you interested in working for me, Catlyn?"

"I love books," I said. "I also want to earn some money for college."

She nodded. "Are those your only reasons?"

"No, ma'am." I didn't have to hide behind the brick wall now, but I did have to be careful. "My brothers are great, and I love them, but I want to become more independent."

She nodded. "If I hire you, how will you get back and forth to work?"

"I'm planning on taking the bus that runs from Farmer's Market to downtown," I said. "Both of my brothers drive, so if I miss it, one of them can drop me off or pick me up."

She gave me a shrewd look. "What are your five favorite novels?"

I thought of my small collection of books. "*Valley of the Horses* by Jean M. Auel, *Pride and Prejudice* by Jane Austen, *Mistress Devon* by Virginia Coffman, *A Wrinkle in Time* by Madeleine L'Engle and *The Long Winter* by Laura Ingalls Wilder."

"Interesting." She seemed to relax. "You can often tell a great deal about someone when you know what their favorite books are. You enjoy stories with strong heroines placed in impossible situations."

"I know heroes are more popular with most people, but I like girls who think for themselves and do something about their problems. Instead of waiting to be rescued by the hero," I tacked on.

"I think I have just the book for you." She opened a drawer and took out a worn paperback with dog-eared pages and yellowed edges. "This is one of my favorite novels." The faded cover showed a dark-haired woman in a cloak, and looked a little like a romance novel. "Don't be fooled by the artwork. The story is quite remarkable."

I felt embarrassed. "I'm sorry, but I didn't bring any money with me."

"Consider it a welcoming gift." She handed it to me. "If you can start tomorrow, the job is yours."

"Really?" All the breath wanted to rush out of me. "But I didn't think…"

"That I'd hire you?" The skin around her eyes crinkled. "You're bright, you've never been in trouble, you know how to use a computer, and you love books. That's all the experience I need." She stood up and held out her hand. "I'll see you tomorrow at three o'clock sharp. Wear something comfortable."

"Yes, ma'am." I shook her hand. "Thank you so much."

Three

I practically floated out of Mrs. Frost's office. As I looked around the bookstore, everything seemed new all over again. I was going to work here. I had the job.

"Cat." A petite redhead waved at me from a table by the window where she was sitting with two other girls.

I grinned and walked over. "Hey, Tiffany." I nodded to her friends Amber and Gwen, who were also on the cheerleading squad at our high school. "Are you doing some shopping?"

"We're hiding from my mom. She's on a Christmas ornament bender for her ladies club swap. I'm about to overdose on red, green and adorably cute." She pushed out the empty chair and patted the seat, inviting me to sit down. "What are you doing in town?"

I sat down, trying not to beam like an idiot and

failing. "I just got a job, working here. I'm going to be inventorying the shop while Mrs. Frost is up north for the holidays."

"Then you deserve a cookie." Tiffany handed me a little decorated gingerbread man. "If you ever need someone to come over and harass you, give me a call."

"Great." I bit into the cookie to hide my dismay. Just like everyone else in town, Tiffany didn't remember me, or that when I first moved here she had harassed me almost daily at school. It hadn't been her fault, but she didn't remember that, either.

"So did you hear about Sunny Johnson?" Amber asked. At my blank look, she pointed at the shop across the street. "Her parents own the Junktique."

"No." I glanced through the window but only saw a closed sign. "I don't think I know her."

"She mostly hangs out with the 4-H'ers," Tiffany said, referring to the tight group of kids at Tanglewood whose parents were all working farmers. "Her boyfriend is Nick Starple. You wouldn't know him; he dropped out last year."

"Anyway," Amber said, "Nick always picks Sunny up at school and takes her home. Only last Friday his car broke down so he couldn't make it, and when Sunny's parents got home that night, she was gone."

I frowned. "Gone where?"

"They say she ran away from home again." Amber looked around and lowered her voice. "She's done it a couple times before, you know, because her dad is so strict and her mom just goes along with it to keep the peace. Lately Sunny has been saying how she and Nick might take off and go up north, like to Maryland or something, where they could get married without their parents' permission."

"It's all Sunny talks about," Gwen assured me. "She hates her parents and she's crazy about Nick."

"Then why would she leave without him?" I asked.

"She wouldn't," Gwen said.

Amber nodded. "Exactly. No one can figure out why she'd take off alone, least of all Nick. She didn't have any money or a car. No one saw her at the bus station, and she hasn't phoned anyone. Not even Nick, and she would definitely call him just to let him know she was okay."

Gwen lowered her voice to a whisper. "What if Nick did something to her and is just trying to cover it up?"

"No way." Tiffany sounded adamant. "I've known Nicky since kindergarten. He acts tough, but he's not a bad guy. The only reason he dropped out of school was to take care of the farm after his dad got sick."

Amber nodded. "Nick's been talking to everyone, trying to find out if anyone has heard from Sunny. One of the shopkeepers thought he saw her talking to an old man near her folks' shop that night after they closed, but he couldn't be sure. Nick swears she would have walked to the shop when he didn't show up, but no one can find this old man. He thinks something bad must have happened to her. Like maybe someone jumped her."

"Or grabbed her," Gwen added. "It's happened a couple times before. That's why we have the curfew."

Just before the Halloween dance I'd seriously thought about running away from home, but in the end I'd decided against it. A girl by herself in a strange place, who had no money, no transportation and no friends, was a walking target.

"I wish I could help, but I've never met Sunny," I said. "I don't even know what she looks like."

"She's pretty average," Tiffany said. "Brown eyes, long brown hair, kinda skinny. She always wears this jacket Nick gave her for her sixteenth birthday. It's pink satin with a white rabbit on the back. Really beyond tasteless, but she didn't care. She loved it."

"That's 'cause Nick always calls her his Sunny Bunny," Amber added wistfully. "I bet she was wearing it that day."

After no one said anything for a few minutes, I decided to change the subject. "So what are you guys doing over winter break?"

"Avoiding our mothers," Gwen said, making a pained face. "They always try to volunteer us for Sparklefest slave duty."

I frowned. "Sparklefest?"

"A very dull and boring annual downtown tradition that starts a couple of days before Christmas," Tiffany said. "The shopkeepers and the mayor like drape the entire town in lights, and then they have a parade on Christmas Day and a bunch of old guys make speeches about the history of Lost Lake. At midnight they turn on all the lights in the park at once, which is the really big thing. They usually have some oldies band play down by the lake, too. It's mostly for the tourists, but we always have to go."

"The food is pretty good," Amber put in. "All the local restaurants and cafés set up booths, and it's become kind of a competition to see who sells out first."

"I'm sure Mrs. Frost will give you that night off," Tiffany added. "That way you can enter the big relay race."

"Sorry, I don't run," I told her. "Unless I'm being chased."

She giggled. "It's not that kind of race. It's the final big thing they have the day after Christmas. They use horses and riders for the relay, out on the old track by the east side of the lake. It's supposed to date back to something that happened like a hundred years ago, when the founding fathers first settled here. Someone set fire to the town, and they had to send messengers on horseback to get help from the farmers before it burned down."

"Really." I felt a little shocked. "I guess it worked."

"Yeah, they saved the day and everyone's lives, so of course we have to reenact it every year." Tiffany faked a yawn and patted her mouth. "Ancient history, if you ask me. I'd much rather go to a dance."

"Yeah, like a winter formal. My older sister goes to one every year at her college," Amber said, and began describing the event.

I recalled the last dance I had gone to, the school Halloween dance that had changed everything. Tiffany and the other girls didn't remember that night, but I did. And I could never think about it at home, so all the details came rushing back into my mind.

Wearing a red dress and dancing with my dark boy. *You look like a grand duchess.*

Looking at the beautiful old ring in my hand, the ring that had brought us together. *You're always with me.*

Listening to someone I thought had been a friend scream at me. *You hurt my Aaron.*

Kneeling beside my dark boy, both of us bleeding. *You have to stop me now, before I become a monster.*

Telling him how I felt, how I had always felt from the night we met. *I did mention that I'm in love with you, didn't I?*

Standing up to my brother, Patrick, when it was over. When he found us together. *I have the right to a normal life.*

Seeing the anger, sadness and regret on Trick's face just before he wiped away my memories. *I'm sorry, Catlyn.*

Tiffany touched my arm. "You okay, Cat?"

"Yeah, just zoning out a little." I wasn't okay, and I wouldn't be until much later tonight when Tiffany, her friends, my brothers and the rest of the world were asleep. When I stopped being sister and friend and got to live my other life, my secret life, the one I could only live a few hours at a time, always in darkness. "I've got to go meet my brother. See you guys later."

———

I expected my brothers didn't think I could get the job working in town, but neither Trick nor Gray seemed surprised by the news. That night at dinner we talked about juggling chores and schedules, and I promised to keep up with my part of the housework.

Gray didn't cook, but unfortunately Trick tried to, which was why I usually made dinner for us. Since I would be at work now, I had been making up ahead of time big batches of pasta sauce, chili and other things that froze well. I'd put out whatever they wanted to defrost before I went to catch my bus, and by dinner time all they'd have to do would be warm it up.

"One thing I do need is a house key," I said as I passed the chef's salad I'd made to Gray.

Trick looked up. "What for?"

"I'm taking the bus home," I reminded him. "I won't get back from work until after eleven. You guys will be asleep."

"I'll wait at the bus stop for you," Gray volunteered.

"You have to get up early to take care of the horses." I saw the way Trick was frowning. "The bus stop is only a two minute walk from the house. One minute if I run."

"I don't like the idea of you walking—or running—home alone that late at night." Trick turned to Gray. "I'll go to meet her at the bus stop tonight, and then we'll switch for her next shift. Whoever stays home gets up with the horses."

Gray nodded.

"Nothing is going to happen to me." When neither

of them reacted, I blew out a breath. "All right. Keep treating me like a helpless baby who can't even cross the street by herself."

"If we were doing that," Trick countered, "you wouldn't have this job at all."

He was right, and I hated him a little for it. "Fine. Whatever." I got up and took my plate over to the sink.

As far as my brothers knew, I had no memory of the first five months we'd lived in Lost Lake, or anything I had learned during that time. Because of this, and a bargain Trick had made to keep things that way, they thought they had nothing to worry about at all.

I didn't tell them I remembered everything because I needed them to go on believing that I was good old oblivious Catlyn. They trusted me now, and believed everything I told them. Especially when I said good-night to them at ten o'clock and went upstairs to go to bed.

Trick still checked on me occasionally without warning, so I did change into my pajamas, brushed my teeth and got under the covers. Sometimes I would read for a few minutes as I listened to the sound of Gray's footsteps as he went to the old garage that we'd converted into bedroom for him, or Trick pouring water into the coffee maker and the faint beeps as he set the automatic timer. Other nights I would just turn out the lights, roll onto my side, close my eyes and begin silently counting the seconds as they crawled by.

Tonight I heard the creak of the stairs under a heavy foot, but when my bedroom door opened a few inches

I smelled sunlight, Gray's scent, not coffee, Trick's scent. He didn't come inside, but he did stand there watching me for a minute before he closed the door and went back downstairs.

Gray never checked on me, so this wasn't a good sign. Telling him the whole fake-crush thing about Sheriff Yamah had been a stupid stunt. I'd wanted him to be afraid, at least for a few minutes, but I'd only managed to make him suspicious.

Because of this, I waited an extra half-hour before I got up and changed into my riding clothes. I also didn't bother tip-toeing down the stairs but went to my window and opened it, taking a deep breath before I climbed over the sill and jumped to the ground.

If I'd been a normal girl, I'd have broken my legs. Instead I landed as silently as my four-legged namesake, straightening and holding still as I listened before I headed for the barn.

As always, Rika was the first one to look over the edge of her stall as I came in, but for once she seemed a little less hostile, and only snorted. Sali whickered to me, her big eyes shining, and tried to walk out of the stall before I'd gotten a bridle on her.

"I know," I said, stroking the warm arch of her neck. "I'm impatient, too." I kept my voice low so as not to alarm the other horses, although the rest of our new stock weren't much interested in me. Flash ignored everyone but Gray, so only Trick's big white stallion Jupiter stuck his head out to give me a you-bad-girl glare.

Over the last couple of weeks I'd trained Sali to carry me on our midnight rides without a saddle or a bareback pad. It took some getting used to for both of us, but I found I actually preferred it. With nothing between us, she responded even faster to my body signals, and riding that way felt more natural to me. Sometimes I even felt like I became part of her, as if when we rode we somehow merged together.

Once we were clear of the barn and the stockyard, I leaned forward to whisper in her ear, "Take me to him, girl."

Sali probably didn't understand the words, but she knew what I wanted her to do whenever I said them, and took off. We both preferred to ride at a running walk, as hers was faster and smoother than any other breed's, but my own impatience got the better of me, and I urged her into a lope as we crossed the road and followed the winding trail into the dense, dark woods across from our farm.

The glow of a few candles lit the windows of the old manor house, and a big black stallion stood tethered outside. Prince turned his head and then shuffled around, his ears perking at the sight of Sali. She came up alongside him, touching his nose with hers before she stood still so I could dismount. Once I tied her beside him I gave both horses a pat and then walked over to the wide stone steps leading up to the front door, and the dark boy waiting there for me.

At five-foot-ten I loomed over most boys my age, but Jesse Raven stood a head taller. People would have called him lanky, at least until they saw him move; he had the slim, tough build of someone who had been riding horseback almost since he could walk. The paleness of his skin made his long, straight hair looked like polished black silk, and when he looked at me the moon threaded amethyst light through the dark strands. He had dark gray eyes that even in the shadows glittered like marcasite, and a face so beautiful sometimes it hurt me just to look at him.

"Catlyn."

He had grown up speaking Romanian and Russian and a bunch of other languages I didn't know, and while he spoke perfect English, his accent added an extra syllable to my name, changing it into something strange and exotic. Despite everything we had been through, seeing him still occasionally made me feel as if I were dreaming. That at any moment I would open my eyes and find myself in my bedroom, and he would be gone.

"Jesse."

"You're late." He held out his hand.

"Better that than never." I curled my fingers around his, shivering a little with how good it felt to touch him. "I've missed you."

"How long have you missed me?" he asked as he drew me inside.

"Nine days, three hours, ten minutes and I made myself stop counting the seconds." It didn't matter how long we were apart; I could feel him every night, almost from the moment he woke. "I got the job in town."

Jesse picked me up like I weighed no more than a kitten and whirled around, laughing with me.

"I never doubted you would," he said as he set me back down on my feet. "But I am glad it is decided."

Getting the job at the bookstore had been the simplest solution to our problem, namely of trying to see each other without my brothers or Jesse's parents finding out about it. Our families regarded each other as natural enemies, and because of that felt they had the right to keep us apart. My brothers and Jesse's parents had taken extreme measures to do just that, too. They hadn't just erased my memories of moving to Lost Lake, meeting Jesse and falling in love with him; they'd made everyone in town forget me, Jesse, and almost everything that had happened since my brothers and I had moved to Lost Lake.

They didn't understand who we were, or why we were together. It didn't matter to Jesse that I was a Van Helsing, the granddaughter of a family of vampire hunters. It didn't matter to me that Jesse was only one step away from becoming a vampire himself. We both knew, almost from the moment we first met, that we were meant to be together. The world might have wanted us to be monsters, but when we were together we were just a girl and a boy who were crazy about each other.

"There is one thing," I said to Jesse. "Either Trick or Gray will be waiting for me at the bus stop every night I work. So you won't be able to drive me home." Which had been part of our original plan when Jesse told me about the job at Mrs. Frost's.

"We will still have thirty hours every week for ourselves." He smiled and touched my cheek. "I think by the new year you will be completely bored with me."

"Oh, sure, that's going to happen." I rolled my eyes. "I have to recite Shakespeare's twenty-ninth sonnet about a hundred times a day just so I don't think about you when Trick is around me."

We knew my oldest brother had the power to make me forget things; what I still didn't know for sure was if he could also read my thoughts whenever he wanted. I suspected he couldn't, because he would have known about me meeting Jesse from the beginning, but I wasn't a hundred percent positive yet. And it wasn't like I could ask my brother about his weird Van Helsing ability, so to be safe I never let myself think about Jesse around him but instead thought of the sonnet.

"I found out something else today that might help us," I told Jesse. "Mrs. Frost told me that she just bought a huge collection of rare books from the estate of a guy who was into the occult. I think we should look through them and see if we can find out anything else about vampires and the Van Helsings." Something occurred to me. "Did you or your parents know Julian Hargraves?"

"We knew the family, of course, but after they came to Lost Lake they kept very much to themselves," Jesse admitted. "Julian never married or had children, and after his parents passed away he inherited their home. Toward the end of his life he became quite reclusive. What are you hoping to learn from his books?"

"I want to know if there's a cure for this. Not just for you," I added. "For me, too."

My ability, which I still didn't quite understand, somehow gave me the power to attract and control cats. Not just the pet-type of cat, I had discovered, but any feline. Before erasing my memory, Trick had told me that all cats responded to my thoughts, but that was the sum total of what I knew.

Paul Raven, Jesse's father, had told me that all the Van Helsing children were born with special abilities that helped them hunt and destroy vampires. He thought I would use mine on Jesse, but we'd already passed that test. Wounded, desperate for blood and nearly out of control, Jesse had begged me in the boathouse on Halloween night to kill him. Instead, I'd given him my blood. At the time I hadn't cared about the consequences—drinking human blood was supposed to be the final step that would transform Jesse into a vampire—but then we'd learned that my blood wasn't altogether human.

My father had been infected with vampire blood, just like Jesse and his parents. And because vampire blood also ran through my veins, drinking it hadn't pushed Jesse the rest of the way into becoming a full-fledged monster.

My heritage meant nothing to me. I didn't want to be a vampire, a vampire hunter, or anything else besides a normal human girl. Jesse wanted to be human again, too. So if there was some way for us to be normal again, I was going to find it.

Do you have to find it tonight?

No, I thought back to him. Since Halloween night, Jesse and I could read each other's minds. Part of a bond that formed between two vampires, it was just one more thing we were not supposed to be able to do.

It also still scared me, so I said out loud, "Let's take a ride over to the lake cabin."

Four

Jesse's parents had given him the land we were riding on, and hundreds of acres surrounding it, which contained dozens of old riding trails, overgrown pastures, empty barns and grain silos and even some abandoned old houses, like the cabin we found by one of the four lakes on the property.

Prince and Sali preferred racing to exploring, but once we took them on the narrow trail they fell into our usual riding positions, Jesse and Prince in the front and Sali and me following behind. Nothing ever bothered us, but sometimes my presence attracted some feral cats, lynxes and other felines to trail after us, so I kept my thoughts clear and calm. Once I had even drawn a Florida panther and her two cubs that lived on Jesse's land to me, and while the horses didn't spook easily, I didn't want to disturb the big cat.

Not that any other, non-feline critter would bother us. Predators instinctively avoided vampires, Jesse had told me, and since I'd never had a run-in with anything I guessed they were the same with half-vampires. Then there was the connection we shared. Sometimes when Jesse and I were together I could almost feel it in the air, as if the two of us being close to each other generated a kind of unseen energy. He had many of the same powers that full vampires possessed, and I had my Van Helsing abilities, which Jesse's father had once told me were still developing.

Into what, I didn't know. Thinking about it only made me dread finding out.

The trees parted away from the trail, and over Jesse's shoulder I saw the sagging roof of the old lakeside cabin, and reined in Sali.

The little lake was hardly more than a pond, but it had an interesting spiral shape. Strips of earth sprouting water grasses curved around the edge and formed some clusters in the center. It reminded me of a creek that had gotten tired of running and curled up for a long nap.

Jesse dismounted and tethered Prince to one of the remaining fence posts, and reached up to help me down. I could swing off by myself, of course, but I liked holding his hand. Once we tied up Sali we walked down by the water. The moonlight lit the surface of the murky water, turning it into silver-white crystal.

"In the spring it won't be this quiet," he predicted as he put his arm around my shoulders. "There will be birds and crickets and frogs, and after dark they become quite loud."

"I don't care." I leaned my head against his shoulder. "I like the sounds they make."

He glanced down at me. "I will remind you of this when the frogs begin their mating season."

We walked over to the cabin, which Jesse had told me had been here since before his family had come to America in the late nineteenth century. Whoever had built it had used enormous oak trees, notching each end before stacking the trunks like Lincoln Logs. More split trunks had been stacked against a V-shaped frame to form the roof. While the walls of the cabin were still sturdy, the split trunks had slowly rotted over the years; many looked to be on the verge of collapsing.

Only a few narrow slots served as makeshift windows, and someone had blocked them with chunks of the same board that had been nailed over the warped latch-string door.

"I want to look inside," I told Jesse, who went to the door and tugged off one of the boards, as easily as if it were made of Styrofoam. "Why aren't I as strong as you?"

He thought about it as he removed the other boards. "You are a girl."

A laugh burst out of me. "That has nothing to do with it and you know it, you chauvinist."

"It was the only answer I could think of. You ask hard

questions." He set the boards out of our way and tried the door, which made a splintering sound and fell inside. A small cloud of dust billowed out around our feet, but nothing came running out.

"I should have brought a flashlight," I said as I peered inside. Because we both had excellent night vision, we never needed them. "Who do you think built this place?"

He breathed in and frowned. "Someone who killed animals. Perhaps a trapper or a hunter."

Jesse's sense of smell, which was as keen as a vampire's, could detect a drop of blood from across a room. Too much blood, especially human, made him shift into his predatory state. I saw his eyes darken, but they didn't turn solid black as they would have if the blood were fresh.

"You don't have to go inside," I told him. "I just want to see if it might work."

"As what?"

"A safe place." I stepped over the threshold and gingerly moved inside.

Except for what the wind had blown in through the narrow gap at the bottom of the door, the interior of the cabin was surprisingly clean. Split logs of wood with their flat sides up formed the floor; time had left a lot of cracks in them, but the wood still felt sturdy under my boots.

"Why do you need a safe place?"

"It's not for me." I turned around to find Jesse right behind me. "It's for you."

His teeth flashed. "All right, why would I need it?"

"I was thinking we could make it into a vault."

Although Jesse had most of the same powers as a full vampire, he also shared some of their weaknesses. Iron and garlic were poisonous to him, and any exposure to the sun's rays burned him like fire. If he stayed out too long in the daylight, he would die. As he nearly had once when we'd been together, and Prince had suddenly bolted, leaving me and Jesse on foot in the woods near dawn.

I'd gotten him to safety in time, but I'd had to take my brother's truck without permission and speed through town to get to Jesse's boat to take him back to Raven Island, where I wasn't welcome. Trick, who at that time still hadn't known about me and Jesse, or why, had grounded me for weeks after that.

Jesse stopped smiling and took my hand in his, threading his fingers through mine. Instead of ridiculing my fairly ridiculous idea, he took a more serious look around. "The roof would have to be replaced and sealed from within, and any gaps in the walls filled. Such renovations would require many materials and supplies. Purchasing them and transporting them here without drawing anyone's attention would be difficult."

"I was thinking that we could put something inside the cabin," I said. "It would just have to be light-proof, and big enough for you to get inside. That way we could leave the outside of the cabin like it is, as camouflage."

He nodded. "We could use a coffin."

I felt annoyed. "Don't make bad jokes."

"I am quite serious, Catlyn," he assured me. "Vampires prefer caves and vaults, as they can be barricaded and safeguarded more easily. However, they have been known to use coffins and crypts as places of concealment and protection when they are caught away from their strongholds during the daylight hours. Humans have great respect for the dead, and never think of looking among them for those who prey on the living."

"You're not a vampire." I couldn't stand the thought of seeing him climb into a coffin. "We'll think of something else."

A block table and chair sat empty by a brick-and-mud fireplace, and against the other wall I saw bunches of long branches that had been lashed together to form a short rectangular bed frame. Some pieces of rotted rope hanging from the branches at regular intervals must have once webbed the frame to support the bedding.

Something drew me to the hearth and the long wooden mantle set into the stone above it. On one corner someone had carefully carved a small heart into the edge of the mantle. On top of that an old, battered tin cup, coated brown with rust, sat next to an equally ancient lantern. The kerosene it had once held had long ago evaporated, but I could see something through the dusty glass that had been wedged behind it. I moved the lamp aside, creating another dust cloud, to expose a flat piece of metal.

I took it down and carefully blew away more dust to expose the image on the surface, which showed a man and a woman in very old-fashioned clothing. "Look at this." I handed it over to Jesse. "It's almost like a photo."

"It is a photograph. These were called tin types. They printed the images on the metal to better preserve them." He studied the couple. "This man is wearing a uniform. He was a soldier. Perhaps he and his lady came here to escape the war between the states." He turned it over. "There are some letters and numbers engraved on the back." He swiped his thumb over the metal to wipe away some dirt. "And three words: 'From Jacob's heart.'"

I touched the carved heart. "He was a romantic guy."

Outside the cabin, Sali uttered a short, plaintive whinny, her way of telling me that she was bored. Prince followed it up with his deeper, rumbling whicker.

I checked my watch, which read 3:20 a.m. "We'd better head back. It'll be dawn in a few hours." I saw him pocket the tin type. "Why are you taking that?"

"It intrigues me. Perhaps I can use it to find out who they were." He gave the cabin a final glance. "And why they made their home here, in such a remote place."

Now he was making me curious. "Maybe they were like us, and this was the only way they could be together."

"Someday we will have more than a secret cabin in the woods, Catlyn." He touched my cheek. "I promise."

———

"Bugs love old books," Trick said at breakfast the next morning. "You'd better find out how she deals with them, because I doubt she uses insect spray."

I shrugged. "She probably shakes them out and swats them with the book."

"Yeah, but you hate bugs," Gray reminded me. "And you don't want to run around the place shrieking. Someone will call your boyfriend."

Trick looked up from his paper. "What boyfriend?"

"He means Sheriff Yamah." I glared at Gray. "With whom I am not even friendly."

"That's another thing." Trick set aside his paper. "I don't want you letting any of your friends from school in the store while you're working. This is a job, not a hangout for winter break."

"I promise, I will not let a single friend from school into the store." I hadn't met Jesse at school, and he didn't attend Tanglewood, so it wasn't a lie. "All my hanging out will be done at other locations, like strip clubs, crack houses and biker bars."

His jaw tightened. "Does the owner have a security alarm?"

"I don't know, Patrick." I folded my arms. "I didn't exactly inspect the place from top to bottom yesterday. I was too busy, you know, trying to *get* the job?"

"Ask her about it," he told me, "and if she does have one, have her show you how to arm it while you're working."

"I don't think old books are at the top of the list of stuff burglars want." I looked at his face. "All right, all right, I'll ask."

Finally my brothers went out to repair the damage

Rika had caused to the training pen, which made me very happy. Being asked questions I didn't want to answer was almost as annoying as listening to advice I didn't need.

I spent the rest of the morning taking care of my daily chores before I went upstairs to tidy up my room and figure out what I was going to wear for work. That was when I realized I had a brand-new wardrobe problem.

Mrs. Frost had said to dress comfortably, which to me meant jeans and a T-shirt. Most of mine were worn, though, and while they were okay for home and school I felt I needed a different look for my job.

The good outfits in my Justin case would definitely be too dressy, and I couldn't borrow anything from my brothers. Why hadn't Trick or Gray been born a girl?

Just as I reached for the newest pair of jeans I owned, I felt a funny twinge inside my head, and glanced at the four old suitcases sitting on the shelf above the hangers. I used them whenever we moved, and they were empty … at least, I was pretty sure they were.

I reached up and took down one, which was light as a feather, but opened it to be sure. The only thing I'd left inside were some balled-up socks that I'd outgrown in middle school. Feeling stupid, I closed the case and put it back. As I did I bumped one corner into the others, which shifted—all except the largest one.

I pulled down the largest suitcase, which was so heavy I nearly dropped it, and lugged it out to my bed, where I opened it. A faint trace of some sweet perfume rose from the inside of the case, which was filled with stacks of neatly folded clothes: blouses, slacks, skirts and a couple of scarves. They all looked brand-new, and were in soft, pretty colors and nice fabrics; most of the blouses had lace cuffs and collars.

None of them, however, belonged to me. In fact, I'd never seen them before now.

"What's that?"

I yelped and whirled around to see Gray standing right behind me. "God, you scared the wits out of me. Ever hear of knocking?"

"The door was open." He stared past me at the suitcase. "Where did you find that?"

"In my closet, but they're not mine." I eyed him. "You or Trick like to dress up like girls?"

"They were Mom's clothes."

That explained the scent; our mother's name had been Rose, and she had always worn rose-scented perfume.

All the anger inside me faded as I reached for one of the pretty blouses. I'd been too young when our parents had died to remember much about my mother, but thinking of her always made me feel a little blue. "She really wore these?"

"Yeah." He came to stand beside me. "Trick's been saving them for you, I guess."

"Not like you guys could wear them, although you might look good in lace." I held up the blouse against my front. "Why didn't he tell me he put them in my closet?"

Now his eyes shifted away. "He probably forgot."

I had seen a few pictures of our mother, who had

been a petite blonde with big blue eyes. I was tall and thin like our father, so I probably couldn't wear any of her slacks, but some of the blouses might fit.

"Gray, are you—" Trick stopped in his tracks when he saw Mom's blouse in my hands. "What are you doing with that?"

"I found it in my closet, so I'm going to wear it to work." I held it up and faced him. "What do you think? Does it say 'responsible employee'?"

"I was saving those for when you grew up." He sounded angry.

"I don't think I'm going to get any taller." I measured one sleeve against my arm. "They should fit me okay now. Any other objections?"

I could tell from his expression that he didn't want me to wear my mother's clothes. From his silence I knew he didn't want to tell me why. I didn't feel sorry for him, though. If my big brother had been honest with me about everything, he wouldn't be in this position.

Gray looked from me to Trick. "Those old books might be dirty, Cat. You don't want to ruin Mom's clothes."

"Dust washes out, Grim. Besides, I'll be wearing gloves and an apron." I was almost enjoying myself now. "Now if you two don't mind, I'd like to get a shower so I can try these on and see how they fit."

They didn't leave, and for a second I thought Trick was thinking of using his ability to make me forget I'd found the clothes. I didn't know how I'd stop him if he tried—or even if I could—but I stood my ground. I knew I'd never been able to prevent him from doing it before, but maybe this time I could punch him before he brainwashed me again.

"You'd better braid your hair," Trick said finally. "You don't want it getting in the way while you're working."

My brothers went back downstairs, but I didn't hear them leave the house. I grabbed my newest pair of jeans and a towel and went into the bathroom, turning on the shower before I walked out into the hall.

I could hear Gray and Trick talking in the kitchen, and because they thought I was in the shower, the talk was probably about me.

If they catch me I'll pretend I ran out of soap, I thought as I carefully made my way down the stairs. I'd already tested each step thoroughly so I could avoid the squeaky spots.

I went to the laundry room, the best spot for eavesdropping, and positioned myself behind the door.

"—not coming back," Gray was saying, "but she's getting suspicious. If you don't quit jumping on her she's going to start asking questions you don't want to answer."

"I'm glad you've decided that this is *my* fault." Trick sounded disgusted. "Why didn't you put that case up in the attic, like I told you to?"

"I thought I did," Gray insisted. "It must have gotten mixed up with hers when we unloaded the truck."

"The damage is done. At least this time she didn't have a flashback." My oldest brother made a tired sound. "We can't make any more mistakes, Gray."

I didn't wait to listen to anymore; I hurried back upstairs and locked myself in the steamy bathroom. My hands shook as I undressed and stepped into the shower, where I leaned against the tiles and closed my eyes.

Trick had a trunk that I was pretty sure had once belonged to Abraham Van Helsing; I'd found it filled with old books and papers about vampires, and some of the iron weapons our ancestor had used. He'd made me forget about it at least twice, and probably more times than that; now I knew he was keeping other things from me.

Why didn't you put that case up in the attic, like I told you to?

I'd never been up in the attic. I didn't even know we had one. Was that something else he made me forget? If I didn't remember anything, why did he sound so worried?

I quickly finished my shower, dried off and brushed out my hair before I dressed. Mom's blouse proved to be only a little loose, and while pastel lavender wasn't a color I ever wore, it looked good on me.

Why would seeing Mom's clothes make me have a flashback? I'd only been about five when my parents had died. I could barely remember them.

I straightened the delicate lace collar, and then reached out to wipe a circle in the steam-clouded mirror. My face looked whiter than usual, while my eyes had gone dark; a sure sign I was going to get a massive headache. I took my bottle of aspirin from the cabinet and dry-swallowed two pills. The bitter taste on my tongue matched my mood as I braided my damp hair.

Frustration made me want to yank my hair out of my scalp. No, what I really wanted was to go down there and tell my brothers that I knew what they'd been doing to me. But if I did that, Trick would erase my memories and move us to another town, someplace where he could keep me completely clueless and cut off from the world.

I'd lose Jesse again, this time for good, and no matter how angry I felt, I wasn't going to let that happen.

Five

My brothers had gone back to the barn by the time I went back downstairs, so I made a sandwich and bagged it along with some fruit and a couple of water bottles. That went with my purse into the red and black plaid backpack I used for school, which I figured would be easier to carry while riding the bus and walking around town.

I couldn't leave without saying good-bye, so I made myself go out to the barn. Gray was holding a section of the pen up for Trick, who was drilling holes in it, but both of them looked up as I approached.

"I'm leaving now," I said in my best cheerful tone. "Want to wish me luck?"

"You won't need any," Gray told me, and even sounded like he meant it.

"Call and check in with me when you're on your break," Trick said.

I gave them a farewell wave and started toward the front gate. Gray caught up with me before I got to it.

"Here." He shoved something into my hand. "You might need this so you don't miss the bus home."

I recognized the old silver pocket watch; Trick had given it to Gray for his sixteenth birthday. Like the St. Christopher's medal I wore, it had once belonged to our dad. I also knew it was Gray's most prized possession. "I can't take it."

"Give it back to me tonight." He tapped my wrist. "And next time, remember to put on your watch." He grinned at me before he strode back toward the pen.

I slipped Dad's watch in my pocket and went through the gate, latching it behind me. I didn't want to hate my brothers forever, and every time I thought I would Gray or Trick would do something to pull me in the opposite direction. It wasn't fair.

Walking to the bus stop didn't take long, and when I reached the wooden-slat bench seat by the sign at the corner I checked Gray's watch and saw that I had another ten minutes to wait.

Our nearest neighbor was another six and a half miles away, so the only thing surrounding the road were fenced-off pastures and fields. Big rounds of feed grass that had been cut and baled sat like giant pencil erasers across one pasture; a small herd of goats wandered scrounging through another harvested field. In the distance I could see slow-moving Black Angus cattle shuffling around a ditch where another neighbor had been burning dead brush and long, twisted branches of black oaks. Just beyond it a tractor stood hitched to a gigantic trailer piled with weathered and broken lumber; he must have torn down an outbuilding or a barn.

A plaintive mew and the brush of fur against my jeans made me look down at a cream-colored cat with dark brown ears, paws and tail. The rhinestone-studded collar he wore was the exactly same shade of blue as his eyes.

"Hey, kitty." I reached down to let him sniff my hand, but he leapt up onto my lap and rubbed his head under my chin. "Nice to meet you, too."

On his collar was a bright new metal tag engraved with the name "Johnson" along with an address on a county road I knew was on the other side of Lost Lake.

I cradled the cat's face between my palms. "Why did you stray twenty miles from home, sweetie?"

I wasn't expecting an answer, but the cat gracefully jumped down and scampered across the road. The reason seemed to be the rumbling sound of a diesel engine coming close, and when I turned I saw the bus into town coming toward my stop.

As the bus's brakes squealed, I shouldered my backpack and took out the change for the fare. The narrow doors at the front of the bus swung open, and I climbed up inside to deposit the coins in the change meter.

The driver, a big man with hair so bright red it was

almost orange, nodded to me and waited until I took a seat in the back before pulling onto the road.

Only six other people were riding the bus into town; two men dressed in town maintenance uniforms, an older woman in a mauve cardigan who was knitting something small, two boys in soccer jerseys and some lanky teen in a black hoodie who was slouched down in the seat in front of me. Everyone glanced at me except the kid in the hoodie, whose face was concealed behind an open photography magazine.

I got comfortable and looked out the window to see if the cat had emerged from the brush, but the sound of the bus must have scared her off. Cats were pretty sensible that way; if she'd been a dog she probably would have tried to chase us into town. I still couldn't figure out what she was doing all the way out here; she'd looked too sleek and well-fed to be anything but an indoor cat.

"The view doesn't get better," a wry voice warned.

I looked at Black Hoodie, who had turned around to talk to me. "Excuse me?"

"You're still living in the creepiest small town in Central Florida." The kid pushed back the hood to reveal her face. I recognized her as Karise Carson, Tanglewood High School's only real Goth girl. Her shorn blonde hair had grown out a little, and she'd switched her black lipstick for a softer, prettier pink gloss, but silver still glittered from her nose and eyebrow piercings. "Why are you resorting to public transport, Youngblood? Your brothers too cheap to drive you into town?"

"I've got a job for winter break at…" I stopped talking to gape at her. "You know my name."

"Sure, you're Catlyn Youngblood." She smothered a yawn. "Got some pics of you, too. You're very photogenic. Real supermodel material."

"I haven't seen you since before Halloween, have I?" I knew I hadn't, but I didn't want to jump ahead of myself.

"Nope." Her eyes gleamed. "I was too tied up to make the school dance. I also missed that nasty flu that went around the day after. You know, the real *tricky* one."

I understood what Kari meant: my brother hadn't erased her memories. "How did you manage not to catch that?"

"Easy." She turned her head and bared her teeth at Mauve Cardigan, who was watching us, and whose mouth puckered with disapproval before she went back to her bootie knitting. "I pretended I already had it. Seek, my boyfriend"—she rolled her eyes over the last two words—"did the same as me, so he's cool, too."

"You haven't told anyone that you didn't get… sick?" As she shook her head, I relaxed a little. "I am so sorry about this, Kari."

"Why? You didn't do it." She finally got up and came to sit beside me. "Seek and I wanted to let you know, but when you came back to school it was pretty obvious you'd gotten a really good dose. We were afraid if we told you, you'd go to your brother, and he'd come after us. Or the sheriff would, now that they're such good buddies. And me and Seek, we're…" she hesitated, and then sighed.

"Okay, I'll admit it. We're stupid crazy in love with each other; we have been since Halloween night. We couldn't risk losing that."

What Trick had done had frightened and angered me, but I'd never considered how it affected anyone but me and Jesse. Now Kari made me realize that he hadn't simply erased the town's memories, he'd stolen bits and pieces of their lives.

"Cat." Kari waited until I looked at her. "I've got to get off at the next stop. Where are you working in town?" After I told her, she nodded. "Sometimes I hang out at Tony's Garage, one block over. It's where Seek works. Maybe we'll run into each other again one night."

"I hope so."

"Until we do, stay healthy, Youngblood." She reached up to pull the stop cord, and then gathered up her things and got off the bus. I watched her through the window as she walked down a dirt road toward an apartment building.

I felt a small surge of hope. If Kari and her boyfriend had avoided being brainwashed, maybe other people had, too. My brother might have a freakish, scary ability, but he wasn't all-powerful. He couldn't control everyone.

Mauve Cardigan, I noticed, was watching me again. I couldn't manage a Kari-glare so I gave her a little smile.

She smiled back.

———

I got off the bus at the closest stop to the bookstore, at the little park in front of City Hall, about two blocks away. My watch said I had twenty minutes before I was to start work, so I wasn't going to be late. Finding out Kari remembered me had been a shock, one that still made me feel a little shaky, so I sat on one of the benches encircling the fountain to drink some water and calm down.

"Ms. Youngblood?"

I looked up at two small reflections of my face in Sheriff Yamah's mirrored sunglasses. "Yes, sir?"

He studied me for a second. "You all right, young lady?"

"I'm fine." No, I was horribly uncomfortable as I remembered how I'd made Gray think I had a crush on the sheriff. *Say something before he arrests you for indecent teasing.* "It's a nice day, isn't it?"

He nodded, and then looked around slowly before showing me my twin face reflections again. "Planning to do some holiday shopping?"

"Ah, no, sir. I'm starting my new job today." And he would want to know where, of course. "I'll be working at Mrs. Frost's shop."

His thick mustache twitched. "Martha Frost rents out her shop to some college test prep service so she can spend the holidays with her grandkids."

"Yes, sir, she has. I'll be taking inventory for her in the evenings." I hoped I looked as innocently employed as I sounded. "I love books, so it should be a lot of fun."

"Is that right." He shook his head, and for a split second I thought he was going to slap the cuffs on me and call Trick. "Not much of a reader myself. I expect it's because I've got to deal with too much conflict in real life."

"My brothers are the same. About reading books, I mean," I tacked on quickly. "Although I got my oldest brother to read Nathaniel Philbrick. He writes history books, mostly about famous ships, but he's not boring at all."

"I'll mention him to the wife, next time she goes to the library." He touched the brim of his hat. "Good luck with the new job, Ms. Youngblood."

"Thank you, Sheriff." I didn't let out the breath I was holding until he walked down the block. "After this it should be a piece of cake."

My nerves weren't going away anytime soon, so I got up and went to the corner to cross the street. Most of the antique stores that shared the same block with Mrs. Frost's shop were open, and seemed to be doing good business, thanks to all the browsing tourists. Some were shopping with kids I recognized from school, and must have been grandparents or relatives who came to Lost Lake to visit for the holidays.

I saw a CLOSED sign hanging in the front door of Nibbles and Books, and the door was locked, but Mrs. Frost was sitting at one of the café tables and came to let me in.

"You're right on time, Catlyn," she said, smiling as she closed the door behind me. "I was just putting together the inventory sheets for you." She took my arm in hers and started walking toward the back of the shop. "First, let me show you where you'll be—"

"*Sunny?*"

The shriek made us both turn around to see a wild-eyed woman standing in the doorway.

Mrs. Frost hurried over to her. "Nancy, I didn't know you were working at your shop today."

"I thought that ... I thought ... " Nancy's face crumpled, and her eyes filled with tears. "I was so sure when I saw ... "

"That's completely understandable, my dear," Mrs. Frost said gently. "Let me introduce you to Catlyn, my new employee. She'll be looking after the inventory while I'm visiting my children." She glanced at me. "Catlyn, this is Nancy Johnson. She and her husband own the shop across the street."

She must be the mother of the missing girl, I thought. "It's very nice to meet you, Mrs. Johnson."

"Why don't you sit down, Nancy?" Mrs. Frost suggested. "I'll make a cup of tea for you."

"No, Martha, I'm not ... I'm sorry I barged in." She gave me another long look before she left the shop as quickly as she'd come in.

Mrs. Frost went to close the door and stood there watching Mrs. Johnson until she disappeared into the shop across the street. "Poor thing. She's beside herself with worry, not that anyone could blame her."

"Has there been any news about her daughter, or what might have happened to her?" I asked.

"None, I'm afraid. Her daughter has run away from home before, but never for so long." Mrs. Frost eyed me. "Do you know Sunny?"

"No, ma'am. We've never met."

"She's a sweet girl. A little headstrong and thoughtless at times, but she has a good heart." Mrs. Frost made a face. "Nancy is having a very difficult time coping, obviously, especially with her husband out searching for the child all hours of the day and night."

I nodded. "I hope she comes home soon."

"As do I, my dear. While I'm gone if you happen to see Nancy"—she seemed almost afraid to finish the statement—"behaving oddly in some way, you should call the sheriff and let him know. His number is on the list by the wall phone in the corner there." She gestured toward it. "Jim will look after her."

"Of course, I will." Hoping I wouldn't have to, I glanced through the window at the Johnsons' shop. None of the lights were on, and their CLOSED sign was still gently swaying in the door.

Mrs. Frost led me to her office in the back, where some of the clutter had been tidied up, and most of the papers removed from the top of her desk. "I've tidied up in here so you'll have some workspace. I'd like you to work Monday through Friday, but if you have some family functions you can certainly work a shift over the weekend. I don't expect you to work on Christmas Eve or Christmas Day."

She went on to explain the simple process I was to use for taking inventory, which involved noting the shelf counts on tally sheets and then inputting the numbers into an accounting program. Mrs. Frost had me practice on one shelf, and nodded as she checked my tally. "Excellent. Once you've finished inventorying the store stock, you can begin cataloging the new stock in the back store room."

That was where we went next, and found stacks of large plastic bins filled with books.

"I've been too busy to sort through these," Mrs. Frost said, sounding slightly apologetic, "so you have your work cut out for you here."

I peeked in the bin she had opened. "Wow. Those look really old."

"Yes, they are. Before you handle any of them, please put on a pair of these." She pointed to a blue cardboard box with an open top, which contained dozens of pairs of white fabric gloves. "They'll help protect the books and your hands."

I thought of what Trick had said over breakfast. I didn't see anything crawling around in the sealed bins, but the light may have made them hide. "Could there be any bugs in them?"

"Sometimes I think silverfish and spiders could survive a thermonuclear war, but in this case I seriously doubt it," she said. "Julian was a tidy, conscientious soul who cherished his collection, and took very good care of every volume in it."

I didn't feel convinced. "I'm sure he did, ma'am, but what should I do if I find something that got past him?"

"Don't use any sprays, as they'll harm the books," she advised. "Either step on them, or bring the vacuum in my office closet with you when you work in here." She hesitated before she added, "I know how tempting it is to be surrounded by books, so you have my permission to borrow anything from the store shelves, as long as you return it in pristine condition. But because Julian's collection is so valuable, I must insist his books remain here."

"Yes, ma'am." I could just imagine my brothers' reaction to me coming home with books on demons and witches. "After I've cataloged them, do you want me to move them out to the shelves and add them to the inventory?"

"No, that won't be necessary. I have a private buyer who intends to make an offer as soon as I send the complete list of titles." She took out a small key ring, and held it out to me. "These are the keys to the all the doors in the shop, and this one"—she separated one that was smaller than the rest—"is for the security alarm system. Let's go out front and I'll show you that next."

While Mrs. Frost demonstrated how to turn the store's alarm system on and off, I felt an odd sensation, as if someone were watching us, and looked out through the window by the counter. Standing inside the door of her shop, Mrs. Johnson was watching, but she wasn't looking at Mrs. Frost or the alarm box. She was staring at me, with that same hopeless expression she'd had when Mrs. Frost had introduced us. I had to force myself to pay attention to the rest of Mrs. Frost's instruction.

"I think that's everything you need to know," Mrs. Frost said. "Do you have any questions?"

"No, ma'am." I checked the window again, but Mrs. Johnson was no longer in sight.

She also looked in that direction. "Was Nancy watching you?" When I nodded, she sighed. "I'm sorry. Don't let her frighten you, she doesn't mean any harm."

"I'm not afraid of her," I said. "But why does she stare at me like that?"

"That's right, you said you've never met Sunny." Mrs. Frost smiled sadly. "She's tall and dark-haired, and has fair skin. From a distance you probably look exactly like her."

Six

When the airport limousine arrived a half-hour later to pick up Mrs. Frost, I helped her carry her suitcases out to the curb.

"I'll call you every Friday afternoon to check in," she said as the driver loaded the cases in the back of the van. "If there are any issues with the shop you can call the landlord. The number is on the wall list."

I frowned. "I thought you owned the building, Mrs. Frost."

"No, dear, my shop and most of the others in town are leased out by Raven Property Management. If you need anything, just call them." She gave me a quick hug. "I'll see you in January. Good luck."

I waved as the taxi drove off, and went back into the store, locking the door. It was hard not to check and see if Mrs. Johnson was staring at me again, but I thought if I pretended everything was normal she'd stop acting so oddly.

Being by myself inside the bookstore felt a little creepy, too. Without Mrs. Frost there it was dead quiet; the only sound came from the café's refrigerator, which hummed, and the air coming through the vents overhead, which sounded exactly like someone whispering. I had a clock radio in my room at home, and I decided I'd bring it with me tomorrow. Because Lost Lake was in the middle of nowhere, it only picked up a few country music stations, but even that would be better than working in the too-loud silence.

I took my bag of sandwiches and water bottles out of my backpack and carried them over to the café's refrigerator. Inside I found a bin filled with soft drinks and a small baker's box with a note on top.

> *Catlyn, here's something to help you celebrate your first job. Enjoy—Martha Frost.*

I took a peek inside the box, which contained a packet of fancy crackers, a bunch of luscious red grapes and an elegant, paper-wrapped wedge of cheese. I didn't care much for sweets, so it was the perfect snack for me. "I like working here already, ma'am."

Once I put everything in the fridge, I went back to the office to get started. I already knew how I wanted to run the inventory, and how many shelves I'd have to count during one shift in order to be finished before Mrs.

Frost returned from her trip. I wanted to allow enough time tonight to look through Julian Hargraves's books and see if he had any about vampires and vampire hunters.

Will you have any time left for me?

I think I can spare you a few minutes. Hearing Jesse's thoughts made me smile for an instant before I recalled what Mrs. Frost had said just before leaving. *You didn't mention that your parents own this building.*

My parents own most of the town, Catlyn.

Yes, but... I wasn't sure why I still felt suspicious, only that I did. *Did you do something to Mrs. Frost to convince her to hire me?*

The only thing I could compel Mrs. Frost to do is tell me that you applied for the job, he assured me. *Or I might make her forget that you did. That is all.*

I felt a little better—and suddenly ashamed of myself. *I'm sorry.*

Don't be. I would rather have your honesty than your suspicions.

I felt a wonderful, warm sensation inside me before his thoughts ebbed away. It was difficult for us to share thoughts during daylight hours. He had told me that he spent the entire day underground, in rooms built under his parents' mansion on Raven Island to protect them from the sun's lethal rays. I knew he didn't have to sleep the entire time he was there, but until nightfall his powers were weaker and much more limited.

Mine aren't. But I was only half vampire, and like the Ravens my father hadn't changed completely. My other half was human, like my mother, and she'd passed along to me her Van Helsing ability.

As I picked up a stack of tally sheets, I wondered for the first time what specific ability my mother had inherited from her parents. In her love letters to Dad she had mentioned being a "finder," the same thing I'd once heard Trick call Grayson. Jesse's father knew a lot about the Van Helsings, but I couldn't exactly call him and ask for more information. Like my brothers, he still thought I had amnesia.

I didn't like to think about whatever I was supposed to be. My ability to control cats and use them like bodyguards and hunting dogs already troubled me. If I wanted to, I could summon every feline in the area and use them like an army to attack whoever I wanted. Jesse's father had practically accused me of being a vampire killer.

I'm not a killer. I'm ... an inventory clerk.

I walked out to the shelves and got started on the count. I stopped only once after finishing the first shelf to retrieve a feather duster from Mrs. Frost's office—some of the books had sat undisturbed long enough to breed baby dust bunnies—but otherwise kept going until I had finished counting the entire section.

As Mrs. Frost had predicted, a few books were out of order, but I didn't find any missing. Counting the books on the lowest shelves was a little awkward, as I had to kneel on the floor, but other than that it seemed like a breeze.

I took out Gray's pocket watch. Surprised to see it was already seven-thirty, I left the clipboard on the step-ladder and went to retrieve my sandwiches and Mrs. Frost's snack from the fridge. I took everything back to the office so I could call home and let my brothers know I had survived the first four hours unscathed.

Trick answered it on the first ring. "Youngblood Ranch, Patrick speaking."

"What happened to 'Hello'?" I asked before I took a bite of my sandwich. "And why are we a ranch? I thought you were going with 'farm.'"

"I kept getting too many cold calls from tractor salesmen." He sounded amused. "How are things at the job?"

"Lots of dust bunnies and shelf shuffling, but the good news is, I still know my ABC's and can count past twenty." I reached for my water bottle. ""How did you manage with dinner?"

"According to Gray, the scorched tomato soup was slightly better than my blackened grilled cheese," he said. "He also made me promise to defrost something you made for tomorrow night."

I grinned. "I recommend the lasagna."

"I'll be waiting at the bus stop," he reminded me before he said good-bye and hung up.

Once I finished eating, I tidied up the desk and carried my trash to the big can outside the restroom, where I went to wash up. I still had to enter my counts into the computer, but I wanted to take another look at the Hargraves collection.

The overhead light in the storeroom was bright enough to work by, but the stacks of bins left hardly any space to work. When I began cataloging the collection I'd have to carry a bin out to the office, or out to one of the tables in the café.

I put on a pair of gloves before I took down the top-most bin on one stack and placed it on the floor. The lid, held tightly in place by two hinged clamps on either end, came off with a faint pop when I released them. A musty odor rose from the books inside and made me wrinkle my nose.

Whoever had packed the bin had put the books inside carefully, arranging them in two layers with the heavier volumes on the bottom. All of the books were hard covers, although some were bound in leather and others in cloth-covered end boards. When I crouched down beside the bin, I could still read some of the titles and authors' names where they had been embossed or stamped on the spines.

"*Pagan Rituals of the Fourteenth Century*," I murmured. "*Alchemists of France. Medieval Manifestations.*" After I inspected the rest but found nothing about vampires, I sat back on my heels. "Of course *How to Cure Vampirism* wouldn't be in the first one."

"No one before you has ever wished to cure us."

I swung around and nearly fell over, but Jesse caught me and helped me to my feet. "How did you get in here?"

His mouth curved as he tucked a stray piece of hair behind my ear. "I know I should have waited, but I couldn't. Not knowing you were so close."

I couldn't help slipping my arms around him and

resting my cheek against his heart. "Where did you tell your parents you were going?"

"Fishing on the lake. They believe it's my newest hobby." He kissed the top of my head before he drew me out of the storeroom. "Show me what you're doing."

I couldn't take him out into the front of the shop, where anyone walking past would see us together, but I took him into the office, and turned on the computer as I described what I'd accomplished so far.

"I've got to enter some numbers into the inventory program, but after that we can start looking through Julian Hargraves's books." I frowned as he sat down in Mrs. Frost's chair. "What are you doing?"

"If I help you, we'll have more time to look through the collection." He opened the inventory program, picked up the clipboard with my tally sheets and, after glancing over both, began entering numbers.

I almost protested, until I saw his fingers blur over the number pad on the keyboard. "Vampire show-off."

"Jealous mortal." A minute later he finished and handed the clipboard back to me as he stood. "Come and check, I know you want to."

I came around the desk and compared the tally sheets to the figures he'd put into the program. They matched perfectly, of course. "The next time I get ten pages of calculus homework, I'm making you do it."

"You'll never learn anything that way," he chided. His smile faded as he looked at me. "What's wrong?"

"Nothing." I made a face. "It's just... Trick always

says the same thing." I ducked my head. "He loves me, you know."

Jesse nodded slowly.

"And I hate him," I said flatly. "All this pretending, and scheming, and sneaking around behind his back, everything we have to go through just to have a little time together. It's not right. You don't do this to someone you love."

Jesse held out his hand. "Take a walk with me. Only for a few minutes," he added.

I scowled. "We can't go anywhere. Someone might see us together."

"Not if we go the way I came in." His eyes gleamed. "Come and I'll show you another of our secrets."

Jesse led me to the shop's back door, but instead of opening it he bent down and pressed his fingers against what looked a knot in the hardwood floor panel. The knot sank about an inch, and then he pressed two more, which did the same. As the third sank down, a four-foot square section of the floor popped up. He caught one side and pulled it up like a hatch, revealing a short ladder that led down into darkness.

"Get out of town." I could hardly believe my eyes. "You have a secret tunnel under the bookstore?"

"The bookstore, and almost every other building in Lost Lake. My parents had our people install them for us after we settled here. We stopped using them after we moved to the island. Or, at least, my parents did." He climbed halfway down the ladder, and then glanced up at me. "It's all right, don't be afraid."

"I'm not." As I climbed down onto the ladder, I felt as if I'd stepped into my favorite Nancy Drew novel, though. "How many more secrets do you have?"

"Only a few."

Jesse waited at the bottom of the ladder, and helped me down as I reached it. We stood in what appeared to be an empty cellar made of brick, although there were no windows and only three old oak doors, one set in the center of each wall. When he climbed back up to close the hatch, the darkness swallowed us for a moment, and then eerie blue lights flickered on.

"The lights switch off when any entrance to the passages is opened," he explained as he climbed back down. "James just installed them for me, in the event I was caught away from the island again before sunrise."

Now the lack of windows made sense. "These are vaults to protect you from sunlight."

"Vaults, storage rooms, tunnels." He gestured toward the door across from us. "I use that one to go to James's house. It leads up into his den."

"I don't want to go there," I assured him.

"That would probably be best." He took my arm to guide me through the door on the right, which opened into a tall, narrow brick passage.

The sound of dripping water and some puddles on the floor beneath our feet made me frown. "Is this place leaking?"

"The water table is high, but James runs pumps to

keep most of it out," he said, and then added, "The only time the passages have flooded was in 2004."

"That was when the four hurricanes hit Florida, I remember." At the time I'd only been eight years old, but my school had collected bottled water and canned goods to send to the victims. "What did you and your parents do?"

"We stayed on the island during the storms, and then came to town at night to help James clear the roads. Prince and I spent weeks herding cattle that had strayed through broken fences." At the end of the passage he opened another old door, but stopped me from walking through it. "This may seem somewhat bizarre to you."

I lifted my brows. "More bizarre than secret hatches, hidden passages and underground vaults?"

"Perhaps."

He actually seemed worried. "Jesse, you don't have to hide anything. You can trust me with any secret."

He nodded, and then pushed the door open wider.

This vault was not empty like the one under the bookstore, but had been made into a real room. Shelves of books and magazines flanked an enormous antique roll-top desk, which held old-fashioned quill pens and an inkwell. On the top ledge of the desk two bronze book-ends shaped like rearing horses held a long row of leather-bound books.

On the walls hung neatly framed photographs in different sizes, each showing different shots of Lost Lake, old houses and various spots around the town. All of them had been taken at night, I noticed, and were quite beautiful. Another, more modern desk took up another corner, and this one held a laptop and a small printer, and over that hung a curio cabinet filled with small birds hand-carved from different woods. Beside one of the bookcases stood a painter's easel and a half dozen canvases faced toward the wall.

I walked over to the paintings, but stopped as I reached for one and looked back at him. "May I?" When he nodded, I turned it over.

The painting was a portrait of Sarah and Paul Raven riding two white horses. Jesse's parents both wore what I recognized as nineteenth-century circus costumes. Behind them I saw a crowd of people in the same period clothing smiling and applauding.

There was only one person in town who could have seen Jesse's parents performing as the Ravenovs. "You painted this."

"I did, last summer." He went to the laptop, booting it up as he said, "I've been searching through records from the Civil War to see if I could identify the soldier who built the lake cabin." He opened a file, which displayed a page filled with the name Jacob along with different surnames. "These are all of the men named Jacob who fought for the Confederacy and survived the war. A total of one hundred twenty-two."

I scanned the list. "Jacob was a popular name." I thought for a minute. "Wouldn't he have taken out a claim or a deed or something on the land before he built the cabin?"

"My parents filed the first recorded deeds when they bought the land," Jesse said. "Before we came here, the area was regarded as unsettled wilderness, and property of the state."

"Maybe he was a deserter, and was hiding out here." It was a wild guess, but it also made sense. My gaze strayed back to the curio cabinet. "Where did you get these?"

"The birds? I carved them." He walked over to the roll-top desk. "I wrote these journals." He gestured at the photographs. "I took these as well."

"You could open a one-guy art gallery," I said, but he didn't smile at the joke. "Why do you keep your art down here instead of on the island?"

"My father dislikes clutter."

He sounded so uncomfortable I suspected there was a lot more to it than that. *Maybe he's shy about showing anyone what he does*, I thought, and went to open the door next to the stack of canvases, but found it locked. "What's in here?"

"It's just a storage room."

I was tempted to ask him to show me what was inside, but I'd been away from the shop long enough. "We'd better go back."

Seven

As soon as we made it back to the book shop I heard the phone in Mrs. Frost's office ringing, which meant she was probably calling to check on me.

Guilt made me fumble the receiver before I answered with a breathless, "Nibbles and Books, Catlyn speaking."

"This is the second time I've called," Trick said. "Where have you been?"

"I was, um, in the restroom." As Jesse came in I held a finger to my lips. "What's wrong?"

"Sheriff Yamah called me. He stopped by the shop thirty minutes ago, but you didn't answer the door."

"I never heard him," I said quickly. "I've been working back in the storeroom. What did the sheriff want?"

"He wanted to make sure you were all right." He

sighed. "Well, at least now I know you're safe. I'll see you at the bus stop. Be careful."

"I will, I promise. Bye." I hung up the phone and hugged myself with my arms. "The sheriff came by the shop while we were gone. He called Trick." A wave of anger came over me, and I knocked a pile of tally sheets to the floor. "I can't even spend a few hours with you without my brother ruining everything."

"Catlyn." Jesse came over and put his arms around me, and touched his forehead to mine. "Nothing is ruined. We will be more careful and stay in the shop. The tunnels are not important. Being with you is all I need."

"I'm glad you feel that way, because we're not going to be able do anything but sit in this shop all winter break and look at each other." A yowling sound from the back of the store made me cringe. "God, not again."

We went to the back door, and as Jesse turned on the outside light I looked through the small square window. Dozens of stray cats had swarmed into the alley, and were mewling and milling restlessly just outside the shop's door.

"Marvelous." I knew my anger had drawn them here; felines responded to my thoughts, and when I was angry, formed my own little private furry army. When I reached to unlatch the bolt, Jesse stopped me. "Jess, you know I have to go out there and send them away or they'll stay here all night."

"I know, but not yet," he said, and touched my temple. "If you are to gain control of your ability, you must practice using it. This is a good opportunity. Give them a command with your thoughts. Tell them to sit."

I felt silly as I closed my eyes and did what he asked. *All felines in the immediate area, please sit.* When the yowling stopped I glanced through the window and saw five young cats sitting on the doorstep, and the rest staring up at me. "It didn't work."

"Try once more," Jesse urged me. "Remember, they have limited minds. Keep your command simple."

This time I kept my eyes on the cats as I thought a single word: *Sit.*

Every cat in the alley dropped their hindquarters. A couple of thin, scruffy-looking toms turned their heads and hissed at each other.

Quiet, I thought, and the cats fell silent. "It's working now." I didn't like it, either. "Why does it have to be cats? Why not polar bears, or killer whales? Why not Dobermans?"

"Vampires do not dwell in the Arctic or the ocean, and they frighten dogs." Jesse nodded toward the cats. "All felines are hunters, and even the smallest and most domesticated retain some of their feral nature."

"You mean they're all natural born killers." I closed my eyes. "Like me."

"We are who we choose to be," he said softly. "I died a mortal, and my murderers tried to bring me back as a vampire. I may never be human again, but no one can

85

force me to kill. You know this because you have made the same choice."

His calmness made me feel ashamed of my self-pity party, which I decided it was time to end. "I think that's enough practice for one night." I looked out at the cats, and as soon as I thought *Leave* they scattered in all directions. "I've still got to go through one of the bins in the storeroom. Want to help me sort out the old scary books?"

Jesse did even better than that; he set up a table and two chairs behind the back bookcases where we could work without being seen from the front of the shop. Then he carried out the first bin and began unloading it. I rolled up my sleeves and got started on the first tally sheet for the collection.

After he set down the first stack of books, he leaned over and gently touched the abrasion across the back of my wrist. "You hurt yourself."

"It's just a rope burn. Rika ran off the other day, and I had to catch her." I told him what had happened, and added, "I know Trick bought her just because she's pregnant and we all need to practice foaling, but I'm not sure it's worth all this trouble."

"Horses are herd animals, and we are not," Jesse said. "Until we gain their trust, they see people as what we are: predators."

"You'd think by now she'd have figured out we don't want to eat her." I set down a stack of books and frowned.

"You've raised a lot of horses. What do you think could be wrong with her?"

"From what you've told me, she is afraid, not lazy," Jesse said. "Has she made a place for herself among the other horses?"

"Well, Sali's our lead mare, and Rika seems to be okay with that. I mean, she doesn't challenge her or pick fights." I thought for a minute. "She knows Jupiter is our alpha horse, but she's never shown any respect to him. Jupe is pretty patient, but eventually he'll go after her to bring her in line. And she hates Flash, which is weird because he's the master of avoidance." I shook my head. "Mostly what she does is run away, which is not normal for a pregnant mare. She runs like the farm is a trap, and we're monsters, and she wants to escape."

"It sounds as if she is obeying her survival instinct," Jesse said, sounding thoughtful. "Horses respond first to danger by running from it. Something is prompting her to flee. When you determine the trigger, then you can understand her fear."

"Everything seems to scare her." I sighed. "Gray has been trying to train her, but she's not responding."

"You should perhaps take her back in the barn to work with her. She will be enclosed there, and cannot see an avenue of escape," he advised. "I would use a bridle with a smooth-mouth snaffle and a short rein. Don't try to make her stand still; that will only aggravate her nerves. Work her from one end of the barn to the other, and see how well she can turn on command. When she does turn, ease up on the reins, and she will know she has performed correctly."

We'd all assumed Rika knew her turning cues, something taught when a horse was saddle-trained. Even if she did know them, I saw the wisdom of repeating the cue training; horses always followed their noses. "Plus she can't charge forward if all she's doing is turning in circles."

"Exactly. Once she lowers her head to rein pressure, and turns on cue each time, then move her outside. Use a round, empty pen and don't hang anything on the railings. Make sure it has dry ground that offers good footing. Horses have no depth perception, so even a small hole or puddle can appear to them as deep as a mine shaft."

It always amazed me, how much Jesse knew about horses. Of course he and his parents had been breeding and training them for more than a century. "Thanks for the advice." I wished I could ask him to come to the farm to look at Rika, but that could never happen. "Hopefully we can get her trained before she delivers, or we may have to take her to the vet to foal." I saw he had opened one of the books and was reading the title page. "What do you think of the creepiness collection?"

"Julian must have spent a great deal of money to build it." He glanced in the bin. "Most of these appear to be older than I am."

"That's why they've survived so long." I picked up a slim volume on ancient astrology and admired the gilded edges. "They really made them to last, back in the day." I realized something and giggled at myself.

"What is so funny?"

"I was going to ask you what your sign is," I explained. "That's also known as the oldest and lamest pick-up line in the world."

"I don't know," he admitted. "I was born on June nineteenth."

"I think that makes you a Cancer." I opened the astrology book and thumbed through it until I found a chart. "Nope, I'm wrong. You're a Gemini."

"Indeed." He leaned close and waggled his eyebrows. "What's your sign, pretty girl?"

I laughed. "I'm an Aquarius, you lecher." I read through the different notations on the chart. "This says we're both air signs, so I think that makes us compatible. Let me check." I flipped through some pages to the section on Aquarius, and stopped as a folded note fell out. I opened it to see Julian Hargraves's name printed at the top, followed by some writing in an unsteady hand:

Born January 27th
Seattle Wash
NMR

I read it twice before I handed it to Jesse. "I guess Mr. Hargraves looked up his sign in the book, too. Kind of a weird coincidence, though."

"Why is that?"

"Well, it's just that my birthday is January twenty-seventh, and I was born in Seattle." I frowned. "Hang on. Trick read the obituary to me from the paper. It said that Julian was born here, in Lost Lake."

Jesse gave me a troubled look. "He was."

———

At ten o'clock I left the bookstore and walked down the block to the bus stop. Jesse couldn't go with me, or let anyone see him leaving the shop, but he promised to watch over me. I didn't realize he meant that literally until I sat down on the bench at the park stop. Across the street I spotted a tall, slim shadow jumping from the roof of one building to another.

I held my breath as he walked to the edge of the building across from the park and stood there looking down at me like some dark guardian angel.

An older woman carrying some shopping bags came and sat on the other end of the bench, and we exchanged tired smiles.

Jesse, someone is going to see you, I thought as I deliberately stared at my sneakers.

I do this all the time, Jesse thought back to me. *After dark, people never look up.*

They'll look if you slip and fall on your head. The sound of the bus coming down the road made me turn my head, and I saw two people standing at the corner. One was Mrs. Johnson, who was staring at me again. The other was a tired-looking man who was talking to her. I couldn't hear what he said, but when he tried to take her arm she shook him off, turned and walked back to her shop. The man followed her inside.

The bus pulled to the curb and opened its doors. Once I paid my fare I sat down in an empty seat behind the driver and looked up.

Jesse pressed his hand to his heart, and then reached toward me. *Until tomorrow night, pretty girl. Sleep well.*

I pressed my hand against the glass. *Be careful.*

The ride home gave me a little time to think about all the night's near-disasters. I hadn't counted on the visit from the sheriff, but I should have known Trick wouldn't be satisfied with one check-in call. Getting a job in town was supposed to give me a little of the freedom I so badly needed, not make me feel as if I'd been moved to another part of my brother's prison.

It hadn't been a complete disaster. Now I knew about the tunnels, and Jesse's surprising talents. It made me wonder what he had put away in the locked storage room, too. As shy as he was about his art it would probably take me some time to convince him to show me more, but I could work on that.

The note in the astrology book had been the creepiest discovery of the night, but since I'd never met Julian Hargraves I knew it couldn't be about me. I certainly wasn't the only person who had ever been born in Seattle on January twenty-seventh, either.

Trick sat waiting on the bench at my stop, and after

the bus took off stood and took my backpack from me. "I should have brought the bike. You look beat."

Seeing him made me feel that way, not that I would admit it. "I'm okay."

As we walked down the road to the farm, he gave me the usual interrogation. I told him about the work I'd accomplished and the little present Mrs. Frost had left me. He didn't comment until I mentioned Julian Hargraves's collection.

"He's that recluse who died back in October on Halloween night," Trick said. "What sort of books did he collect?"

"Just a lot of old stuff." I wanted to kick myself for mentioning it, but it was too late now. "I always wondered why rare book shops smell funny. Now I know it comes from the books."

By the time we reached the house I was yawning, and as soon as we went inside I headed for the stairs. "See you in the morning."

"Cat, would you come into the kitchen for a minute?" my brother asked. "I have something for you."

Inside the kitchen there was a small red-and-black box sitting on the table. I could have sworn I'd never seen it before, but at the same time it looked familiar.

"Is it an early birthday present?" I guessed.

"More like a late one." My brother used a little key sitting on top of it to unlock it, and lifted the lid. Inside were little black velvet compartments, each holding different bejeweled stick pins and brooches. "This was Mom's."

I reached in and took out a gold pin in the shape of a flower that had petals made of garnet around a center topaz. "I remember this." I held it up against my blouse in a spot over my heart. "She wore it right here."

He nodded. "Dad gave her a flower pin every year on their anniversary. He couldn't afford diamonds, but she didn't care."

"It's nice that you saved them," I said, picking up a gleaming silver rosebud and admiring the tiny crystals that had been placed like drops of dew. "She would have liked that."

"They're yours." When I stared at him, he added, "As you're so fond of reminding us, you're the only girl in the family."

I didn't know what to say. "Why are you giving them to me now?"

"They'll look pretty on the blouses you wear to work." He came over and kissed the top of my head. "Go to bed now and get some sleep."

I carried the jewelry case upstairs, and then sat looking through the pins for a few minutes. I always wore the only jewelry I owned, a silver St. Christopher's medal that had belonged to my dad. I'd been forced to give back to Jesse the ring he'd given me on Halloween night, although he'd told me he would only keep it until I turned eighteen, when Trick would no longer be my legal guardian.

Sometimes I thought about the future, hazy as it was. Someday I would leave Lost Lake with Jesse, and find another place for us, far way from our families. In some of those dreams we got married and had children, just as my parents had. In others I convinced Jesse to change me to be like him and his parents, so we could be together forever.

Now, looking at Mom's pretty pins, I realized how difficult it was going to be when that day came. Despite all they'd done to me, I loved my brothers. Jesse felt the same about his parents.

I knew our families had their reasons for their mutual hatred—while trying to protect Trick, my mother had once tried to kill Sarah Raven—but Jesse and I had never been a part of that. We might have been born to be enemies, but when we met all we had known about each other was that we both loved to ride at night. We'd fallen in love just like any normal boy and girl. If anything, our natural feelings proved that the Youngbloods and the Ravens didn't have to be enemies.

Mom and Dad would understand, I thought as I put my mother's pins back in the jewelry case. *But they're gone, and no one cares what Jesse and I want.*

I took off my St. Christopher's medal and added it to the case before I took it over to my dresser. When I opened the bottom drawer, I saw the shorts I kept there were no longer as neatly folded as I'd left them. I straightened and looked around my room, and realized everything was a little out of place. My brothers had searched my room again while I was at work.

We can't make any more mistakes, Gray.

The sound the drawer made as I slammed it shut echoed in my heart.

Eight

My new job did have one positive effect on me; as angry and disgusted as I'd been after discovering my brothers had again searched my room, as soon as I got into bed and my head hit my pillow I fell asleep.

I knew I was dreaming when I opened my eyes and found myself alone in the tunnel under the bookstore. Water dripped in slow motion as I followed the passage to Jesse's room, but when I stepped inside everything was gone.

"Jesse?"

I heard a rattling sound, and saw the knob on the padlocked door turning, first one way and then the other. As I started walking toward it, the room began to stretch as if it were made of rubber. The knob began to shake, and something banged on the other side of the door, first slow and then faster and harder, until the sound made me cover my ears, and then something soft hit me in the face.

I grabbed the pillow, yelping as I pulled it away from my head and sat up.

"About time." Gray was standing next to my bed. "Come on, you've had eight hours. Get up."

I glanced at my clock radio, which read 8:14 a.m. "Good morning to you, too," I said as I rolled over and showed him my back. "Now go away."

"Having a job doesn't mean you can sleep through your morning chores," Gray informed me.

"No, God forbid I not get the laundry done before noon." I dragged myself out of bed and pulled on my robe.

"Use some bleach this time; my socks are starting to look dingy." He then ducked to avoid the pillow I threw at his head. "Girls can't throw worth a—*ow*." He rubbed the spot on his shoulder where the boot I threw after the pillow thumped him.

"What was that about girls?" I asked as I went around him and headed for the bathroom.

After I showered and dressed I went downstairs to find Gray setting the table for two. "Where's Trick?"

"He had to go pick up some stuff at the hardware store." He thumped a bowl down in front of me. "Hot or cold cereal?"

Trick must have told him to make breakfast for me, I thought, and grinned as I deliberately lounged in my chair. "Oh, I don't know." I knew how much Gray hated to cook. "I'm more in the mood for French toast, bacon and some fresh-squeezed orange juice."

"How about I make you toasted raisin bread, maple-raisin oatmeal, and a big glass of prune juice?" he countered.

I shuddered. There was nothing on earth I despised as much as raisins—except maybe prunes. "Cold cereal. Hold the mummified grapes."

Gray might have been allergic to the stove, but he sliced up a banana for my cornflakes and didn't hog all the milk. I did my part by clearing and washing up after we finished. I expected Gray to tromp out to the barn, but he sat and pretended to read the paper. He did the same thing whenever he needed to talk but didn't know how to dive into the conversation.

"Those stalls aren't going to muck out themselves," I told him as I put the last glass in the rack to dry and came over to take the paper from him. "So what's on your mind?"

"Nothing." He hunched his shoulders. "Okay, there's a guy who has a strawberry farm a few miles down the road. He's looking for some hands to help get the fields ready for planting."

"I already have a job." Then I got it. "But you don't, and now you want one. Is this a sibling rivalry thing?"

"Trick has spent a lot of money buying new stock and getting the farm back in shape," he said. "With the vet bills, the extra feed, all the stuff we've done to the barn, there can't be much left."

I hadn't thought things were that bad, but our big brother never talked about our financial situation. "He's going to sell Rika after she foals."

He shook his head. "Not as wild as she is. You know Trick. He doesn't want to pass the problem on to someone else. He won't touch our college accounts, either."

"If we run out of money, then he'll have to. Or he'll just go get a full-time job," I said, and then saw Gray's expression. "You think he's already looking for one."

"I know he is. This is the fourth time he's gone to the hardware store this week, and he's been taking the paper with him." He opened the paper to the classified section. "This morning he forgot it."

I saw several listings circled with a pencil; all of the ads were for different office positions. "Okay, so we should talk to him about this when he gets back."

"You know how he is," Gray said. "He won't admit we're going broke, but he's worrying himself sick. His insomnia has gotten so bad he went to the doctor and got sleeping pills."

"No way," I said. "Trick hates taking pills."

"Go look in his bathroom," Gray said. "The bottle is on the top shelf of his medicine cabinet." He heaved a sigh. "I thought if I got a job first, he'd feel better about letting us help. Or maybe we could just pay some bills and stuff."

"We don't have the checking account, he does," I reminded him. "I think if we start buying groceries out of the blue, he'll figure out that we know he's having money trouble."

"Then what do we do?" he asked. "Nothing?"

"No." I didn't have any immediate answers, though. "Let me think about it." I glanced at the wall clock. "It's getting late. I'll come out and help you with the horses."

Between the two of us we got the horses fed and turned out half of them so we could clean their stalls. I went outside to fetch the barrow we used to haul the soiled bedding and saw a rider coming up the road toward our property.

Some of the local trainers would take their students out on trails around our farm, but this girl was riding alone. Her mount, a pretty golden buckskin mare with black stockings and a glossy dark mane and tail, wore an English saddle, and trotted like they were circling an arena.

She looked so small atop the mare that I thought at first she might be a lost kid, but when she dismounted and led her mount through our gate she showed no hesitancy.

"Where's the barrow?" Gray asked as he came out, and then noticed our visitor, who had led her horse up the drive and was coming across the lawn toward us. "Who's that?"

"I don't know." I walked out to meet the girl, who was barely five feet tall, and had short curly black hair and pretty brown eyes. "Hi. Can I help you?"

"That's my line," she said, her crisp voice adding a little snap to the words. "I'm Mena. My dad sent me over." When I frowned, she added, "Dr. Marks is your equine vet, right?"

"Yes, he is." She definitely wasn't twelve, but she couldn't be much older than me. "Do you work at the clinic?"

"When he drags me in on Saturdays, or any other day one of the techs calls in sick." She led the buckskin over to a post. "Mostly I'm too busy training."

I still wasn't clear on why Dr. Marks had sent her to the farm. "Did he give you something to deliver?"

"He didn't call, did he?" She shook her head. "He's so busy in the spring that he forgets. I show horses, and I've worked with some Arabians, so he wanted me to take a look at your mare." She glanced over my shoulder. "Who's the professional wrestler?"

"That's my brother Grayson." I took her over to introduce them, and watched them size up each other.

"I don't know," Gray said. "You're pretty tiny to be handling Rika."

I stared at him. "Gray."

Mena seemed amused. "I'm stronger than I look, big guy." She cuffed his shoulder before she headed into the barn. "So where's her stall?"

My brother and I went in and took her down to the end stall, where Rika immediately stuck her head out and laid her ears back as she whinnied a warning.

"Talkative little brat, aren't you?" Mena circled around her, keeping out of nipping range. "Have you got her to tie quiet?"

"Not all the time," I admitted. "She's going to foal soon, and we didn't want to stress her out by working her too hard."

The girl nodded, still studying the mare. "So you're a *pregnant* talkative little brat." She reached for the door latch.

Gray beat her to it. "Not a good idea, kid."

"Really. How many Arabians have you trained?" Mena asked sweetly. "Any at all?"

Gray scowled. "She kicks."

"I can dodge." She pulled open the stall door and went inside.

Rika backed up until her hindquarters hit the wall, and then she tossed her head and reared.

"Hey, now, none of that." Mena grabbed her halter and brought her head down so they were eye-to-eye. "You may be bigger, but I'm a brat, and I know all your tricks." My brother and I watched as the girl ran her hands over the mare, feeling the muscles in her shoulders, legs and neck. Rika only shied a little when Mena checked her ears, but the girl ignored her.

"She's in decent condition." She pulled on a pair of thin leather gloves before she pushed back Rika's lips and nudged her teeth apart.

Seeing that small gloved hand reach into Rika's mouth made me cringe. "Mena, maybe you shouldn't... " I stopped as Rika responded by licking the girl's fingers. "Holy cow. She likes you."

"It's my size. They think I'm a snotty little filly." She

patted Rika's shoulder before she came out of the stall. "I also have a secret weapon that no horse can resist."

"Sure you do." Gray smirked. "What is it? Horse hypnosis?"

"Molasses." She tossed him a small plastic packet, which he caught reflexively. "I put a little on the fingertips of my glove."

Mena went into the tack room, where she looked at everything, and then asked me to show her how we were mixing Rika's feed.

"That reminds me, Dad said you should increase her concentrate now." She took out a little notepad and scribbled down some ratio numbers. "Have you checked where she's foraging?"

As I told Mena about our weeding routine, we walked out to the back pasture. She inspected one partially eaten hay bale before she studied the graze around it, and then climbed up on the fence and sat on the top railing to look at the side of the barn, where Gray was washing Flash.

I joined her. "So what do you think?"

"He needs some manners, and a haircut, but he's kind of cute." She saw my expression. "Oh, you mean the mare, not your brother. Her sire and dam were probably show horses, and there may have been others in her herd, but my guess is she was never trained. Or she could have just been starting when the VBE happened."

That was something I'd never heard of. "The VBE?"

"Very bad experience," Mena said. "I think someone

scared the crap out of your mare, and not just once. They did it so often that she may never stop trying to run away."

Of course I'd heard of horses being ruined for life, but the thought of someone doing that to a mare as young and beautiful as Rika made my heart clench. "Maybe we can still gentle it out of her."

"I thought the same thing about my first show horse," Mena told me. Her expression turned wistful. "He was a dream to ride. Quick, smart, loved the arena. A real gentleman. Every time he took a fence I felt like we were floating over it."

"He sounds like a great first horse."

"He was." Her smile slipped. "There was just one problem. Whenever my trainer led him to a gate, he'd freeze, dig in or try to rush it, like it was his first turn out after six months in the barn."

"Gray's horse didn't like gates when we first got him," I said. "And he still hates trailers."

"My horse didn't just balk at gates. He seriously freaked out every single time he came within ten feet of one," she told me. "Once he even bucked me off, and came close to trampling my trainer."

I caught my breath. "That must have been awful."

"My dad bought him from a breeder, so I thought it was me. My trainer drove herself nuts trying to work it out, too." Mena sighed. "Finally my dad called the breeder, who told him how to handle it. He said to punish the horse every time he balked at a gate, and that would keep him in line. Then we knew. To that horse, gate equaled punishment. We worked with him for another year, but the behavior was too ingrained. I never showed him again."

I understood what she was trying to tell me. "Do you think Rika's that far gone?"

Mena shrugged. "It's hard to say. Foaling might settle her down. Not even the best vet—or his darling perfect daughter—can fix everything, but we can try. Tell me what happened the last time she bolted."

I described how Gray had put Flash in with Rika that morning, and how Rika had reacted by breaking down the pen and taking off. "When Sali and I found her, she was lathered and exhausted, but she still tried to get away from us."

She nodded. "With frightened horses it's always run back to the herd first. Safety in numbers. She's so young she's probably still looking for her mother, too. Which is good, because she might make your lead mare her surrogate."

I didn't know if I agreed. "She seems to hate all the other horses."

"She doesn't know them," Mena corrected. "I know you're worried about her temper, but the only way she can form bonds within the herd is to socialize with them. Start by turning her out with Sali and a couple of the other mares for an hour or two. Use one of your bigger pastures so they have room to run her around."

I chuckled. "I don't think Rika needs any help with that."

"The mares will keep her trotting. It's how they enforce the ranks. It's also good exercise for her, but don't leave her out too long. Once she accepts the females, then introduce the males one at a time, starting with the gentlest." Mena jumped down from the fence.

"Rika's owner moved out of state, and we can't reach him," I mentioned as we walked back to the barn. "How can we figure out where her training went wrong?"

"It won't be easy," she said. "Since she's bolting every time she has a shot at freedom, the fear factor is consistent. It could be a sound or a smell, but odds are it's something that is a constant in her daily environment. Something she sees or senses like my jumper's gate. It could be a piece of equipment, something you do as part of her care routine, or even one of your brothers."

"I wish horses could talk."

"They do," Mena said, and smiled as she went over to Sali's stall. "Like this cutie here. You're just a big flirt, aren't you, girl?" Sali lowered her head to nuzzle Mena's neck. "See? She gives away free kisses to total strangers."

"Horses don't kiss." Gray wheeled in the barrow we used when we mucked out the stalls. "Are you guys done? I've got work to do."

Mena frowned at him. "Is it me, or is he this unfriendly to everyone?"

"It's him," I told her.

She dug her fingers into her back pocket, and produced one of her father's colorful business cards. On the back she jotted down a number and handed it to me.

"That's our home number, if you need to talk. Or if your brother ever gets over himself and wants to ask me out." She raised her voice. "I like going on trail rides, picnics and seeing movies, by the way."

"Thanks." I glanced at Gray, who looked like Rika had kicked him in the head again. "He's a little shy."

"That's okay. I'm not." She walked out of the barn.

I went to the door to watch her ride off, and after a minute my brother joined me. "There is something wrong with that girl," he told me.

"She says what she thinks. I like her." I held the business card up under his nose. "Are you getting over yourself, or should I sell this to you at a later date?"

"Shut up."

———

My new job kept me too busy to brood much over my problems. Each afternoon before the sun set I focused on inventorying the store's shelf stock and filling out the tally sheets, and then had my meal break. Jesse usually arrived right after that, and did his part by entering my counts into the computer. Once he'd gone through all the sheets, he'd bring out a bin from the storeroom and we'd tackle that together.

I did borrow one book from Mrs. Frost's shelves, one I had to keep in my backpack in case my brothers decided to search my room again. I'd never read Bram Stoker's *Dracula*, but I knew he had written a character in the story based on Abraham Van Helsing, a real nine-teenth-century vampire-hunter. Since Stoker hadn't even bothered to change his name, I was hoping to find out more about the first Van Helsing from the book.

I had very mixed feelings about Julian Hargraves's collection. Some of the books fascinated me, especially those with detailed illustrations of fantasy creatures, but others seemed a little silly. A few even made me angry.

"From the way they describe these dogs, they probably had rabies or some other kind of disease," I said to Jesse after I read a passage on hellhounds in a book about demonic animal possession. "So getting rid of them was a good thing. But I don't get why black cats had such a bad rep. It's just a fur color."

"Black is the color of night, the time when people sleep, and are at their most vulnerable," he told me. "It may be the reason mankind learned to control and use something as dangerous as fire. So they could light up the darkness."

"Okay, so black isn't anyone's favorite color, but why pick on cats?" I argued. "I bet it's just because they've never sucked up to humans the way dogs do."

He laughed. "Perhaps."

At home Trick brought down from the attic our small box of Christmas house decorations and put them out, which made the old farmhouse seem a little more festive. We never went all-out the way some families did during the holidays, but it was nice to see the old stockings hanging from the mantle, and the lighted wreath on our front door.

One night when I came home from work I saw something I didn't expect in one corner of our living room.

"There's a tree inside the house," I said to Gray, who had walked me home from the bus stop.

"I know, I went with Trick to the tree farm to get it." He sounded vaguely disgusted. "He wants us to help him decorate it tomorrow."

"Oh." I knew what Christmas trees were, naturally, but we'd never had one before this. "Is he going to make us go to church, too?"

"I don't do church." Gray trudged off to his room.

I went over to inspect the tree. At six feet tall it seemed like the right size, and it made the whole room smell like pine, which I also liked. Wedged in between some branches I found a little empty bird's nest, which charmed me. The bottom of the trunk sat in a big, dirt-filled metal bucket, which didn't make sense to me until I brushed back some of the dirt and found the tops of the tree's roots.

"It's a live tree," Trick said from behind me. "After the holidays we can take it outside and plant it."

"That sounds nice." I got up. "Why did you decide to put up a tree for Christmas this year?"

"I thought about it when you and Gray were younger, but we were usually moving during the winter holidays so the two of you wouldn't miss school." He reached out to pluck a piece of straw caught in a cluster of needles. "This is really the first year we have a permanent home."

"I didn't realize that," I said. Then, before I could stop myself, I asked, "Can we really afford it?"

A shuttered look came into his eyes. "Of course we can."

"Let me rephrase." This may not have been the best time, and I didn't know what I was going to say, but I was already halfway there. "Did you find a job yet?"

Trick regarded me as if I'd just confessed to moonlighting as a stripper, and then the light dawned. "You looked through the newspaper."

"Before you get mad, let me point out that Gray did the actual snooping," I advised him. "I'm pretty sure he's also applied for a job plowing fields at a strawberry farm."

My brother shook his head. "I need him here, especially when I...no."

"I'll let you talk to him about it." I took my first pay check out of my back pocket. "Here's my first contribution to the avoid-foster-care fund." I handed it to him. "If you're a smart shopper it should cover our groceries for a week."

"You're not going in foster care, either of you." He tried to give it back to me, and glared when I wouldn't take it. "I can take care of us, Catlyn."

"I never said you couldn't." I tried to sound cheerful. "Besides, you know how cold weather affects Grim's appetite. The horses may not be safe."

He tried going remote on me again. "I don't need your money. If I don't find work soon, I'll sell the Harley."

"I didn't know there was a huge market for cranky motorcycles that break down every other week." I gave him an innocent look. "Pardon me, my mistake."

"Classic Harleys always break down. It's part of their appeal." He sat down on the end of the couch and held my paycheck, looking at it as if he'd never seen one. "If I can't find a buyer for it, I'll sell it to a repair shop for parts."

"Okay." I knew how much it hurt him to say that. "So what happens when *that* money runs out? Do we sell Flash, or Jupe, or some of the new stock? How much do you think you can get for Sali, assuming you can pry her reins out of my white-knuckled hands?"

He didn't reply, and his expression grew bleak.

I went to sit beside him. "Look, Trick, Norman Rockwell might never have wanted to paint us, but we're still a family. I know how hard you've fought to keep us together. Let me and Gray help, at least until you find a job, or we fix the problem with Rika."

He gave my check one last glance before he folded it and put it in his pocket. "I'll pay you back every dime of this."

"I'm sure you will. You should also talk to Gray before he worries himself into two jobs." I smothered a yawn and stood. "I think it's time for me to turn into a pumpkin."

"Wait, there's something I wanted to show you." Trick took a folded flyer out of his pocket and handed it to me. On it was printed MISSING above a picture of a pale, dark-haired teenager. "Do you know this girl?"

At first I thought it was Sunny Johnson, until I read the information written under the grainy photograph. "Melissa Wayne. No, I've never heard of her." The name sounded vaguely familiar, though, and I studied the picture again. "Wait, no, I think I have seen her. She was in my Ceramics class. Everyone calls her Lissa; that's why I didn't make the connection." I looked at him. "What happened to her?"

"Two days ago her parents dropped her off at their church to help with the youth group's annual toy drive," Trick said. "She never made it to the meeting, and no one has seen her since."

Nine

The Sunday edition of the *Lost Lake Community News* ran a brief article on the front page about Melissa Wayne's disappearance, along with a tip line number to call with any information and an open invitation for the community to join a prayer vigil at the Wayne family's church.

"The article says the police recovered some evidence at the scene," I mentioned to Trick when we talked about it over breakfast. "They wouldn't give the reporter any details, though, so it must be bad."

"It's probably something they have to use for the prosecution." He took the classified section from the paper and glanced at Gray, who was staring down at his bowl. "Is it too lumpy, or are you feeling sick?"

Gray started to say something, looked at me, and then began eating his oatmeal.

I knew my brothers had already talked the day before about our financial situation, so it wasn't that. "I thought I'd work with Rika in the barn for an hour today. Any objections?"

"You can try, but if she gives you any grief, you put her back in her stall," my brother said. "Grayson, you keep an eye on them."

"What?" Blonde hair flew as Gray jerked up his head. "I have to stand there for an hour while she leads that nag in a circle? No way."

"I've got business in town, and no one works alone with that mare," Trick said flatly.

"No problem, I don't have to—" Before I could finish my sentence Gray got up, dumped his half-eaten oatmeal in the trash and dropped his bowl in the sink before he stomped out the back door. "Hmmmm. Maybe he got *all* the lumps this morning."

"It's all right." Now Trick got up and dumped his oatmeal. "I'll talk to him later." He went to the window and looked out at the barn. "Cat, I'd like you to do something for me."

"I'm not making breakfast for Grim," I told him. "If he doesn't want oatmeal, let him eat cold cereal."

He swung around to face me. "Don't get too attached to Rika."

"Sali is my best girl," I reminded him. "But I've got a big heart, and maybe in a year or two Rika will take second place. It's not like she's going anywhere, right? You're not going to sell her, so … oh, no." I realized what he meant. "You can't put her down. She just needs some time and TLC."

"I hope you're right, and she turns around," he said slowly. "But I can't sell a dangerous, aggressive horse, and I can't afford to keep one, either. The way she is now, she's worthless."

"What about her foal?" I demanded. "After it's born, it's going to need a mother."

"There are breeders in the area who keep nurse horses," he said, referring to mares who were bred every year so they would keep lactating, and provide milk for orphaned foals. "If we have to, we'll board the foal with one of them until it's weaned."

I knew what it was like to grow up without a mother. To deliberately kill a helpless baby's mother … "That's horrible."

"What if Rika loses it while she's with her foal, and ends up trampling it?" he countered. "It wouldn't be the first time something like that happened. How would you feel if you knew we could have prevented it, and didn't?"

I knew he was right, even if I didn't want to admit it. "Let me work with her in the mornings. Please. I won't get too attached. She deserves a chance, at least."

"Dr. Marks has to evaluate her after she foals," Trick said. "If her behavior is still the same, I'll have no choice.

As long as you understand and accept that, until then you can keep working with her." He picked up his keys. "I'll be back in a few hours."

Once Trick left I flew through my chores so I could get out to the barn and Rika. Naturally she wasn't happy to see me, and I knew my agitation would only make her more nervous, so I left her in her stall and began breaking down a bale of bedding.

Gray came out from the tack room and watched me for a minute. "He told you about Rika."

"Yes, he did." I shoved the pitchfork into the center of the bale. "I think he forgot we're supposed to be breeding horses, not killing them." When Gray took the pitchfork from me, I swiped at it. "You're messing with my therapy."

"You'll only give yourself blisters." He set the pitchfork to one side. "You knew that girl Melissa, right? She was in your art class."

He wanted to talk. I wanted to scream. "Yes, she was, and no, I didn't."

He kicked some loose straw back at the bale. "I know something about her disappearing."

My eyes widened. "You *what*?"

He looked up at the roof. "There was this old guy, and he fell on the sidewalk in front of the church, right after her parents left. She tried to help him. Then she just walked away with him."

"Gray, you saw it?"

"She dropped her purse. That's what the police found."

He swallowed hard. "So I should call that tip line, right? I can give them a description of the old guy."

I couldn't believe Gray had been an eyewitness to Melissa Wayne's kidnapping. "If you were there, why didn't you say something? Why didn't you call 911 immediately?"

"I wasn't there." His voice dropped low. "I dreamed about it, the night she went missing."

I was about to yell at him for making the most sick, tasteless joke I'd ever heard, but then I remembered something he'd said to me, something I wasn't supposed to remember. *My dreams come true.*

I had to force myself to play skeptic. "Why would you believe something you dreamed really happened?"

"Because my dreams come true," he said, in an eerie echo of my memory. "Not all the time, and sometimes they're all mixed up, but this one ... it felt like the real thing."

"If you tell them that you dreamed it, they'll never believe you." I thought for a minute. "You can make an anonymous call from a phone booth. Say you were driving by and didn't realize it was Melissa you saw until you read the paper this morning."

"I'll call from the pay phone at the gas station," he said. "But you can't tell Trick about this."

"Go." I pointed toward his truck. "If you don't go and call them, right now, I'll do it myself from the house phone. Then you can explain this to Trick and the sheriff."

"I knew I shouldn't have told you," he said, and tromped off.

I watched him from the barn door until his pickup disappeared down the road. "Idiot." I was so angry I could have kicked Rika in the head. My brothers and their obsession with secrecy had gotten completely out of control. What if this "old man" my brother had seen in his dream had already hurt Melissa, or taken her out of the state? If not for Gray being a coward, she might be back home with her parents.

I walked back to Rika's stall. "Sorry, girl, I'm cancelling manners class for today."

The mare put her head over the stall and looked at me with sad eyes.

"It sucks, I know." Without thinking I went over to give her a pat. "We'll try again tomorrow morning, and show those boys that they're wrong about you, and why are you doing that?" I stared as she nuzzled my palm, just as gently as Sali would. Her ears weren't laid back, she didn't nip me and she seemed as gentle as a lamb. "Did my other idiot brother give you a tranquilizer?"

Rika lowered her head and gave my shoulder an unmistakable, let-me-out nudge.

"I know I'm going to get grounded for this," I told her as I took her halter down and unlatched the stall door. "So when you kick me in the head, make sure you finished me off as soon as I drop."

Rika stood patiently as I put on her halter and attached the lead rope, and then politely shuffled out of the stall. She glanced at Sali before she lowered her head again.

I pushed up her head and looked into her eyes, which

appeared bright and normal. "Okay, you're not drugged." She could also see that the doors were open on either end of the barn, but didn't take a single step toward freedom. Slowly I released the rope, turning her loose, but she still didn't move. "Um, this is usually when you run to the other side of the farm."

As if she understood—and disagreed with—me, she snorted and waggled her head.

"Or not." I caught the rope and gave it a tug. "My mistake. So, how do you feel about walking outside with me? If you're good, I'll give you an apple cookie."

Rika perked up as soon as we emerged from the barn, but she didn't try to yank the rope out of my hand or buck or any of the other nonsense I'd come to expect from her. She stopped and waited as I unlatched the back pasture gate. I quickly stepped to one side, expecting her to knock me over to get to freedom, but she turned out as nice and polite as Sali would.

I closed the gate and stood watching as she trotted down on fence, had a good look around and then checked out the feed bucket before dipping her head to nibble on some grass.

"Why couldn't you do this when … " I stopped as a thought occurred to me. I couldn't remember a single time I'd ever been alone with Rika, except when Sali and I had ridden out to catch her. Which aside from a couple of visits from Dr. Marks and his daughter, had been the only times I'd ever seen her behave.

You know why she keeps running away.

"No. It can't be that simple." I grabbed the gate and went into the pasture, securing the latch before I faced the Arabian. I let her see the rope in my hands so that she knew I wasn't holding a treat to lure her before I whistled.

She came over to me, as if I'd called her to me a million times.

I still wasn't convinced. I wasn't going to climb on her back; although the books said pregnant mares could be ridden until they foaled, I couldn't assume she'd been saddle-trained.

But I can find out. I climbed over the fence and headed for the tack room. Rika came over as I perched my saddle on the fence and gave it a sniff.

"We'll try the blanket first," I told her as I stepped through the gate and approached her on her right side. Most horse owners believed the old myth that a rider should always keep to the left side, but Trick had taught me and Gray to regularly switch around so the horses would be comfortable being handled from all sides.

From the puzzled look Rika gave me she was also accustomed to being handled from the left, but she didn't fuss or move as I placed the blanket over her back.

I stepped back and went to grab my saddle. "If you keep this on, you get two apple cookies."

I saddled her the same way I would Sali; not being rough but not treating her like glass, either. When I reached under her belly she nickered a little, but that was all the protest she made.

I didn't buckle the girth strap, but straightened and stood back. "That's my favorite saddle on your back, and you're going to stand there all day with it on, aren't you?"

Rika lifted her head, and her ears flicked before she laid them back.

I glanced over my shoulder to see Gray's truck coming back up the drive. "Blast it, I thought he'd take longer."

Rika backed away from me, her muscles bunching as she pawed the ground and then wheeled around, sending the saddle and the blanket flying. She ran to the farthest end of the paddock, and trotted back and forth along the fence as if searching for a gate she could kick open.

Gray appeared on the other side of the fence. "Are you crazy? Trick told you not to work alone with her."

"That's the problem," I told him as I picked up the blanket and shook it out. "Did you call the police?"

"Yeah. I had to hang up because they were asking me too many questions." He gazed at the Arabian. "How did you get that saddle on her?"

"It's my saddle, so it only smells like me and Sali." I handed the blanket over the fence. "She likes girls. I imagine it's the other smells that are driving her crazy."

"What's smell got to do with it?"

"Everything." I retrieved my saddle and hoisted it over. "She isn't afraid of the other horses, or the barn, or anything on the farm. She's not scared of me or Mena, and she behaves whenever Dr. Marks is here. Rika isn't dangerous, Gray."

"Then why does she run away?" he pointed out.

"Simple. There are two things on this farm that terrify her." I looked up at him. "You, and Trick."

Ten

While I was riding the bus into town the next afternoon, I thought about everything I had to tell Jesse. So much had happened that I started running a mental list: Jesse and Mena had been right about Rika being afraid (of my brothers), Gray had psychic visions in his dreams (was that part of his Van Helsing finder ability? I needed to ask Jesse what he thought), and (if Gray was right) Melissa Wayne had not been grabbed outside her family's church, but had gone willingly with the kidnapper.

I also used the opportunity to read a little of *Dracula*, the novel I'd borrowed from the shop. I skipped through a long, droning introduction by some modern critic I'd never heard of to read the first page, which had been written as a journal entry. It was mostly a travelogue about traveling around Europe on a train. It seemed almost as boring as the intro, although I did smile when Jonathan Harker complained about the spiciness of a dish made with lots of paprika.

Someone sat down next to me, but by that time I was so caught up in the story that I didn't pay any attention until I heard a distinctive click.

I looked into Kari Carson's camera lens. "What happened to 'Hi, Cat, can I take your picture?'"

"Shoot first, worry about law suits later." She grinned and shifted position. "Plus you photograph like a Vogue cover girl, Youngblood."

I held up my book to block her from taking another picture. "Does that mean I can charge you a thousand dollars an hour?"

"No. What are you reading?" She cocked her head to see the front cover. "Ah, Bram Stoker, who never met a diary or letter he didn't like. I used to read that book whenever I couldn't sleep. Knocked me out better than a sedative. So anyway, how do you like being a working girl, in the non-prostitute sense of the term?"

I told her a little about my job, leaving out only the fact that Jesse Raven was my boyfriend and came every night to help me. I liked Kari, but I wasn't ready to confide all my secrets in someone who worked for a subversive underground newswire being secretly passed around our school.

She listened without comment until I mentioned the collection, and then she looked around the bus before she asked, "You know what happened in the cemetery last month, right?"

I thought for a minute. "I remember my brother saying someone vandalized a grave."

"That's the official story. Aka a complete lie." She unzipped her backpack and took out a plain spiral notebook, opening it before she handed it to me. "Seek made it the lead story for the winter break edition."

I read the headline. "Lost Lake has a grave-robber?" I put down the notebook. "Seriously?"

She nodded solemnly. "Whoever broke into the Hargraves tomb stole all three bodies inside. Now Mom and Pop had been there for like fifty years, so they were only skeletons, but they'd just had old Julian's funeral the day before. He was probably still pretty juicy."

"Oh, gross." I cringed. "Did you have to tell me that?"

"The public has the right to know all the gruesome details." As the bus stopped to pick up more passengers, she slid down in her seat and pulled her hood forward to conceal her face. In a lower voice, she said, "Seek and I are investigating the break-in. We thought it might be some kid pulling a really nasty prank, but so far this looks like an inside job."

I frowned. "I don't understand."

"Julian was the last of the Hargraves, you know. When they put him in there, they were supposed to close up the tomb for good." Kari pressed some buttons on her camera before she showed me the LCD screen. On it was an image of a huge marble tomb, the front of which stood open. "See the edges?" She pointed to them. "Bare marble. They were never sealed. Whoever stole the bodies just had to push in the front panel."

Something was wrong with the picture, but I couldn't tell what. "Did Seek run this photo in the Ledger?" I touched the notebook. When she nodded, I realized something. "Your boyfriend is the editor of the Lost Ledger?"

Kari winked. "I cannot confirm or deny that statement."

Which meant yes, I thought. "Can I show this to someone?"

"Sure, as long as you tell me what you find out." She took out a pen and wrote a phone number on the corner of one blank page. "I'll be home every morning through New Year's. Or come over to Tony's Garage the day before Christmas Eve." She looked up. "Oops, this is me." She reached over me to tug on the stop cord. "Don't work too hard, Youngblood. Santa's elves will picket you."

Kari's warning made me feel a pang of guilt; I hadn't given a single thought to what I would give my brothers for Christmas. Gray always gave us T-shirts, black for Trick and white for me, but he made up for his lack of imagination by recording Christmas movies for us all to watch. Trick always liked to surprise us with something special; last year he had found a beautiful black leather saddle for Gray, and had given me a gorgeous red and white fountain pen along with six bottles of fancy-colored inks.

My usual thing was to make a batch of Gray's favorite cookies and put a tin of them in a basket with a book, a mug and some hot cocoa mix. I did the same for Trick, except I made him an apple pie instead of cookies. Neither of them ever complained, but I wanted to do something different this year.

Then there was my dark boy. Jesse couldn't eat food, which ruled out baking, and since I'd handed over my paycheck to Trick I didn't have a lot of money to spend on a store-bought gift. I didn't even know if Jesse and his parents celebrated Christmas.

I stopped in front of the bookstore and glanced across the street. I'd never been inside the Junktique, and on impulse I crossed the street to look in the windows. The Johnsons displayed lots of little holiday-themed oddities, like Christmas tree salt and pepper shakers, and cookie jars shaped like snowmen and angels. I put up my hand to shield my eyes from the glare of the sun on the window, and saw Mrs. Johnson standing on the other side.

I dropped my hand, smiled uneasily and turned to go back to the bookstore.

"Catlyn." She came out and held the door open. "Would you like to come inside?"

"No, ma'am." That sounded so panicky I added, "Thank you, but I have to get to work." She looked so disappointed that I felt even worse. "Maybe just for a few minutes."

Mrs. Johnson followed me into the store. "Are you window shopping for any particular reason?"

"I might need a gift for a friend." I looked around the

shop, which was crammed with all sorts of old and interesting things. "He, uh, likes art."

"Come this way." She went around a big table stacked with vintage linens and led me to a wall with various old paintings. "The framed oils are rather expensive, but we have a few watercolors."

"They're very nice." I'd actually been thinking more along the lines of art supplies versus finished art.

"They are." She took out a rag and dusted the edge of one frame. "Did you have any classes with my daughter?"

The abrupt question flustered me. "Um, no, ma'am, I didn't."

"Sunny's very friendly. It's why she's so popular at school." She put away the rag and straightened one of the paintings. "Maybe you sat with her at lunch one day."

"I'm sorry, but I never met your daughter, Mrs. Johnson." I pretended to check my watch. "I should really be getting to work."

"I know she told her friends where she was going that day," she continued, as if she hadn't heard me. "They won't admit it because they're afraid of getting in trouble, but they know. I can see it." She turned to me. "You have the same look in your eyes, Catlyn."

"Nancy." The man I'd seen arguing with her near the bus stop appeared and took Mrs. Johnson's hand. "We should close up and go home early tonight. This young lady can come back another time." He gave me a direct look.

"Of course I can." I forced a smile. "Thank you for showing me the paintings, Mrs. Johnson."

"Anytime, dear." Sunny's mother wandered off, leaving me alone with the man.

"I'm Catlyn Youngblood," I said. "I work across the street."

"You're the girl Martha hired, of course. I'm Nancy's husband, Jack." He sighed. "I'm sorry if my wife frightened you. She's … not herself."

"You don't have to apologize, sir," I assured him. "I shouldn't have bothered her."

"Let me walk you out." As he did, he looked back a few times, and as soon as I left he turned the OPEN sign over to CLOSED and pulled down the door blind.

I hurried across the street and let myself into the bookstore. Only when I'd locked the door behind me did I let out the breath I'd been holding. "No more window shopping," I told myself as I went to take care of the alarm.

———

The unnerving encounter with Sunny's mother left me with a jumpy feeling I couldn't shake. I didn't understand why at first, until I took my tally sheets into Mrs. Frost's office and switched on the computer. That reminded me of the day in the school media center, when Barb Riley had sabotaged one of the computers and almost got me in trouble for it. At the time I hadn't known how disturbed

Barb was. Seeing me with Aaron Boone on Halloween night had somehow pushed her over the edge, and she'd attacked, almost killing Boone and Jesse in the process.

The way Mrs. Johnson had talked to me about Sunny had made her sound a lot like Barb when she'd talked about Boone. I was no shrink, but even I could see that Sunny's mother was seriously losing her grip on reality.

Although Jesse had been taking care of the computer data entry part of my job, I needed something to focus on, and so I sat down and got started on the first tally sheet. Working with the numbers helped me stop thinking about the dreadful events of Halloween night, and I decided to keep working until Jesse showed up.

An hour later I finished entering the counts from the last sheet, but still, no Jesse.

He told me that he might not be able to come every night, I thought as I went to the fridge and retrieved my dinner. *His parents must have wanted him to stay in tonight.*

Seeing Jesse almost every day had spoiled me, and I refused to sulk. I called home to check in with Trick, who told me that from now on either he or Gray would be picking me up at the store.

"I haven't had any problems walking from the store to the bus stop," I reminded him. "I'm also not stupid or careless."

My brother wouldn't budge. "This is how we're going to do it until they find those girls."

Once I tidied the office I went back to the storeroom

to look at the bins. I really didn't want to work on the collection by myself, but I was already two days ahead of schedule on the shelf counts.

I walked back out and stood over the tunnel hatch. To avoid getting caught Jesse and I had been staying in the store; I hadn't been back down in the tunnels since that first night.

He never told me I couldn't go by myself, I reasoned, and thought of the storage closet in Jesse's underground vault. *Maybe I can see what sort of art supplies he already has, so I'll know what he doesn't need.*

I took care to go down the ladder slowly—the last thing I needed to do was fall and knock myself out—and followed the tunnels in the direction I thought would lead me to Jesse's vault room. To my surprise I didn't get lost or take a wrong turn; my feet seemed to know the way there.

Once I walked inside Jesse's work room, I felt immediately better. I could almost feel him there, as if he'd spent so much time in that place that he'd left behind an imprint on every object in the room. Even picking up the jacket he'd left draped on the back of his desk chair gave me a little thrill, especially when I held it up to my nose and smelled the sweet-spicy scent he'd left on the material.

"When you start sniffing his clothes," I told the shelf of carved birds, "you know you're stupid in love."

I had forgotten one thing: the door to the storage closet was locked. For the first time I also realized how strange that was. If no one but his parents and Sheriff

Yamah knew the tunnels existed, why did he have to lock up anything down here?

"It's just a closet," I told my overactive imagination. "Not Bluebeard's secret room of ex-wives."

I looked through the drawers and cubbyholes of his desk, but didn't find a key. Then on a hunch I searched the pockets of his jacket, and found a ring of keys, all the same size and brand.

"Here we go." I took them over to the storage closet and began trying them one after the other, until I found the right one and popped the lock.

"Catlyn?" Jesse's voice echoed down the tunnel.

"I'm in here," I called back. I took off the padlock, but found the door knob jammed. "Not having much luck snooping through your stuff, though." I rattled the knob, working it back and forth. "This place is like an underground Fort Knox."

I felt a rush of air behind me, and then a cool hand covered mine.

"I'm sorry I'm late." He drew my hand up to his mouth and kissed it. "What are you looking for?"

"I can't tell you." I grinned up at him. "You'll have to wait until Christmas morning." Finally I felt the knob turn all the way. "What have you got in here, anyway?"

"Catlyn, don't—"

A light came on inside the closet as the door opened, and then I saw it wasn't a closet at all, but another room that was the same size as his work room.

A crowded room, I thought as I looked at the long

rows of painted canvases leaning against the walls. He had installed wide shelves on the walls to hold more canvases, although these paintings were stacked face-down in tall piles. The shelves marched all the way up to the ceiling.

"They are not very good," Jesse said, and took my arm. "Why don't we go back to the shop?"

He sounded upset, and I was almost willing to believe that he was simply being shy about his art. But something told me not to go. "What's in those crates over there?"

When he didn't answer, I pulled away and went to look inside.

Birds, carved out of wood, filled the crate. Some had been painted, others left bare, but they looked just like the birds on the shelf in the other room.

I saw something behind the crates, and walked between two of them to a big steel cabinet. "Is this where you keep your supplies?" I was almost afraid to look inside.

"Catlyn, it's not what you think."

I made myself open the door, and caught a book that fell out as soon as I did. It fell open in my hands to reveal Jesse's elegant handwriting covering both pages. I closed it and went to put it back on one of the shelves, which like the others was crammed with more journals. I knew it took me six months to completely fill a journal; Jesse had finished hundreds.

Maybe that's why there's so much. I came out to look at him. "How long have you been storing things down here?"

"Too long."

I didn't understand why he sounded so disgusted. "Jesse, why didn't you want me to see any of this?"

"I don't paint or carve anymore. It upset my parents." He wouldn't look at anything but me. "I still keep a journal, but that isn't … part of this."

"But this is amazing." Why would Sarah and Paul object to what he'd done? He must have spent years filling this room. "What have you been painting, anyway?"

"Nothing of importance."

"Well, I still want to see." I went over to one shorter stack and picked up the canvas on top, turning it over. It showed Jesse's parents performing their circus act. "I've seen this one before." I looked at the next painting, which was the exact same scene, as was the next, and the one after that.

I stopped looking through the paintings after seeing ten more copies of the same scene. "Jesse, are they all like this?" He nodded. "Why would you paint the same over and over?"

"It is something else we share with vampires," he said slowly. "We sometimes become obsessed."

"You mean, like obsessive-compulsive?"

He nodded. "Those who attacked and changed us had caves filled with gold and jewels and other treasures they'd taken from the humans they'd killed. Ordinary human thieves would simply sell everything they'd stolen, but not the vampires. It was as if they could never take enough to satisfy their strange need for it."

I studied the racks of paintings again. "And this is your version of that."

"I've always been able to overcome a compulsion and stop myself after a time. But sometimes"—he gestured at the paintings—"sometimes it takes many months."

I walked out of the room and gently closed the door. Then I looked down at the other keys on the ring. "Are there more rooms like this?"

"No. Once I conquer the compulsion, I destroy whatever I've accumulated." He eyed the door. "I stopped painting last summer, and I had planned to burn these." He shook his head. "Since meeting you I haven't thought about them at all. Until you reached for the door, I'd forgotten they were there."

"You never have to hide anything from me." I looked around his work room before I met his gaze. "If this happens again, tell me. Maybe I can help."

"You have already." He touched my cheek. "Nothing has taken hold of me since the night we met. Being with you has changed my life."

I wanted to believe him, but I remembered how many times he had come back to the farm, as if he couldn't stay away. "What if I'm your latest compulsion?"

"I have considered that," he admitted. "I know that if I were only obsessed with you, nothing could keep me away. I'd have no choice but to spend every waking hour with you." He picked up my hand and pressed it against his heart. "I never enjoyed any of my obsessions. I've feared and despised them, and fought them until I finally freed myself. You were nothing like that. From that first night you were a part of me, the other half of my heart."

"You know I feel the same about you." I brought his hand to my heart. Whenever we touched, our heartbeats changed rhythm, as they did now, until they beat together in sync. "I love all of you, Jesse. The good, the bad, even the obsessive-compulsive."

He kissed me. "There is something I wanted to show you tonight."

I went with him back into the tunnel passage, where he led me down to the very end. There the walls widened into a room filled with mechanical equipment and another ladder leading up to a grate.

Jesse jumped up to the top of the ladder, pushed the grate aside and then turned to beckon to me. "It's up here."

I followed him up through the opening into a narrow, cylindrical space made of rough wood. He pushed against one spot, which swung out like a hatch. As I stepped through, I saw we'd been inside the hollowed-out trunk of an enormous black oak. It had been chopped off about six feet from the ground, and used to form part of an archway engulfed in vines. Big hedges flanked a stone path that wound around overgrown flower beds before it branched off in different directions, some toward the lake and others into the woods.

I looked around. "What is this place?"

"It's called the Jester's Maze." Jesse guided me over to

a small shrine made of stone and shells. Inside the shrine stood the statue of an old-fashioned clown riding backward on a big white horse. "That is Stanas, one of the circus performers who came over to America with us. He built the tunnels under the town for my parents. He created this maze, too, in secret, as a tribute to the girl he loved." Jesse gestured to another shrine across from the clown's. A delicate bower of shell-flowers protected a sculpture of a girl holding an armful of wildflowers. The girl seemed to be smiling at the clown.

"That's so sweet. Did they get married here?"

"No." His expression turned sad. "She was killed during the attack on our caravan."

"How awful." I glanced at the hedges. "He must have worked on this a long time."

"Years. The paths go from the gardens to the woods and keep going for miles." He crouched down to brush some dead leaves from the statue. "When my parents discovered what he had done, Stanas told them that whoever solved his maze and found its heart would discover a great treasure he'd hidden there. But no one ever has."

"Have you looked for it?"

"A few times," he admitted as he stood, and his expression turned rueful. "I've never been able to locate the center on my own. Perhaps there is none, and Stanas had the last laugh on us all."

"That seems like a lot of trouble to go to, just for a practical joke." The temptation to follow the path into the maze was almost irresistible, but I imagined the phone in the store ringing off the hook. "Come on, we have a bunch of creepy old books to catalog."

Eleven

As we worked our way through another bin of Julian Hargraves's books, I told Jesse about what had happened over the weekend.

"My parents are very concerned about these missing children," he mentioned. "My father and I checked some of the unoccupied houses in town tonight. That is why I was so late."

"Gray told me that he dreamed of Melissa Wayne being abducted." I related the details of what he'd said and how I'd forced him to report it anonymously. "Do you know if the sheriff has any idea what happened to these girls?"

"James believed the Johnson girl was a runaway, but now that the Waynes' daughter has vanished, he is not as convinced." Jesse frowned at a book he'd taken out of the bin. "This will not open."

"Don't try to force it. The pages may be stuck together." I looked at the book, which had unmarked covers and a leather binding that looked older than it felt. "No title. Okay." Gently I ran my fingers around the edges. "This isn't paper. It's some kind of plastic."

"Is it a bookend?"

"I don't think so." I felt a seam at the bottom and turned it over, locating a tab. When I tugged it the entire bottom came off. "It's a book safe."

"What is it safe for?"

"Not that kind of safe. The kind you keep valuable stuff in." I reached in and pulled out a tissue-wrapped package, which I carefully opened to reveal another, smaller book. "Hmmmm. Why would you hide a book inside a book?"

"It's not a book." Jesse picked up the smaller edition and opened it to show me the writing on the pages. "It's a journal."

I got up and looked inside the bin. "There are more of them in here."

We unloaded the bin, which contained twelve more book safes, all with journals hidden inside.

"Julian wrote these; he signed his name inside the covers." Jesse put them in order by the date of the first entry. "He began writing these two years ago."

"Should we read them?" I thought of how I would

feel if someone had found my journals, and felt a pang of guilt. "Or maybe we should put them back."

"I don't think Julian would have any objections." Jesse opened the last journal, which was half-blank, and skimmed through it until he found the final entry. "He stopped writing them last October." He read the page. "He was very ill. His assistant thought he was dying." He frowned. "He didn't want to go to the hospital. He fired the assistant for calling his doctor to the house."

"No one likes to go to the hospital," I reasoned as I picked up the first journal. "Maybe this is why he left the collection to Mrs. Frost. He didn't trust anyone else."

"Julian was a devoted recluse," Jesse said. "He likely didn't know anyone else."

The first words written in the earliest journal weren't in English, so I showed him the page. "Do you know what language this is?"

"It's German. He quoted a line from Gottfried Bürger's poem 'Lenore.'" He met my gaze. "In English it says, 'The dead ride quick at night.'"

"Wait a minute." I got up and went to my backpack, and brought the book I'd been reading to the table. After I flipped through the pages, I found the passage I recalled. "Bram Stoker quoted almost the same line in his book. See?" I pointed to the page.

Jesse compared them. "They are the same line. The English is different because Julian used the Ayres translation, but Stoker quoted Rossetti's."

"You know a lot about this poem."

"When I was human, Gottfried Bürger's ballads were very famous. Some considered them the finest ever written in German." He hesitated, and added, "Just after we were changed, my parents read everything they could find about vampires. Some scholars believed Bürger witnessed or learned of a vampire attack in a graveyard, which inspired him to write 'Lenore.'"

"Supposedly Stoker did the same thing." Seeing the line from the novel written in the dead man's journal was just too much of a coincidence for me, though. "Is it possible that Julian knew about you and your parents?"

"My parents and I have never had any personal contact with the Hargraves family," he told me. "They were not our people, so they were never included in our circle of trust."

"Maybe Julian found out about you anyway," I said. "He lived here all his life, which was pretty long, and there are things you can't hide. Like the fact that you and your parents don't age. If anyone would have noticed, it would have been him."

He looked worried now. "He did live here more than a century."

"I think we need to read these journals and find out what he knew." I checked my watch. "You'll have to do the reading part. I can't risk sneaking them home, and besides, Gray will be here to pick me up in ten minutes." I explained how Trick had vetoed me taking the bus home.

"Good," Jesse said, surprising me. "I have been worried about you walking to the bus stop at night."

"You've been standing on top of buildings watching over me," I reminded him as I put the journals back in the bin. "There isn't a girl in this town as safe as—" A hammering sound from the front of the shop interrupted me. "Oh, wonderful, he's early."

I went to the front of the store, but the person banging on the door wasn't Gray. It was Mrs. Johnson.

My steps slowed as I saw how wild she looked, but I forced a smile and walked up to the door. "Mrs. Johnson, hi."

"Open this door," she demanded, jerking on the handle. "Now."

"I'm sorry, ma'am, but I can't let anyone in the store." I took a few steps back and glanced at the phone. "Why don't I call your husband? I'm sure he's worried about you."

That seemed to calm her down. "That won't be necessary." She turned and went to a little station wagon parked at the curb and drove off in it.

I retreated to the back of the store. "That was the mother of one of the missing girls," I told Jesse. "She thinks I know something about it, and she's a little crazy, but she's gone now."

"You handled it very well." He kissed my brow and picked up the bin. "I will read through these tonight. Don't leave the store until you see your brother's car."

After Jesse left with the journals, I put away my paperwork and went around to shut off the lights. Then I stood by the front door and watched for Gray, and when I saw his headlights I set the alarm and let myself out.

A blur rushed at me from one side, and as I saw the hands reaching for my neck something hot and angry billowed up inside me. I brought up my arm and knocked away the hands before I grabbed my attacker's upper arms and shoved as hard as I could.

Mrs. Johnson went down on her backside and slid four feet down the sidewalk. She scrambled back up and shrieked, "Where is Sunny? Tell me!"

"I don't know." As she came at me again, I made a gliding movement to one side, circling around her. How I did that, I didn't know—my body was calling the shots, not me. "Mrs. Johnson, please, stop."

She turned around, panting now. "I'll make you tell me." Her hands curled into fists. "I'll beat it out of you."

"No, ma'am, you won't." Gray stepped between us, and caught Mrs. Johnson's wrists as she tried to hit him. "You leave my sister alone now."

The woman stared up at him, and then collapsed against him, sobbing hysterically. Gray glanced at me. "Go inside and call the sheriff, Cat."

———

It only took Sheriff Yamah two minutes to arrive at the store, but by then Gray had managed to calm down Sunny's mother. He led her to his patrol car, and locked her in the back before he came to talk to us.

I briefly described the strange way Mrs. Johnson had been acting since meeting me, and how she had tried to get into the store earlier. "I don't know why she thinks I know something, but I honestly don't, Sheriff," I added. "I've never even met Sunny."

"Nancy's been under a terrible strain," he said, glancing at the patrol car. "I'll take her home and have a talk with Jack." He turned to Gray. "I appreciate you taking care of this."

Gray nodded, and then walked with me to his truck. "You okay?"

"Yeah." I wondered if the complete calm I felt was my own form of hysteria. "Thanks for saving me as usual."

"She won't give you any more trouble," he said, as if she were nothing more than another bully at school.

No one ever picked on me after Gray had a talk with them, and now he'd done the same thing with Mrs. Johnson. He'd confided in me about his dreams; maybe he could do other things. "How do you know she won't?"

"I just do." He got in and started up the truck. "You'd better tell Trick about this."

Yet another good reason for my big brother to make me quit my job; I'd been attacked by the grief-crazed owner of the shop across the street. I slumped back against my seat. "Do I have to?"

"If you don't," he warned, "the sheriff will."

Fortunately when we got home Trick was asleep, and the next morning he left before I woke up. I made my own breakfast before I tackled my chores, and when the housework was done I went out to the barn to talk to Gray.

I saw two box fans whirring just outside the end stall

that Trick had mucked out and sprayed down the previous morning. The strong smell of varnish made me cover my nose as I got close to the stall and looked in.

My brother wasn't putting down new bedding, but was swiping a wide paint brush back and forth over the wall panels. "Whew. Can't you wait until spring to do that?"

"Not unless you want to foal Rika outside." He bent to dip the brush into the tray of clear varnish he had sitting on a stool. "We can't keep the wood clean unless it's sealed."

I picked up a bottle of Tek-trol, which we used to disinfect the stalls every couple of months. "Good idea." I saw that along with the bedding he'd cleared everything out of the stall, including the feed bucket. "Are we going to starve her, too?"

"Trick doesn't want anything in here when she delivers," he told me. "It's to protect the foal from bacteria until he nurses for a day or two. And don't put any fresh bedding in here until we know Rika is ready to deliver."

"We should get a foal alarm," I said, remembering a little electronic kit that included a sensor that hung from the mare's tail, which sent a signal to a monitor the owner kept in their office or home. Even with an alarm, it wasn't going to be easy. "The vet said there's like a dozen mares foaling this month. What if he can't get to us, and we have to do this on our own?"

"Then we do it." Gray set down the brush and took the bandanna from his back pocket to wipe the sweat from his face. "She'll be all right."

"This is her first time foaling," I reminded him. "She's not going to know what to do. Neither do any of us."

"Breeding means foaling." He hesitated before he added, "That show girl stopped by this morning. She said she'd come over and help."

My brows rose. "That show girl? Are you referring to Mena, your arch-enemy?"

He moved his shoulders. "She's okay. For a pushy girl who think she knows everything about horses."

"I'm pretty sure she does, actually. She also seems to like you a lot." I observed his lack of reaction. "You should feel flattered. Not that many people like you."

"I'm not interested."

Oh, yes, you are, I thought. "I was going to make a big batch of meatballs and sauce to freeze for future meals. I can leave some in the fridge for you guys to have for dinner tonight."

"I'm tired of pasta," my brother complained. "Trick overcooks it so much it tastes like mush, even with your sauce. Anyway, he was going to grill something tonight."

"Make something else, then," I suggested. "Heat up the sauce and meatballs in a pan, put them on hoagie rolls with some provolone cheese, and you've got meatball subs. Versus eating whatever Trick turns into charcoal on the grill."

"Thank you," he said, and he meant it.

"No problem." I decided to take advantage of his improved mood. "Can I ask you something?" He gave me a wary look before he nodded. "Last night, when Mrs.

Johnson jumped me, did you see what happened? I mean, what I did to her?"

"You didn't do anything wrong," he said. "You didn't hurt her."

"The thing is, I've never been in a fight," I lied. I had been, with Barb Riley, but I wasn't supposed to remember that. "I didn't know what to do. So she should have been able to beat me into the sidewalk. Only she didn't, because I pushed her away."

"You were defending yourself."

"Gray, I pushed her so hard she almost ended up on the next block. I'm not that strong." I saw him avert his eyes. "Am I?"

He shrugged. "It was probably the adrenaline."

"I also moved so fast she never laid a hand on me. Is that adrenaline, too?" I waited, but he didn't say anything. "Okay. What if the adrenaline kicks in again and I hurt someone?"

He gave me a strange look. "Do you want to?"

"No."

"Then you won't." He went back to varnishing.

I wanted to hit him, but as angry as I was I probably would have knocked him over to the next farm. "You know, every time you do something stupid, I stand up for you. I explain things for you. I've probably kept you from being grounded for like half your life. And if you've forgotten, I even helped you with the weird dream thing the other night. So how can you just ignore me like this?"

He dropped the brush and turned on me. "You're

strong because you've been riding since you could walk. You move fast for the same reason. Last night that lady scared you, and you reacted. Neither of you got hurt. So now you know you'll be okay in a fight." Before I could say anything, he glared. "That's all I can tell you. Which you could have figured out on your own if for once in your life you'd use your brains instead of running your mouth."

I swallowed hard. "You're not supposed to yell at me. House rules."

A crash outside the stall startled both of us. Gray's expression changed, and he grabbed me, shoving me behind him. I stumbled and almost hit the wet-varnished wall but caught myself in time. I was about to yell back at him when I looked over his shoulder and saw Rika rearing just outside the stall. Behind her I saw the remains of her stall door, lying in pieces on the floor where she'd kicked it out.

Rika eyed Gray and made an awful screeching sound as she reared again, this time bringing her hooves against the side of the stall.

I started forward. "It's okay, girl. I'm okay." When Gray tried to stop me, I shrugged him off. "She isn't going to attack me. *You're* the one she wants to trample."

I eased out of the stall, talking in a low, soft voice as I approached her. Once she focused on me, she stopped attacking the stall and put herself between me and Gray.

"Come on, girl." I took hold of her halter and tugged her toward the end of the barn. "Let's both get some fresh air." Out of the corner of my eye I saw Gray starting to follow us. "No, don't get near her. Stay in the barn. I'll be right back."

On some level Rika had decided to trust me, because once we emerged from the barn she didn't try to jerk free or run. I put her in the bathing pen and gave her a minute while I looked her over. I didn't see any injuries from her tantrum in the barn, but once she seemed more at ease I felt her legs and belly.

"You make a great bodyguard," I told her as I went around her front, checking her mouth and shoulders. "But in a fight with the barn, honey, the barn usually wins."

Her belly still hung low with the foal, and I didn't see any show of blood or fluids that would indicate she'd aggravated herself into delivering early. We'd still have to keep an eye on her—or I would, I mentally corrected myself. As far as I was concerned only I was going to handle the Arabian.

When I went back into the barn Gray met me at the door. "She's all right, and I don't think it affected the foal. We should call Dr. Marks, though, and see if he wants to take a look at her anyway."

"I've never heard of a horse getting in the middle of shouting match." He shook his head as he surveyed the damage she'd caused. "You really think it's me?"

"You, or she hates the smell of varnish." I went over and picked up what was left of her stall door. "God, look at this. If you hadn't been inside the birthing stall, she might have killed you."

"Why?" Gray demanded. "I've never hit her, or hurt

her, or even yelled at her. Why would she think I was going to? I wasn't even in her stall."

I went still. "That's it. She thought you were going to hurt me."

He measured the distance between the stalls. "No way. From that angle, she couldn't even see us."

"No," I said thoughtfully. "But she could hear you yelling at me."

Twelve

Trick arrived home from his job hunting just as Dr. Marks finished examining Rika, and after getting a brief explanation from me spoke to the vet.

"She has some minor bruising, but the foal wasn't injured, and I don't think we're looking at an early delivery." He came out of the pen and nodded toward the barn. "She caused a lot of damage in there. I'd like to know what got her that agitated."

What he meant was, he wanted to know what Gray and I had done to her. I would have told him my theory, but I wasn't sure he'd believe me.

"It was my fault, sir," Gray said. "My sister and I were working in the barn, and I shouted at Cat."

Dr. Marks actually chuckled. "Horses don't care for people yelling at them or around them, but I don't think

Rika would bat an eyelash over it. Old Man Hargraves did nothing but yell at his horses."

"I didn't buy her from Mr. Hargraves," Trick said.

"Not directly, you didn't," the vet agreed. "When Old Julian got sick he boarded out his horses; when he passed away his estate manager let the stable owners make offers. Doug Palmer bought her, and was probably planning to use her as a brood mare, but after he lost his stallions he gave up, sold out and moved back up north."

"Sir, what happened to Mr. Palmer's stallions?" I asked.

The vet's expression darkened. "Some lunatic drifter got into his barn one night and used a knife on them. By the time Doug went out the next morning, five had bled to death. The other two died a day later."

The thought of someone killing horses just for fun made me want to throw up. "Was Rika hurt?"

Dr. Marks shook his head. "Whoever did it wasn't interested in the mares." He looked at Gray. "You might want to search the stalls and see if there are any snakes hiding in the bedding. That might be what caused this. Oh, and wear protective gloves in case you run into a coral snake or a pygmy rattler."

Trick walked the vet back out to his car while I helped Gray clean up the last of the mess in the barn.

"She really did a number on this." He sorted out a couple boards that were still mostly intact. "There's not enough left to even cobble it back together."

"We can take the door off the birthing stall," I said.

"It's the same size. I'm sorry I got in your face before and made you yell. You're right, I don't always think things through, and I should."

"I wasn't exactly using my intellect." He dumped the wood into the barrow. "Man. I never saw a horse go ballistic like that."

Trick came back in, stomping mad. "Nice work, you two. Tell me why I shouldn't ground you both until New Year's."

"Um, you can't do everything by yourself," I pointed out. "Sali and Flash would miss us terribly. Also, it's almost Christmas, and we're really sorry."

After I nudged him Gray said, "Yeah. Sorry, bro."

"This isn't funny, Catlyn. Both of you could have been trampled." Trick turned his evil eye on Gray. "And you. Whenever I leave here, I trust you to look after your sister, not put her in danger."

Gray looked prepared to start yelling again. "Oh, is that what I'm doing?"

Whatever they weren't saying hung between them, big and ugly, and for once it didn't annoy me. Not when it made them look like they hated each other.

"You know, we never got to decorate that tree in the house." My brothers didn't say anything, so I added, "I wouldn't mind taking a break and stringing some popcorn. How about you guys? We could play some Christmas music, only we don't have any. I know, we could sing some carols. Ah, do we know any carols?"

Trick was the first to quit the brother glaring contest. "I'm not singing, but I can decorate."

"Do we get to eat some of this popcorn?" Gray wanted to know.

We left the barn open to air, and I sent my brothers ahead to the house so I could lead Rika from the pen to the pasture where the others were grazing. I knew Trick would be watching from the kitchen window as I turned her out, and I was glad she behaved as nicely as she had the day Gray left me alone with her.

I didn't trust my brothers alone for too long, so I went to the house and got busy making the popcorn in the kitchen. I hadn't given much thought to what else we could use for decorations, but when I brought the pan of popcorn out to the living room I found Trick unpacking some ornaments from one of the boxes we'd used for moving.

"We had a secret stash of Christmas tree stuff?" I asked as I set down the pan and surveyed the brightly colored globes. "Pretty."

"Mom had a tree for us every year," Gray told me, and then glanced at Trick. "You were too little to remember it."

Trick produced a glittery star. "Gray, this goes on top. Cat, there's a sewing kit in there you can use for the popcorn."

The way we muddled through the tree decorating would have been funny, if anyone had felt like laughing. We had ornaments but no hangers for them, so Trick had to unbend and rebend a few dozen paper clips to serve as replacements. Gray decided to test an old string of lights he found and in the process tripped a breaker, shutting off all the power to the front room. Stringing popcorn, I discovered, was possibly the most boring holiday activity ever invented.

The tree only added to the joy by shedding needles every time we touched it, until a small pile formed around the base. But despite our lack of decorating prowess, my brothers and I finished the job, and stood back to admire our handiwork.

Trick frowned. Gray didn't say anything.

It was up to me, then. "That is the saddest-looking Christmas tree I've ever seen."

"It's not so bad." Trick reached out to adjust one of my uneven, pitiful-looking popcorn strings. "It looks ... "

"Dismal?" I suggested helpfully. "Depressing?"

"Dead," Gray put in. He demonstrated by grasping one of the branches and running it through his fingers, and then letting the needles fall onto the pile on the floor. Not a single needle was left on the branch.

Trick bent down and checked the dirt in the bucket. "Bone-dry. Didn't you guys water it?"

Gray lifted one shoulder. "You never told me to."

"Me, either." I saw one of the ornaments sliding off a sagging branch. "Uh-oh."

The ball fell to the floor. As we watched, a tiny shower of needles rained down on top of it.

"I think we killed the living Christmas tree." A giggle escaped me, and I clapped a hand over my mouth before I offered a muffled, "Sorry."

"I don't think it's funny." Trick sounded stern, but his lips twitched. "I paid fifty dollars for this thing, and now it's just one big tumbleweed."

Gray studied it. "Maybe it was dead when we got it."

"It could be a Christmas tree scam," I said hopefully.

"After the holidays we could chop it up and resell it as firewood," Gray said.

"That's a good idea," I said. "I mean, it's already been seasoned, right?"

Trick started laughing, and it had been so long since I'd heard that deep, wonderful sound that it set me off. Gray resisted for another thirty seconds before he joined in, too.

Finally I caught my breath and wiped my eyes. "This is the best Christmas present ever," I told Trick.

He gave me a skeptical look. "A dead tree is all it takes to make you happy?"

"No." I smiled at him and Gray. "But you guys do."

———

That afternoon at the store I found a note waiting for me on Mrs. Frost's desk blotter. Jesse hadn't signed it, but I recognized his hand writing, as well as the meaning of the one line he had written:

You should come and see the paintings as soon as you can.

I put down the note and gnawed at my bottom lip. I wasn't crazy about going into the tunnels while it was still daylight, but Jesse wouldn't have left a note if it wasn't important. To cover myself, I called home.

"I'm going to take my dinner break early and use it to do some Christmas shopping," I told Trick. "I won't be long, but I didn't want you to worry."

"Stay right around the shop," he said. "Eat something, and be sure to get back before dark."

"I'll only be an hour," I promised.

I turned off the store lights, mainly so Sheriff Yamah would assume I wasn't working if he drove by, and then went down through the hatch. I didn't know what I'd been expecting when I walked into the work room, but it wasn't to see Jesse sitting at his desk and reading one of Julian's journals.

"What are you doing here?" I said. "The sun hasn't set; shouldn't you still be on the island?"

"I spent the night in the vault." He rose and came to give me a hug. "Aren't you pleased to see me?"

"I'm always happy to see you," I assured him, "but where do your parents think you are?"

"Here. I told them I wanted some time alone. They believe I am still pining for you." His smile faded as he held up one of Julian's journals. "You were right. Over the years Julian did notice that my parents and I were not growing older. He decided ten years ago to find out why."

All the breath went out of me. "Oh, no."

"He frequently referenced his 'findings,' as he called

them, which apparently were the facts, dates, places, and every other bit of information about us that he could learn," Jesse said. "At first he secretly watched us himself, from a distance, and then as he grew older and frailer he hired men to follow us."

I couldn't believe it. "So he knew everything."

"Not precisely. Some of the conclusions that he drew from his findings were wrong, such as the nature of our affliction." He opened the journal to a passage he had marked, and handed it to me to read.

The boy and his parents never eat or drink, so they must have evolved past the need for nourishment, or they are subsisting on some energy source unknown to me. Since they are always acquiring new cattle and horses, and those are the only living things they will tolerate in their presence, I believe the answer lies with how they are using the animals. I have ordered some books on animal ritual sacrifices and their effectiveness. I am also searching for any literature on the transfer of life energy and souls from one being to another.

"He thought you were sacrificing cows for their souls?" I shuddered. "What a nasty mind."

"There's more." Jesse took the journal from me and added it to the pile on his desk. "He knew about us."

"Us? As in you and me?" When he nodded, my eyes widened. "How?"

"Julian sent his assistant to watch the old manor house. He knew I often went there while I was out riding. He assumed—correctly—that I wanted privacy." He caressed my cheek with the backs of his fingers. "The assistant saw you when I brought you there. He assumed you were an immortal, too, and that we were indulging in some sort of mystical courtship. From the way he describes it, he believed that we were some sort of Romeo and Juliet."

In a way, I guessed, we were. "Did he think my brothers and I were sacrificing cows?"

"Julian never discovered who you were or where you lived," Jesse assured me. "He ordered his assistant to take photos of you, but the one night that he tried, Prince got loose and scared him away."

I remembered that night only too well; Jesse had gotten stranded at the old practice barn. "That's why Prince ran. He wasn't spooked. He was chasing off a peeping Tom." I stared at the journal. "The nosy old man almost got you killed, and for what? Just to write a bunch of nonsense in his journals?"

Jesse picked up another journal. "He wrote about that as well." He hesitated before handing it to me. "It's on the third page."

I flipped past the first pages and began reading.

Time is slipping away faster than ever. I can feel my mind fading as well; I must write down everything or I forget it completely within an hour. I must be

helped from bed in the morning, and if I sit too
long in any one place I fall asleep. I can't even enjoy
food any longer, for the doctor won't permit me to
eat anything I want. I dream of steak and potatoes
and a bottle of wine, but my assistant brings me
only soup and pureed fruit and tea.

I'm well aware that I am dying a little every
day. I remember how mother and father were, just
before I lost them. I will not go as quietly as they
did. I refuse to give up hope. It's all I have left.

This last year I've come to understand how
wrong I've been. All my life I believed I was happy,
but I was only deluding myself. Because I never
allowed myself to care for anyone but myself, I have
no wife to love, or children to carry on my name.
No one has ever called me their friend. How can I
realize this only when there's no time left to fix my
mistakes?

I will continue my research. I know the
immortals have learned how to live forever, that
it is possible to avoid death altogether. If only I
can stay alive long enough to discover their secret.
Somehow I must.

I closed the book. "I'm not going to say 'that poor man.'" I glanced at Jesse. "No matter how much I want to."

He took my hand in his. "It does not excuse what he did, but it does explain why."

The old man's sad, desperate words still hurt my

heart, and made me get up and slip into my dark boy's arms.

"You're upset." He rubbed his hand over my back. "I shouldn't have let you read that."

"No, I think it was good for me. Kind of a reality check." I caught a strand of his silky black hair, and moved it so that the light brought out the amethyst glints. Jesse's hair would always be this color, even when mine turned gray. "Someday I'm going to be old. I don't think about it too much, but it will happen. And you'll still be like you are now."

He kissed the top of my head. "It won't make any difference to me, Catlyn. You will always be my lady."

"While eventually I'll have to tell everyone that you're my boy toy," I tried to joke, but my heart wasn't in it. I looked up at him. "What do you think I'll write in my journal when I'm as old as Julian?"

He pretended to think for a minute. "You'll write, 'I spent the day with the one I love. The garden is blooming, the horses are playing tag in the pasture, and the grandchildren are coming to visit us this weekend. I have never felt happier.'"

"The one I love sounds great, and so does the garden and the horses, but grandchildren?" I wasn't sure how to wrap my mind around that concept.

"Your parents had children," he reminded me. "Someday I hope that you and I do the same."

I thought about having kids as often as I did being old, which was basically never. If Jesse and I did have a baby, it would probably inherit characteristics from both of us. If Jesse's father was right, and all Van Helsings were born with special vampire-hunting abilities, the kid would get stuck with that. I'd gotten my dark hair and pale skin from my father, and possibly some of his vampire strengths—I already knew I could jump two stories without hurting myself.

"You do want children, don't you?" Jesse asked, dispelling my thoughts.

"I can't think that far ahead." I made a face. "Grandkids will want to call me Nana, won't they?"

"I'll insist on it."

Reluctantly I left his arms and regarded the stacks of journals. "What are we going to do with these now?"

"Considering how much information Julian amassed about me and my family," Jesse said, "I must ask that you not return any of these to the collection."

I hadn't thought about that, but I nodded. "I'll catalog the book safes as empty. I'm just glad we discovered these before Mrs. Frost sold off the collection." I got up and stretched. "Imagine the field day someone would have with Julian's 'findings.'"

"He didn't record them in his journals." Jesse's eyes narrowed. "He only mentioned them."

I looked up at the ceiling. "We've got to look through the rest of those bins and find them." When he didn't follow me to the door, I turned around. "Don't you want to know what else he had on you and your family?"

"It's not necessary. Last night I searched through the

remaining bins in the storeroom, to ensure we had found all of the journals." He gave me a bleak look. "Catlyn, there is nothing else but books in those bins."

"You checked each one to make sure they were real?" When he nodded, I began to pace. "Mrs. Frost said he was very secretive, and what information he had on you, he definitely wouldn't want to share. Maybe he hid his findings somewhere else."

"He never left his home, so they must still be there," Jesse said. "I'll have to go and search it tonight."

"I'm going with you." I recalled the promise I'd made to my brother. "But I can't, not tonight. I have to get back to the store."

"Tonight is the only chance we'll have," Jesse said. "All of his property—including the contents of his house—is scheduled to be sold at a public auction being held at the estate. I know because my parents asked Lawrence to place bids for them on the house and land."

I closed my eyes. "When is the auction?"

"It starts at noon tomorrow."

Thirteen

Tony's Garage occupied one corner of the block behind the bookstore, and as I walked toward the office door I could hear clanking and banging sounds coming from behind the closed doors of the service bays. I glanced up to see Jesse watching me from the roof, and offered him a wan smile before I went inside.

No one was in the office (which was cluttered beyond belief) so I walked through the adjoining door out into the garage. "Hello? Anyone here?"

A heavyset man rolled out from under a pickup truck. "Help you?"

"I'm looking for a friend of mine," I told him. "Karise Carson?"

"It's okay, Tony." Kari emerged from behind some

shelves of car parts. "She's cool." She glanced over her shoulder. "She's no snitch, either."

My jaw dropped as Connor Devlin, one of Tanglewood's most popular jocks, stepped out into the light. "Oh, my God. You're Seek?"

"I think I'd better plead the fifth." He winked at me. "Nice to meet the other legend."

"I'm not a legend." I sighed. "I'm in trouble again." I turned to Kari. "I need a favor. Kind of a huge one."

After I explained what I wanted to do, she nodded. "Not a problem. So when I talk to him, do you want me to be me, or some shiny glee clubber who goes to church regularly, has made the chastity promise, and would never, ever get you into any kind of trouble whatsoever?"

"You don't have to lie about who you are," I said, making Connor laugh. "Sorry. I meant, be you. Just don't volunteer any extra info."

She looked pleased. "I knew there was a reason I liked you, Youngblood. You're smart and honest, even when you're lying through your teeth."

Connor walked with us back to the bookstore, although he first put on the black hoodie I'd seen Kari wearing to cover his head and face.

"Kari, don't let anyone see you from the front windows," he said when we reached the back door. "I'll wait out here."

"Don't get abducted," Kari told him. After we went inside the store, she said, "Cat, I'd appreciate it if you wouldn't mention Connor's secret identity to anyone.

Principal Deaver would expel him like instantly, and then his parents would probably ship him off to some boot camp or military academy. If they didn't have him committed first."

"My lips are sealed." I gave her a wry look. "I can't believe Connor is running the Ledger. I mean, he's …" I couldn't think of an analogy. "He's Connor Devlin."

"I had a problem getting my head around it, too, until I realized he's Zorro." At my blank look, she said, "You know, rich, entitled golden boy by day; rebellious, secretive whistle-blower by night." She grinned at me. "That's why no one ever suspects him. Connor Devlin can't be the editor of the Lost Ledger. The universe would implode first."

"Well, I never would have guessed it was him." I was still puzzled, though. "How did you and he end up getting, you know, involved?"

"Oh, that." She waved a hand. "He's been totally in love with me since the fifth grade. I'm not kidding. I'm the boy's reason for living." She sighed. "And now he's mine."

"Wow." My heart melted a little, and I wanted to ask her a couple thousand questions about how they were coping with being so different, but Jesse was waiting somewhere nearby for me. "Okay. Are you ready to do this?" When she nodded, I went to the phone and dialed home.

"Youngblood Farm," Trick answered.

"Hey, it's me, back from shopping, safe and sound." I grimaced at Kari. "While I was out I met a girl who was in my Ceramics class at school, and she invited me to come over to her house to hang out."

"Tonight?" Trick asked. "What about work?"

"I can work Saturday night to make up for it," I said, which was true. "Please, Trick? Kari's really nice. She's right here if you want to talk to her."

Kari plucked the receiver out of my hand. "Mr. Youngblood? Hi, this is Kari. I know this is all kind of last minute, but I could use Catlyn's help with my laptop. Every time I boot it up, I get the scary blue screen, and I don't know what to do." She listened for a minute. "Yes, my folks will be there." She eyed me. "Sure, we'll be glad to give her a ride home." She nodded. "Got it. Great, thanks so much." She handed the phone back to me and gave me a thumbs-up.

"I want you home by midnight," Trick told me when I got back on the line. "You can call me if you need some computer advice."

I winced. "Thanks, I will. See you later." I hung up the phone and heaved out a breath. "He bought it."

"Yeah, I'm pretty sure he did," Kari told me. "But even over the phone, he's one scary dude. I know I wouldn't want him catching me in a lie."

"It'll be okay." On impulse I hugged her. "I really appreciate this, Kari."

She patted my back. "Always happy to acquire new blackmail on someone." She drew back. "He's going to ask you what was wrong with my laptop. Tell him that an Internet virus corrupted my start-up program, and we had to wipe my hard drive and restore the factory settings. Also, mention how much I whined about all the photos I lost because I never backed them up."

"Whoa." I gave her an admiring look. "You're really good at this."

"That actually happened to my laptop last year, so it's one hundred percent believable." Kari wagged a finger at me. "Never tell a lie unless you back it up with a truth. Like Tony would love for you and a date to attend the teens and tacos party at his place on Christmas Eve. Now, what part was the lie?"

"Tony's not serving tacos?" I guessed.

"He's not serving anything. He doesn't know about it." She grinned. "He'll actually be up in Brooklyn visiting his mom. So we'll have the place all to ourselves." She glanced around the store. "Unless, of course, you don't want us to meet this incredibly mysterious boyfriend."

"That would not be fair, would it?" Jesse said from behind her.

Kari yelped and whirled around. "Hey, that's not…" her voice trailed off as she looked from his boots to his face. "Man. Oh, man. Am I glad I'm taken." She grinned and held out her hand. "How you doing? Karise Carson, excellent liar."

"I'm very well, thank you," my dark boy said as he clasped her hand. "Jesse Raven. Excessively grateful."

"You are excessively pretty much the total package, dude. Plus you're a Raven, which I think makes you richer than God." Kari gave me a sideways glance. "I'm curious. Has he been in love with you since the fifth grade?"

"Not quite," I said. "We don't have a lot of time, Kari, so…"

"…I should get out and leave you to it. Gotcha." She turned to Jesse. "Cinderella has to be home by midnight. Also, make sure nothing bad happens to her, or I will personally deliver a full confession to Sheriff Yamah and Patrick Youngblood. After I find you and kick your amazingly handsome ass all over town, of course."

I walked Kari out to the alley, where Connor still stood keeping watch. "Thanks, guys. I owe you."

"Yes, you do, and I will collect." Kari regarded her boyfriend. "I met her guy, and he's cool. By the way, he makes you look like a hunchback with one eye and a harelip."

Connor bent over, cocked his head to one side and leered at her. "Why would you think that, my pretty?"

After we all laughed, and I promised Kari (again) that we'd be careful, I went back into the store. In Mrs. Frost's office Jesse sat working on her computer. On the monitor was an image of some type of construction diagram.

"This is the floor plan for the ground level of Hargraves's mansion," he told me, and pointed to one section at the back. "He had this addition constructed thirty years ago."

I blinked. "How did you find that?"

"I have access to the database at City Hall." He opened another window and read a document. "According to the papers his builder filed for the permit, it was intended to serve as a new library." He read further down. "Julian designed it with steel doors, a dedicated generator and an independent alarm system." He glanced at me. "Whatever he had in this room, he considered it extremely valuable."

"That has to be where he hid the rest of his journals with his findings," I said. "But we can't break into a house with an alarm system."

"If it were active, we could not." Jesse printed out a copy of the floor plan. "I called James and told him I wanted to look through the antiques at the mansion so I can instruct our property manager which to acquire tomorrow at the auction. He has disarmed it for tonight."

I didn't know whether to feel relieved that we would have easy access to the mansion, or angry at James Yamah for being such a hypocrite. "We'd better get going."

———

Julian Hargraves's mansion sat atop the highest point of elevation in Lost Lake, a place I told Jesse that some of the kids at school referred to as "Haunted Hill."

"Why do they call it that?" I asked as he drove up the long road to the front gates. Then I saw the house, which was old, huge and painted gray, and could have served as the setting for just about any haunted house movie. "Never mind."

Jesse parked right in front of the gates, which weren't locked, and scanned the area. "This was a beautiful place when Julian's parents were alive. They kept the house painted white and surrounded it with flower beds." He pointed to a neglected-looking wooden swing hanging from one of the black oaks. "Mrs. Hargraves would sit out there at night with Julian and read him stories. Sometimes I would stand behind the hedge there so I could listen, too."

"Why did he let it get like this?" I asked as I followed him up the brick drive.

"I'm not certain," he admitted. "After his parents died Julian stopped coming to town, and soon he never left the house. James came to check on him, but he behaved normally and insisted he was well." He took my hand as we walked up the steps to the front door. "Some said his loss had forever broken his heart."

I looked down over the trees. From here I could see all of Lost Lake, including Raven Island and the roof and some of the windows of the enormous building that occupied the center.

"That's your house down there." I could also see the docks and part of what appeared to be a lighted trail through the trees. "If he used binoculars or a telescope, he could probably see whenever you left the house or the island."

"At home we never bother to stay out of sight," Jesse said. "We've never suspected anyone was watching us." He tried the door, which was locked, and then went to the window. It looked as if it hadn't been opened for years, but he removed the dirty screen panel and forced up the bottom half.

I heard the window latch inside pop off. "Someone is going to notice the window was opened."

"I know how to fix it so they will not." He climbed over the sill, and then held out his hand. Once I was inside, he picked up the screen panel, putting it back in place before he closed the window.

I picked up the broken latch and handed it to him. "You can't fix this."

Using his inhuman strength, he bent the metal of the catch and the latch straight before he put them back together so they looked like all the other latches. "If anyone tries to open the window, they will assume it broke as they made the attempt."

"That's mean. Necessary, but mean." I took in the room around us.

A thick layer of dust covered every surface; even the white cloths draped over the furnishings were gray with it. What must have once been a beautiful crystal chandelier sagged overhead, suspended by two wires in a shroud of cobwebs. The embossed wallpaper curled around the edges and seams and vanished under big dark stains in the upper corners where water had probably leaked through from the roof. Dead bugs littered the badly gouged hardwood floors in between little piles of desiccated rat droppings.

I expected the house to smell as awful as it looked, but the air felt cool, and smelled only faintly musty.

"Mrs. Frost said they fumigated they place. They

must have aired it out after that." I saw how dark his eyes were. "What's wrong?"

He breathed in and then frowned. "I cannot say. The chemicals the exterminators used were strong. They are masking all the other scents inside the house." He put his arm around me. "Stay close, Catlyn. Something here feels very troubling to me."

Jesse and I walked out to the main hall, which split off in different directions. Here the floors had been tiled in marble, but tracked-in dirt, cracks and chips marred the smooth stone. I couldn't even tell what the original color had been.

A pair of heavy steel doors at the end of the hall led into a room so dark not even my excellent night vision could pick out any details. Jesse reached across me to flip on a switch, and overhead lights flickered on.

However much Julian Hargraves had neglected the rest of the house, the library looked as pristine and spotless as if it had been built yesterday. Empty bookcases lined all of the walls, each with glass-fronted panels with individual locks. A giant, old-fashioned wood desk sat at one end, and leather chairs, small tables and floor lamps made little reading islands on either side.

The room might be a hundred times cleaner than the rest of the place, I thought, but it smelled unpleasant, as if something old and damp had been left somewhere to mildew.

Facing the desk was a large oil painting of an older

couple sitting in a gazebo; I guessed from the fifties style of their clothes and the white version of the mansion in the background that they were Julian's parents.

Jesse walked around the room, looking into the bookcases before he stopped at the desk to check the drawers, which turned out to be empty. "There is nothing left in here."

"That we can see," I amended as I looked down at the big Persian rug covering the center of the floor. One edge had a faint curl to it, while the others were perfectly flat. I reached down and pulled it back, exposing the tiles. They had been cut and inlaid with a gray metal that formed a gigantic number eight.

Jesse came to kneel down beside it, but as soon as he reached to touch the metal he drew back his hand. "This has been fashioned out of iron."

Iron (or weapons made out of it) was one of the few things that could harm or even kill vampires, a weakness Jesse and his parents had also acquired after they were attacked and changed.

I didn't have the same problem, so I touched it carefully. The metal didn't budge, but the metal-streaked marble ovals in the center of each end of the eight looked slightly newer than the surrounding tile. As soon as I pressed my fingers in the center of one oval, it sank down slightly, and something under the floor made a mechanical sound. At the same time, one of the bookcases to the left of the desk creaked. I pushed against the oval again, but it didn't budge.

"Try pressing both sides at the same time," Jesse suggested.

When I did that, both ovals lowered into the floor, the mechanical sound grew louder, and the bookcase swung out away from the wall, revealing a dark empty space behind it. We went over to look inside, and saw something like a walk-in closet with files, books and wooden boxes crammed into five deep shelves.

"A bookcase safe." The musty odor smelled stronger now, and I held my breath as I stepped in and took out one of the file folders. Inside were photographs of Sarah Raven kneeling beside a bed of flowers. I handed it to Jesse. "Jackpot."

Something crunched under my sneaker, and I looked down to see an open prescription bottle, and tiny white pills scattered on the floor of the closet. I bent down to pick up the bottle and read the label. "This was Julian's. It's nitroglycerin. He must have had a heart condition." I set the bottle back on one of the shelves.

Jesse drew me away from the closet. "Something violent happened here. I can smell traces of blood." He started to say something else, and then shook his head.

I put my hand on his arm. "Tell me what it is."

"I can also smell us." He looked down at me, his eyes solid black now. "Your scent, and my own." He nodded toward the closet. "It's coming from inside there."

"But we've never been here before tonight." I looked

all around the shelves, until something inside me focused my attention on a wooden box that had fallen to the floor. Dark stains and smears mottled the outside of the box, and when I touched it I felt an instant sense of recognition—and revulsion, because the stains and smears were dried blood.

I couldn't bring myself to open it, so I handed it to Jesse, who slowly lifted the lid. A large plastic bag had been left in the box, the inside of it also stained with dark red splotches. At the very bottom of the bag I saw something, and forced myself to retrieve it.

Jesse's blood had once soaked the broken piece of oar in my hand. I knew this because on Halloween night I had pulled it out of his chest.

I closed my fist around it. As I did, I heard my heart beat in my ears like a drum, pounding hard but at the same time slowing. A chill spread through me, icy and terrifying, as everything in front of my eyes blurred and changed. Lost Lake spread out before me, its waters silvered by moonlight, and on the banks I saw a highwayman and a duchess standing together, smiling at each other.

That's me on Halloween night, I thought dreamily. *And Jesse.* I couldn't understand why everything looked as if I were seeing it from inside a small box, until my breath fogged the glass in front of my face. Not a box, but a window.

"Catlyn?"

I knew Jesse was speaking to me, but I could hear

him only faintly, as if from the other side of the house. "He was there. In the boathouse."

"What do you see? Who was there?"

"He waited," I told Jesse. "When you came into the boathouse after Barb stabbed you on Halloween night, he hid in the shadows." I smiled a little as I felt a twisted pleasure spread over me. "You were wounded and weak. He enjoyed seeing you like that…"

"Catlyn."

The images faded, and I snapped back to the present. "Oh my God." I dropped the piece of oar and rubbed my hand against my jeans, frantically trying to get rid of the awful sensations it made me feel.

Jesse grabbed my hands and held on to them. "It's all right, Catlyn. Don't be afraid. You had a blood vision."

"What?" I stared at him, horrified. "I'm not psychic. I don't have visions."

"You are in part psychic," he corrected, "and it was a blood vision. Vampires can use blood to see the past. My parents and I can do the same in a more limited way. Since your father was like us, he must have passed on his ability to you."

I stared at my hand. "But I've never been able to do that. Why would I start now?"

"Our bond." He picked up the broken wood. "This was stained with my blood. You must have been responding to that." He put it back into the bag, and some of the darkness faded from his eyes. "You said that someone was there in the boathouse. Who was it, Catlyn?"

Someone walked in the room, and I spun around to see Sheriff Yamah standing a few feet away.

"I'd like to hear that, too, Jesse." He eyed me. "But first, young lady, I'd like to know why *you're* here."

Fourteen

Despite Kari's coaching, I couldn't think of a single lie that would explain why I was with Jesse. I couldn't even come up with a decent excuse as to why we were searching Julian's library.

Fortunately, I didn't have to.

"Julian Hargraves knew about us, James," my dark boy said. He took one of the files from the hidden closet and brought it to the sheriff. "He had us watched, and followed, and photographed."

Yamah took the file, opening it and flipping through the pages. As he did, he began shaking his head. "You're mistaken. Old Julian never left this ..." he stopped speaking as soon as he saw the first photograph of Jesse's mother.

I took pity on him. "He noticed that the Ravens weren't aging. Up here he could watch the island without anyone knowing about it. He hired men to follow Jesse and his parents and take pictures of them, and report on what they did whenever they left the island. He even knew about me. He was hiding in the boathouse on Halloween night."

Yamah closed the file and looked past us at the closet. "It's all in there?"

"I believe so." Jesse gave him a pointed look. "We have not yet had time to look through everything."

"I'll take care of it." Yamah sighed. "But this girl should never have been involved in this, Jesse. You should have come to me."

This girl. The words made anger simmer inside me. He spoke as if I were no one and nothing.

"Catlyn found Julian's journals," Jesse told him. "If not for her, I would never have discovered what he had done to me and my family."

"Keeping your family safe is my business, son." Yamah regarded me. "I'll take you home now, Miss. You can explain all this to your brother."

"No." All the emotions I'd been holding back roiled inside me, seething and dark red and ugly. "I'm not going anywhere with you. I haven't done anything wrong."

He tilted his head back to look down his nose at me. "Breaking and entering is against the law."

"Is it legal to deliberately turn off a security system for a property you don't own?" I countered. "How about helping to erase three months of someone's life? Or covering up the fact that a high school boy was shot on Halloween night?" I heard a yowling sound, but I was too furious to stop. "I wonder, what would they charge you with, Sheriff, if they knew you helped a vampire hunter brainwash an entire town?"

Somewhere in the house glass shattered, and Yamah glanced briefly over his shoulder before he said, "Your brother said you would never remember anything about that night."

"My brother?" I smiled. "Was wrong."

Yamah yelped as a river of small, furry bodies poured into the room. "What in God's name…"

My whole body lit up from inside as I released more and more of the power inside me, drawing more of my cats to me. I could feel them leaping through the hole they'd smashed through one of the windows, first the wild things that lived on Julian's land, and then the pets who had escaped from their owners' houses. Bobcats came from the woods, their spotted fur bristling as they rubbed shoulders with the alley cats from town. They flooded into the library, some coming to surround me but most forming a deadly circle around the sheriff. Their eyes, like glittering jewels, fixed on Yamah's pale face, but not one made a single sound.

Their power reflected back to me, strengthening me, and for the first time I understood why my Van Helsing ability might be the deadliest of all. I didn't dream the future or make others forget the past; I was a hunter, as wild and lethal as my small warriors. They knew this, and for me, they would do anything.

"Don't move, James," I heard Jesse say, just before I felt his hand touch my hot face. "Catlyn, look at me."

I didn't want to, not now that I'd finally let go. I loved Jesse, and we belonged to each other, and no one was going to take him away from me. The weight and pain of all the months I had pretended and kept silent fell away from me, freeing me from the fear that had trapped me. I wasn't afraid of the sheriff anymore. My cats covered every inch of the floor, and they were ready.

All it would take was one thought from me, and they would silence James Yamah forever.

Jesse gently turned me toward him, but I saw no anger in his beautiful gray eyes. Instead there was something like sorrow and understanding, as if he knew exactly what I wanted to do, and how good it would feel if I did. "We chose life over death, Catlyn. We must always do that, or we will become monsters."

Of course he knows about the terrible urge inside me, I thought. *He's been fighting it every day since he was changed.*

Slowly the heat inside me receded, taking with it the irrational hatred I felt for the sheriff. I looked down at the cats my emotions had summoned, and as their heads turned toward me I reached out to them. *Leave us now.*

As silently and quickly as they came, the cats dispersed. In a few seconds we were alone again with Yamah, who had gone very pale, and walked over to sit down heavily in one of the chairs.

I knew I should apologize for scaring him, but he'd

done the same to me too many times now. In my eyes, we were even.

"What am I going to tell your parents?" Yamah finally asked Jesse.

"Nothing. Julian is dead, and this is over." My dark boy gestured toward the closet. "Take all the records out of here tonight and burn them."

"It's not as simple as that, and you know it." The sheriff dragged a hand through his hair. "My family has served yours for generations, and I am as loyal as the rest of them. But I'm sworn to your father, Jesse, not you. It was your father who worked out this truce with Youngblood after Halloween night; I have to tell him that you broke it by refusing to honor your part of the agreement by staying away from Miss Youngblood."

A loud, startling sound came from the handheld radio mic clipped to the epaulet of the sheriff's uniform, and he unclipped it to answer it. "Yamah."

"Sheriff, dispatch just received a call," a man said over the radio's speaker. "Another girl's been abducted. She was visiting her grandmother at the nursing home over on Center when a man came into the room. The nurses said she just walked out with him."

Yamah's knuckles bulged as he pressed the response button. "Who was taken?"

"Ross Hamilton's girl, Becca."

As the sheriff issued terse instructions to begin a search of the area for the girl, I turned to Jesse. "Why didn't she try to run away from the man?"

"I'm not sure," he said. "Perhaps the kidnapper threatened to harm her grandmother if she didn't go with him."

"Put out a description of Becca," Yamah was telling his deputy. "She's five-nine, about a hundred twenty pounds, long dark hair, fair skin, dark blue eyes." As he said that, his eyes shifted to me. "Call in everyone off-duty, and ask the fire department if they can spare some men to help with the search. I'll be at the station shortly."

"Do you have a description of the man who took her?" Jesse asked.

"That we do." The sheriff's expression turned to disgust. "The nurse who saw him says he's young, dark and handsome. Becca's grandmother swears he's a wrinkled, bald old man." He stood. "You'll both have to come back to the station with me. I'll call your father from there, Jesse, and see what he wants me to do about the two of you."

"If you do that, Catlyn and I will not be coming to the station," Jesse said. "We will leave Lost Lake tonight, and our families will never see us again."

"You think you can just leave town?" Yamah uttered a bitter sound. "Think about who her brothers are—they will come after you. So will your parents, for that matter. If that happens, someone is going to die."

"You're sworn to protect the Ravens, Sheriff," I said. "That includes Jesse, doesn't it?"

He didn't say anything, but his expression wavered.

"James, please," Jesse said. "Nothing is more important

to me than being with Catlyn. When the time is right, we will tell our families about us. I promise you this."

Yamah rubbed his eyes in a tired gesture. "You don't give me much choice. I'll keep quiet about this, but I want something in exchange."

"What is it?" Jesse asked.

"I think there's a fully turned vampire in Lost Lake," the sheriff said. "He's the one who is responsible for taking the kids."

Jesse went still. "A vampire took the missing girls?"

Yamah nodded. "It's why none of the descriptions of him match, and why the girls go with him without a fight. He's able to cloud and confuse human minds." He turned to me. "You're the vampire hunter, Miss Youngblood. So in return for my silence, I want you to find him. Find him, and kill him."

———

While the sheriff began removing all of Julian Hargraves's secret files from the library, Jesse and I left the mansion. Yamah's belief that a vampire was abducting the girls was almost as outrageous as his demand that I hunt him down and kill him. I hadn't agreed or disagreed; I'd been too shocked to speak. Jesse had hustled me out of there before I'd really had a chance to think about it.

By the time we reached Jesse's car, my head cleared and I finally reacted. "He's crazy. I can't hunt a vampire. I certainly can't kill one."

"You don't have to," he said as he helped me into the car. "I will take care of it."

"What happened to choosing life over death?" I asked as he got in on the other side and started the engine.

"Vampires are not alive."

I had to think about that for a minute. "Okay, but if that's true—"

"I am the same," he finished for me.

That I would never accept. "I don't think so, Jesse."

"I died a human death, Catlyn." His mouth thinned. "Vampire blood reanimated me, but my body no longer functions as yours does. I do not age or scar. I cannot be harmed by disease or injury. The vampire blood that changed me allows me a semblance of life, and as long as I consume blood it will continue to do so, but I am not alive. It is why we are called the undead. A vampire is death undone."

"I don't believe that. You're not a vampire." A thought occurred to me. "If you were dead, you wouldn't have a heartbeat."

"Like the rest of me, my heart is animated and sustained by vampire blood." He folded his hand around mine. "It is a mimicry of life, part of the vampire's lure. My heart beats so that you are fooled into believing I am alive."

"How can vampire blood do that?" I demanded.

"I wish I knew. I only know what destroys it." He nodded toward the sky. "Exposure to the daylight causes the vampire's blood to break down, which is why sun is so lethal to us. Without the vampire blood to sustain us, our bodies rapidly age and wither. It happens so rapidly that we literally catch on fire."

"Don't remind me of that." I saw that we were half-way to the apartment complex where Kari lived with her mother. "Anyway, it doesn't matter. I can't kill anyone, dead or undead, and you're not going to, either," I added before he said anything to the contrary. "But maybe I can find the missing girls. Wouldn't that be good enough for the sheriff?"

"If James is correct, and a vampire is responsible for taking these girls," he said carefully, "you may not wish to find them."

"You think he's killed them."

"He would have to feed on them, and eventually they would die of blood loss." He hesitated, and then said, "What I meant to say is that he cannot be alone. Vampires are clannish creatures, Catlyn. They are drawn to each other. When there are no others they can find, they are compelled to make more of their kind."

Now I understood. "If he's by himself, he may have turned the girls into vampires, too."

"It is their way." He made a turn down an old road that led past some cottages and mobile homes before it wound around a large apartment building.

I saw Connor waiting on his dirt bike at the entrance to the lot, and returned his wave. "There's my ride home."

Jesse put the car in park before he turned to me. "I will do some hunting and see what I can discover. Can you meet me at Kari's taco party on Christmas Eve?"

"I'll try." Suddenly we were too far apart, and I flung myself at him. "I don't care about vampire blood or reanimation. You're not dead. You're alive."

He folded his arms around me, and rested his cheek against the top of my head. "You make me feel as if I am."

"We'll find a cure for this, and when we do, you're going to be human again," I promised him. "We'll finish growing up together. You have no idea how much fun it's going to be while we get crow's feet and gray hair, and kids start calling us 'sir' and 'ma'am.' We're going to have kids, and grandkids, and spend the last years of our lives in rocking chairs on a front porch. I'll have too many cats, and you'll complain about taxes, and … " my throat hurt too much for me to finish.

"We will be together. Always." Jesse lifted my chin, and kissed away a tear from my cheek. "I love you, Catlyn."

I pulled away and got out of the car before I sobbed all over him, and made myself walk over to Connor. "Thanks for waiting." I used my sleeve to mop up my tears, and felt a wrenching sensation as I heard Jesse drive away. "I was having a girl moment."

"You're allowed." He handed me a spare helmet. "Everything okay?"

"Ask me that in another life." I put on the helmet,

clipped the chin strap together, and then climbed onto the back of his bike.

I'd ridden on the back of Trick's Harley more times than I could count, so I wasn't worried about riding with Connor. His bike, while smaller, seemed a lot faster and much more maneuverable, and probably was a blast through these hills.

Instead of using the road that passed the farm, Connor drove into the woods in front of Kari's apartment building.

"It's almost midnight," he called back to me over his shoulder. "This is faster."

I gave him a thumbs-up, and then looked ahead at the old trail he was taking. Jesse and I had never ridden out this far, but I knew it crossed his property. Connor would be able to drop me off practically at my front door.

Something big and fast-moving darted in front of the bike, making Connor swerve to avoid it, and I grabbed his waist as we wobbled and almost toppled over. He righted the bike just at the last minute and stopped an inch away from the massive trunk of an old oak, and flipped up his visor.

"Did you see that?" he asked me.

Before I could answer a horse came barreling out of the brush, its eyes wild and its legs churning as it reared. I realized it was Rika the minute I saw her swollen belly, and jumped off the bike, tearing off the helmet as I got between her and Connor.

"Turn the bike off," I told him as I held out my hands. "Rika, it's me. It's okay."

The Arabian dropped down, her ears pricking at the sound of my voice, and then she glared at Connor.

I approached her slowly, still talking to her in a soothing voice. "You're okay now, it's all right. This is my friend, Connor. He's not going to hurt you."

Once I got hold of her halter, I stroked her neck and rubbed her shoulder, bringing her head down to mine. "Connor, I'm going to have to walk her back to the farm. Wait for a few minutes before you start up the bike; the sound probably spooked her."

He dropped the kickstand and took off his helmet. "I'll walk with you." As I started to tell him no, he said, "I promised Kari I'd make sure you got home okay. I am not going back there and telling her I left you alone in the woods with a runaway horse. I value my life too much."

"Okay, but stay where she can see you," I warned him.

Together with Connor I led Rika across Jesse's property, stopping at the old Ravenov manor house to let her rest and have a little water. While she drank, I checked her over, but found no injuries to indicate she'd broken out of her stall.

"I don't understand how she got loose," I said to Connor as I retrieved a lead rope from one of the posts and tied it to her halter. "She's kept in the barn all night. They must have forgotten to bring her in." As soon as I got home I was going to give both my brothers a piece of my mind.

"There have been a lot of strange things happening with horses around here," Connor told me. "You've heard about the ones that were killed, right?"

I nodded. "Our vet told us about Mr. Palmer's stallions. He was the guy who sold Rika to us before he left town."

"It's not just Palmer's horses," Connor said. "I've been getting all kind of weird reports for the Ledger. From what I've pieced together, these two guys have been going around the farms, sneaking into barns. Sometimes they attack the horses with knives. Other times they turn them loose and run them off. No one knows why."

I thought of the descriptions Sheriff Yamah had gotten of the man who had abducted Becca Hamilton. "Is one young, and the other one old?"

He looked astonished. "Yeah, how did you know?"

"Whoever has been hurting the horses may be the same guys who are taking these girls." I told him about the call the sheriff had gotten earlier, and the descriptions of the two men. "Has anyone recognized the guys hurting the horses? I mean, are they local, or maybe a couple of pickers?"

"No, but there is one thing. Mr. Palmer went to Ringers' Tavern the night before he left town," Connor said. "He was pretty upset, and started knocking back shots like they were going to be outlawed tomorrow. He told some guys there that he saw who attacked his horses. He said it was a ghost."

"There's no such thing as ghosts," I assured him.

"Well, if there is," he said, "Palmer said this one looked just like Old Man Hargraves."

Fifteen

Connor stayed with me as I put Rika back into the barn, which was where Gray found us as he rode in on Flash.

"You found her." He dismounted and led the grumpy palomino back to his stall before he joined us. "She all right?"

"She was," I said as the Arabian began pawing the ground. "Keep your distance." I led her into her stall, taking off her halter before I came back out and latched the door. "What did you do? Leave her outside all night?"

"Trick put them away after dark," he told me. "He must have forgotten to throw the latch."

"Was the barn door open when you came out here and found her gone?" As Gray nodded, I asked, "Do you think he left that open, too?"

Gray started to say something, and then looked at Connor. "What's he doing here?"

"He gave me a ride home." I introduced them, although it was hard to keep the irony out of my voice. Gray knew exactly who Connor was, and Connor hadn't been forced to forget my brother.

"Nice to meet you," Connor said before he turned to me. "I've got to get back before my girlfriend calls in the Marines. Talk to you later."

Gray waited until Connor left before he started on me. "How do you know him, and why is he bringing you home?"

"You caught me. I'm having a wild affair with Connor Devlin and his girlfriend." I uttered a blissful sigh. "Do you think Trick will mind me being part of a threesome?"

My brother scowled. "You're not doing that."

"You know, you're right. I'm not. Connor is a nice boy who just gave me a ride home. Deal with it." I walked out of the barn.

At the house I expected to see Trick waiting for me, but as Gray came in he told me he'd gone to bed.

"Lucky for you," he added. "If he'd seen you with that boy, he'd have gone ballistic."

"I'm sorry," I said in my best insincere tone. "Am I not allowed to have friends?"

"That guy is not your friend," my brother said. "And you didn't go shopping tonight."

"No, I didn't," I confessed. "I actually broke into an empty house to search it for hidden documents. When the sheriff caught me, I almost killed him." I batted my eyelashes at him. "But I was able to blackmail him into keeping his mouth shut, so no real harm done."

Gray looked uncertain. "You're not funny."

"I'm not joking." I went upstairs.

As tired as I felt, I had trouble falling asleep, and when I finally drifted off I dreamed of horses being chased through the woods by a maniac who kept changing back and forth from an old man to Jesse. As he attacked me, Rika suddenly appeared and began trampling him, but he wouldn't die. It seemed so real that when he turned and came at me with the knife I woke up and almost screamed.

My clock radio said it was only five a.m., but no way was I going back to sleep. Instead I took a long, hot shower, and once I'd dressed I went downstairs to start breakfast.

My pancakes weren't going to win any prizes, but it felt good to cook and work off the anxiety left over by the nightmare. When my brothers got up an hour later I had the table set and breakfast ready.

"Morning," Trick said as he made a beeline for the coffee maker. He eyed the full pot I'd made for him. "My birthday is in July."

"I couldn't sleep." I took out some orange juice and filled the glasses I'd set out on the table. "Rika got loose last night."

"What?"

"I found her in the woods across the road." I briefly

described what happened, and I didn't bother to lie about Connor bringing me home. "Did you forget to latch her door?"

"I don't think so." Instead of jumping on me for riding home with a boy, Trick looked at Gray. "What were you doing out there, riding around in the dark on Flash?"

"I found Rika gone when I went out to groom him," he said, giving me a resentful look. "I didn't think she'd wandered that far."

"Right. Like Rika would never go anywhere once she got loose." I brought the sausage I'd cooked over on a plate and thumped it down in front of him. "You're an idiot."

"Catlyn." Trick came over and sat down. "I thought Kari's parents were bringing you home."

"Nope, I rode in on the back of Connor's dirt bike. He took me through the woods." I forked a couple of pancakes onto my plate and grabbed a sausage patty from the pile Gray had shoveled onto his plate. "Yet strangely, nothing bad happened to me, and I was able to catch Rika." I looked at both my brothers. "Isn't that absolutely incredible?"

Trick put down his coffee mug. "If you have something on your mind, Cat, maybe you should just come out and say it."

Here was my chance. I could tell them that I remembered, that I knew what they had done, and how Trick's brainwashing hadn't worked. I could detail all the times Jesse and I had met in secret at the bookstore, and what we'd discovered about Julian Hargraves. I could even tell them what I'd promised to do for the sheriff.

The moment I did, Trick would grab me and use his ability to make me forget all of it.

He might do worse this time. Pain pounded inside my temples as if my conscience were taking a hammer to the inside of my skull. *He and Gray might go after Jesse.*

"Kari invited me to a party in town on Christmas Eve," I said. "I'd like to go, but I'm not going to ask. You'll just say no like you always do." I slammed down my fork. "I can't have friends. I can't get a ride home from a nice boy. I can't have a life. Something terrible might happen to me, right?"

Trick regarded me as if I'd grown another head. "Why don't you ask and find out?"

I folded my arms. "Can I go to Kari's party?" Before he replied I warned, "It's at night, at the garage where Connor works. I'm told there will be tacos."

He sipped some coffee and opened the paper. "Will there be any adults there to chaperone?"

"Probably not." I saw pictures of the first two girls who had gone missing on the front page of the paper, and seeing them side by side made me notice again how much they resembled each other. *They could be sisters.*

"I'm not crazy about you going to an unchaperoned party," Trick said, "but as long as we drop you off and pick you up at a reasonable hour, you can go."

I forgot about Kari's party as I looked across the table

at Gray. "Do you know a girl at school named Becca Hamilton?"

He nodded. "She was in my Trig class."

Yamah's description of Becca came back to me, but I wanted to be sure. "What did she look like?"

"I don't know. Tall. Skinny." He shrugged. "Average."

She's pretty average, Tiffany had said when she'd described Sunny Johnson to me. *Brown eyes, long brown hair, kinda skinny.* When I'd first seen the photo of Melissa Wayne in the paper, I'd presumed it was another picture of Sunny. Then I remembered what Mrs. Frost had said on my first day at work, when I asked her why Sunny's mother had kept staring at me. *From a distance you probably look exactly like her.*

"Gray, does Becca have long dark hair and pale skin?" When he nodded, I took the paper out of Trick's hands and folded it over to show Gray the photos of the two other missing girls. "Does she look like them?"

"I guess." His gaze shifted from the paper to my face, and he frowned.

I got up and went to the phone, but I didn't know the number to the sheriff's office. I also didn't know what I was going to say to him. I didn't think he'd believe me if I told him what I'd confirmed about all three girls. They didn't just resemble each other.

They all looked like me.

———

Jesse didn't come to the store for the rest of the week, but each afternoon I found a pale white rose waiting for me on Mrs. Frost's desk. I missed him, and knowing he was out hunting the vampire every night kept me in a constant state of fear and worry, but I knew I couldn't help him with this. A part of me was glad I didn't have to find out just what sort of vampire hunter I might be.

To keep from brooding I threw myself into finishing the store's inventory, which I finished the day before Christmas Eve. That afternoon I hauled the rest of the bins out of the storeroom and began cataloging the remaining portion of Julian Hargraves's collection.

Without Jesse there it was slow, dull work. I no longer found any of the books fascinating, not now that I knew why Julian had been so obsessed with the occult, so I hurried through each bin. That was probably the reason I found the letter the old man had written to Mrs. Frost; in my haste I dropped an enormous book on ancient Egyptian rituals, and as soon as it hit the floor the envelope tucked inside slipped out.

No name had been written on the outside, and the envelope had never been sealed. I opened the flap and took out the single page, unfolding it to read:

My Dear Martha,

I am sure you will find this as you are making up a catalog of my books; you would not sell off the collection without first having them appraised.

That is why I have hidden my journals within the collection, so that you might understand my struggle against death. You must read these first, and then you will understand the rest of what I write here.

I have recovered some of the blood belonging to the immortal girl, and tonight I plan to use it in an ancient ritual of rebirth. My findings have indicated that her blood will reverse the aging process, and restore me to a state of youth that will never end.

I am willing to share my rejuvenation with you. You can be eternally young with me, and we can have the love that life denied us. Come to me as soon as you have read everything. I will be waiting for you at the house.

Yours,
Julian

Blood. Immortal girl. Rebirth. The words kept leaping off the page into my face, and I groped for a chair as I read the letter a second time, and then a third.

Julian had seen me and Jesse in our costumes in the boathouse on Halloween night. He'd witnessed Barb's attack and he'd hidden when Jesse had stumbled into the boathouse. He'd seen me come in, and how I'd pulled the broken oar out of Jesse's chest. We'd both been hurt, and Jesse's blood had soaked the floor … but why had Julian thought it was mine?

The sound of someone knocking and calling my name at the front of the store dragged me out of those dreadful memories, and I pushed the letter under a stack of books before I went out to see who it was.

Tiffany Beck stood outside the shop, and as soon as she saw me she waved frantically. "Sorry to bother you at work," she called through the glass, "but I come bearing gifts. And a desperate request."

I went over and unlocked the door. "Hey. Come in."

"Can't." She lifted the two bundles of gift bags she was holding. "I'm on begging and groveling duty. My mom's in charge the Sparklefest relay race, and we need more riders to sign up. I know you and your brothers have horses, so do you think you guys might want to enter the race? Please, please say yes."

"My brothers will probably say no, and I'm trying to finish up the inventory at my job." I saw the disappointment in her eyes. "Sorry."

"It's all right. Last-minute begging and groveling hardly ever works anyway." She made a face. "You would have had to dress up in a riding habit costume, and they're pretty awful."

"What fun." I was so glad I had my job as an excuse. "Are you riding in the race?"

She nodded. "Mine is green and white, with like yards of tatted lace. I look like a great big toad draped in a doily. Gotta run." She hurried down to the next open shop.

Costumes...

I went back to my work table and turned over one of the blank tally sheets to make a list.

Julian Hargraves
- *Sees me with Jesse down by the lake.*
- *Takes blood he thinks is mine from boathouse.*
- *Writes letter to Mrs. Frost about using blood.*
- *Dies the same night.*
- *Body stolen from tomb after funeral.*
- *Palmer's horses are killed.*
- *Sunny Johnson talks to an old man before she runs away.*
- *Melissa Wayne is kidnapped by an old man.*
- *We find Julian's journals.*
- *We search Julian's library.*
- *Becca Hamilton is kidnapped by an old man or a young man.*

It was all right there in front of me, everything going back to that night in October. The only connection between every event was Julian Hargraves or an old man.

I picked up the book in which I'd found the letter to Mrs. Frost, and began skimming through it. It was older than I'd realized; the copyright date was 1901. I didn't recognize the name of the publisher or the author, but the title was fairly straightforward: *Ancient Egyptian Death Practices and Rituals.*

I skimmed a couple of chapters on the various ways the ancient Egyptians had embalmed and preserved their dead, and stopped when I found a section on ceremonies. At first the author covered the different types of funerals given for those who had died, but then he moved on to a chilling account of a prince who had tried to cheat death by drinking the blood of his human slaves. When this didn't work, he began kidnapping and draining the bodies of foreign dignitaries who came to pay homage to his father, the King.

> The only time the existence of this prince was ever recorded was in the personal journal of a visiting ambassador's personal physician. In his account, the physician provided details of an ominous blood ritual, during which the prince used the hollow fangs of a snake to pierce his own veins and introduce the blood of his victims into his own body.
>
> In his account the physician noted that after the ritual had been completed, the prince took on a much younger appearance, as if infusing himself with the victim's blood had somehow reversed the aging process. There was a terrible price for tapping this ghastly fountain of youth, however, for over time the prince became addicted to blood, and could not eat or drink as other mortals did. Nor could he tolerate the heat or light from the sun. Force to live in the bowels of his father's

palace by day, the prince would roam freely at night, terrorizing the city and surrounding villages in his endless quest for more victims upon whom he could feed.

Not a great deal is known about this ancient vampire prince, except that shortly after his evil practices were discovered he vanished, and all mention of him was removed from the royal family's records and tombs. To this day, no one knows his name, or what became of him.

I set down the book and took out the letter Julian had left inside it. *I have recovered some of the blood belonging to the immortal girl, and tonight I plan to use it in an ancient ritual of rebirth.* I glanced at my list, and then realized what might connect all of the events together.

"You look very serious."

I clapped my hand over my mouth to smother a shriek, and then rushed to Jesse, who stood holding a white rose in his hand. I wanted to yell at him for scaring me, but I was too happy to see him. "Thank goodness you're here." I hugged him, and accepted a kiss along with the rose. "I need to know something, and this is going to be a very weird question, but bear with me, okay?"

He smiled. "You can ask me anything."

"Then here goes," I warned. "If someone took some of your blood, and injected it in their own veins, would it change them from human to vampire?"

He looked bewildered. "I would never give anyone my blood, Catlyn. It is too dangerous to humans."

"I know that. I'm not saying you did," I assured him. "But if someone found some of your blood, and did that, what would happen to them?"

"It would poison them, and they would die," he said, frowning. "Catlyn, why are you asking me this?"

"I'll explain, but just one more question," I begged. "What if the person was already dying when they injected your blood? Would it change them?"

"It is unlikely." He thought for a minute. "To create a vampire, you must first kill them as a human. This person would have to be very close to death for the process of change to be triggered. They would have to be within moments of dying."

I thought of the bottle of pills we'd found scattered in the bottom of the hidden closet. "Like someone who was having a heart attack because he deliberately didn't take his medication."

"Now will you explain this to me?" Jesse asked.

"I think you'd better read this first." I handed him the letter.

Once Jesse read the letter, I showed him the passage in the book, and then the list of events that I'd written.

It only took Jesse a few seconds to put it all together. "Julian took my blood from the boathouse that night."

I nodded. "He somehow knew how to re-create the

ritual that the Egyptian prince used. Julian didn't die on Halloween night, Jesse. He used your blood to turn himself into a vampire."

Sixteen

On the morning of Christmas Eve I stayed in the kitchen baking my gifts for my brothers while they were out doing their usual frantic last-minute shopping. I hadn't been able to think of anything new to do for them, so I fell back on what I did every year. I also made some mini red velvet cupcakes to take to Kari's party, which boosted my festive mood a little. I'd be able to give Jesse his gift tonight.

For Gray I baked a big batch of chocolate chip cookies, and put them in a basket with a football-shaped mug, some hot chocolate mix and a copy of *Glass Houses* by Rachel Caine. For Trick I broke with my tradition and made up a pan of old-fashioned gingerbread, a little jar of lemon glaze and some packets of decaf coffee stuffed in a Harley mug. I also gave him a copy of *Carrie* by Stephen King.

I knew the tone of my gifts would worry them, which gave me a certain amount of sour amusement. I didn't think I could keep my secret much longer anyway, not now that Sheriff Yamah knew Jesse and I were together.

While I baked and basketed and gift-wrapped, I hummed "Deck the Halls" under my breath. I would have sung it if I'd known all the words to it, but humming worked nicely to keep my mind on task.

Using the impending holiday as a way to keep from thinking about Julian Hargraves and the missing girls felt pretty cowardly, but there was nothing I personally could do about it. Jesse had taken everything I'd found along with my list to the sheriff. He'd also been going out with Prince at night to search Julian's property and check the basements of empty houses and every other place a vampire might use as a sanctuary.

"You are the one Julian has been hunting," he had told me when I'd offered to go with him. "Until James and I find him, you are in danger."

I hated being left out, but I knew he was right. I wanted to help find the girls, and stop Julian, but if we were right he might attack me the moment he saw me. Jesse could heal from almost any type of injury; I couldn't.

I knew all that in my head, but my heart still argued with me. *I'm the vampire hunter. What if I'm the only one who is able to find him? What if those girls die because I'm too afraid to try?*

"I don't even know how to try," I told my whiny heart as I picked up my gift baskets and took them up to my room. Once I hid them in my closet, I took out the shoebox where I'd put Jesse's gift.

I'd found an old map in one of the *National Geographic* magazines Trick had thrown in the recycle bin, and used that as the wrapping paper. I didn't have any ribbon that matched, so I tied it with a piece of jute and tucked in the knot a twig of Florida holly from the bush that grew out near the fence between his land and ours.

I went out to the barn to check on Rika, and ended up saddling Sali and taking her for a ride. Frost had turned all of our pastures brown, and some of the trees had shed nearly all their leaves. I knew when spring came everything would green up again, but until then our land would remain bleak and depressing.

I needed to go somewhere else, somewhere I felt happy. "Let's ride out to the lake cabin, girl." I touched my heels to her sides.

Eager as always, Sali took off toward the front gate.

Following the path Jesse and I had ridden so many times by myself felt odd, but the sunlight streaming through the canopy of trees lit up the woods and brought out the colors I could never see as well at night. We passed a miniature maple, and the blazing red of its tiny leaves against a cluster of nobby-trunked, deep green pines made me smile. Even nature found a way to dress up for the holidays.

I dismounted as the trail narrowed and led Sali the rest of the way to the little lake. In the sunlight the cabin looked much older, but now I could see how strong the walls had been built, and even the remnants of a little stone path that led around the lake.

I tied Sali out front before I went inside. The light that came through the windows formed glowing, slanted columns that interlaced with each other over the split-log floor.

Jacob and his lady had lived all alone out here. I didn't know how I knew that, only that it felt right. No family, no friends, and probably no children. Like me and Jesse, all they had needed was each other. I could sense the love that had dwelled in this place; I had from the first time we had come here.

I went to the hearth, and touched the heart carved into the mantle. "I'm afraid," I whispered. "I don't know if we can do what you did. Leave everyone behind to be together, just me and him. It's one thing to say it, but to actually go, and never come back, never see them again…I don't know if we're that strong."

I pressed my forehead against the mantle, and blinked back the tears. I wasn't going to cry, not in this place. When my eyes cleared, the sunlight crept around me, causing the ashes in the hearth to glow like a little girl's blush.

Ashes aren't pink.

I knelt down and reached into the ashes, stirring them until I found a bit of burned cloth. Then I found part of a sleeve, and a melted piece of fake white fur, and some blackened metal buttons.

Someone had brought Sunny Johnson's jacket here, to our cabin. Someone who had burned it.

I lifted the sleeve, blowing off the ash before I examined it. A dark splotch marred the fabric, and when I touched it the stain flaked off onto my finger, leaving behind a lighter spot on the fabric. It looked like an old blood stain.

Vampires can use blood to see the past. My parents and I can do the same in a more limited way. Since your father was like us, he must have passed on his ability to you.

I curled my fingers over the stain and closed my eyes, drawing on my anger and focusing it on the fabric in my hand as power surged inside me.

This time the vision came in a blur of movement and color that slowly coalesced into shapes: A teenage girl wearing a pink jacket. The streetlight that shone down on her dark hair. A pay phone. The purse through which the girl searched for something.

A voice echoed inside my head, scratchy but kind. *Do you need some change for the phone, Miss?*

I thought I had some. The girl sounded nervous.

Her fear pleased me, and made me feel stronger. My eyes fixed on the girl's throat.

The old voice said, *I can give you what you need, my dear.* A gnarled hand offered some quarters.

The girl drew back. *Thanks, but I think I'll just walk down to the sheriff's station and call my mom from there.*

An ugly anger rose inside me. She wasn't supposed to resist. *Don't you recognize me?*

No, sir. She turned as if she meant to run off.

I couldn't let her get away, not until I was sure.

Don't do that. The old hand seized the girl's arm, the long fingernails scraping over her forearm. *Stop fighting me. You want to go with me. Don't you?*

The fear faded from the girl's expression, and her voice went flat and dull. *I want to go with you.*

That's good. The old hand pulled down the sleeve of the pink jacket, covering the scratches on the girl's skin. *We have so much to talk about, you and I. You must tell me how to complete the ritual.*

I opened my eyes, dropping the fabric as I backed away from the hearth. I stumbled and almost fell as I wiped my hand off on my jeans, and then I had to run outside. Sali whickered to me, and I heard her shuffle as she watched me double over.

I threw up until my stomach was empty, and still it took another minute before I stopped heaving. Feeling the old man's twisted emotions made me want to scrub out my brain with soap, but at least now I knew one thing for certain. Sunny Johnson hadn't run away from home. She'd been taken, like the other two girls.

My head throbbed as I went back into the cabin. I felt too sick to attempt another blood vision, but I could try again later, when Jesse was with me.

I picked up the stained fabric and shoved it in my pocket before I searched the rest of the cabin. The vampire had left nothing else behind but a trace of the same musty, moldy scent I had detected in the library.

Julian hadn't expected Sunny to resist him, and when she had he'd done something to her to make her stop.

He'd told her what to do and she'd done it, as if she'd never felt afraid of him at all. As if he'd made her forget to be frightened … the same way my brother could make people forget things …

Realizing that Julian Hargraves and Trick shared the same ability made things seem very simple and clear. I couldn't turn my back on Sunny Johnson or the other girls that greedy, selfish old man had taken. Not for another minute. No matter what it might cost me.

No one else was going to suffer in my place.

————

That evening Gray finally showed up, tired and cranky, to take me over to Kari's party. He said Trick was still shopping, but he wouldn't look me in the eye.

I accepted the lie in silence as we drove into town. My brothers and their endless schemes no longer interested me; I had more important things to deal with.

It seemed like everyone in Lost Lake had converged on the town, for people jammed the sidewalks. All of the merchants had kept their shops open late, and the local restaurants had set up little booths and carts everywhere to sell food. In the park I saw families spreading blankets and setting up chairs around the fountain, behind which a small stage had been set up. Kids chased each other around as they waved glow sticks and flash lights.

Gray made his way carefully through the crowded streets until we reached Tony's Garage. Teenagers mobbed the place, and salsa music poured out from the open doors of the garage, which had been turned into a buffet and dance floor.

"Kari forgot to mention that it was a costume party," I said as I watched a pirate whirl around a belly dancer. "I guess I'll just have to be a high school girl." I saw a flicker of yearning on my brother's face, and said, "Why don't you come with me?"

He watched Tiffany Beck and Aaron Boone, who had worn matching togas, walk in front of the truck, and his hand tightened on the steering wheel. "I don't have time."

"You can't spare an hour to have some fun?" I asked.

Gray turned his head away. "I'll be back to pick you up at eleven."

"Fine." I picked up the box of cupcakes and my purse and climbed out of the truck. As soon as I shut the door, Gray took off.

"Hey, Youngblood, over here," I heard Kari call over the music.

I saw a Las Vegas showgirl standing in the door to the office, and only when I got close did I realize it was Kari. "Wow." I took in her scanty, sequined outfit. "You look amazing."

"You think so?" She patted the long curls of her blonde wig, from which peacock feathers sprouted. "I have a terrible urge to do high kicks and shimmy my upper parts."

A monk wearing a hooded robe and a full face mask appeared beside her. "Don't ask her to show you," he said in Connor's voice. "She's beautiful and smart, but she dances like a bear on a trampoline."

"Hey." Kari elbowed him. "Watch it." She took the box of cupcakes from me. "Oooh, red velvet. They'll go great with the tacos. You're my new best friend. Come on, I've got a costume for you." She dragged me into the little lavatory in the corner.

A few minutes later we emerged, with me in a pair of too-big coveralls and one of Tony's striped shirts. Kari had stuffed my hair up under a Tanglewood ball cap and fixed a black domino mask over my eyes.

"Why are we wearing costumes to a Christmas party again?" I asked as she led me out into the garage. I looked at the sign she pointed to draped across the parts shelves, which read "Halloween Do-Over." "Oh." I frowned at her. "Are you trying to start some trouble?"

"Always," she assured me. "Also, just FYI, no one knows who my monk is, and I'd like to keep it that way." She grabbed a short, skinny boy dressed up as Einstein. "Denny, meet Cat. Cat, this is my friend Denny, who is the best salsa dancer at Tanglewood High."

"I am?" Denny squeaked.

"You are now." She gave him a little push toward me.

I took his cold, clammy hand in mine. "It's okay," I told him. "I'm the *worst* salsa dancer at Tanglewood."

"Really?" He regarded the packed dance floor, and then looked for Kari, who had disappeared. "Okay," he said grimly, squeezing my hand like a soldier about to go into battle. "Let's do this."

Someone put on a fast beat, and Denny and I did our best to keep up with it and not laugh ourselves silly. When the next song started, he traded places with Aaron Boone, who handed off Tiffany to him.

"I'm not much of a dancer," he told me in a loud voice as he took my hands. "My girlfriend just steers me around."

"I can do that." I tugged Aaron to one side to avoid a collision with another couple.

The last time Boone had danced with me, which he no longer remembered, he'd been an excellent dancer. Had my brother taken away his ability to dance along with his memories? What if he'd done the same thing to me? Was that why I didn't know how to hunt vampires? Had he taken that away from me, too?

"I'm not that bad, am I?" Aaron asked me.

"No." I made myself smile up at him. "But I am."

I traded Aaron back to his very grateful girlfriend, but asked Denny if we could get something to drink. He led me over to a big metal bin filled with bottles and cans of soft drinks sitting in partially melted crushed ice, and after asking what I wanted fished around until he produced a bottle of peach tea.

As I took a sip, I saw a tall, slim figure appear on the other side of the dance floor. He wore riding clothes instead of a highwayman's costume, and the mask Kari had given him was red instead of black, but for a moment time reversed itself, and I was back at the Halloween Dance.

"You okay, Cat?" Denny asked. He looked over at Jesse. "That your boyfriend?"

"Yeah." Remembering my manners, I thanked him for dancing with me. I noticed a petite girl standing alone in one corner and looking wistful as she watched the other kids dancing, and pointed her out to Denny. "There's someone who'd like to meet the best salsa dancer at Tanglewood."

"Well, that's me." He grinned and headed toward the girl.

I started toward Jesse as he came to me, and we met in the middle of the crush of kids dancing. I took his hand and led him toward the back of the garage, where I found a more private spot behind the parts shelves.

"You look adorable," he said.

"Kari's idea." I glanced down at my coveralls and gave him a wry look. "Want me to check your oil, sir?"

"Perhaps another time." He plucked the hat off my head and drew my hair down around my shoulders. "That's better."

I needed to tell him about what I'd found at the cabin, and what I'd figured out about Julian having the ability to use mind-control, but I wanted this moment for us. I took out the map-wrapped package I'd slipped into the pocket of the coveralls and handed it to him. "Merry Christmas, Jesse."

He smiled as he touched the sprig of holly. "You didn't have to buy me a gift."

"I didn't buy it," I said. "Go on, open it."

Jesse untied the string and carefully unfolded the map to reveal the two books inside.

"They're my journals," I said. "Everything I've written since I got my memory back."

He looked uncertain. "But these are your private thoughts. You should keep them."

"They're all about you." I tried to smile. "I've been hiding them from my brothers since I got my memory back; they never thought to look in the barn. Whenever I felt frustrated, which was ten times a day, I wrote in them. There are some poems I wrote about you, too."

"You wrote poetry for me?" He sounded awed.

"I wrote everything, Jesse. Everything I felt and thought and knew about you." I didn't want to tell him the rest, but I had to. "I never considered how dangerous that could be until we found Julian's journals, and all the stuff he collected while spying on you. I didn't mean to, but in a way I did the same thing he did."

"No, Catlyn," he said, and touched my cheek. "Julian didn't care about anyone but himself. All you have done since we met is try to protect me."

I swallowed hard. "Anyway, that's why I decided to give them to you. If something ever happens to me, I don't want my brothers or anyone else to find them and use them to hurt you."

"I will keep them safe." He took an envelope out of his pocket. "My gift for you seems suddenly inadequate."

I frowned as I opened the envelope and took out the multi-page document inside. My name and Jesse's had been typed in at the top, along with a lot of legal jargon and a state seal. "This looks official."

"It is. It's the deed for the lake cabin," he said. "It's in your name now."

My jaw dropped. "You're *giving* me the cabin?"

"The cabin, the lake, and the fifty acres surrounding it. I would give you everything I have," he said, "but I think it would make the county tax collector suspicious."

"I can't believe you did this." I laughed and hugged him. "You really want me to have the cabin?"

He kissed my forehead. "I think Jacob would be pleased to know it's yours."

"All right, who's messing around back—oops, sorry." Peacock feathers swayed as Kari turned around. "Um, when you guys are through having your private moment, can you come into the office? My monk and I have some info we need to pass along."

"We'll be right there," I told her. When she left, I said to Jesse, "I was just out at the cabin today." I told him about finding the remains of Sunny's jacket, and how I'd used it to have another blood vision. "I'm almost positive Julian has the same ability that Trick does. I don't know how that's possible, but he's making the girls forget to be afraid of him. That's why Sunny went along with him willingly."

"That is a Van Helsing ability." He frowned. "He could not have acquired it from using my blood."

"Maybe some of my blood got mixed up with yours in the boathouse." Someone switched off the music, and

I heard Kari calling me over a bunch of protesting voices. "Stay here."

I walked out into the garage, and stopped as soon as I saw Trick standing in the center of the dance floor. My heart sank as I saw Sheriff Yamah beside him.

The party, it seemed, was over.

Seventeen

I kept my innocent face on as I approached my brother. "I thought Gray was picking me up at eleven." I glanced at Yamah. "Is there a problem?"

The sheriff shook his head slightly, as if to tell me not to say anything more.

"Someone broke into the barn while we were gone," Trick said, his voice colder than I'd ever heard it. "Jupiter's been slashed, but the vet patched him up, and he thinks he'll pull through."

I couldn't breathe. "What about Sali?"

"She's fine. The bastard didn't have time to hurt her or anything of the others." Trick sighed. "Rika's stall is in pieces, and so is the barn door and the front gate. From the tracks it looks like she took off again."

"We'll find her." I turned to Kari. "I'm sorry, I've got

to go home." I glanced down at my makeshift costume. "I'll bring these back when I can. Would you say good-bye to everyone for me?" I shifted my eyes toward the parts shelves.

"No problem." She touched my arm. "Let me know if we can do anything to help."

Trick had come along with the sheriff in his patrol car, so Yamah drove us back to the farm. On the way I got more details from my brother about the break-in and the attack on Jupe.

"The gash on his neck was pretty deep, and he lost some blood, but it could have been worse." His jaw tightened. "Dr. Marks stitched him up, and took him to the clinic to watch him overnight. I'd be there, but I have to ride out and find Rika."

"I think you'd better let me do that." Before he could say anything, I added, "She won't come anywhere near you, and you can't lasso her in the woods. Besides, if you scare her more than she already is, you could make the foal come too early."

"Then we'll let her go," he said flatly. "I don't want you riding through those woods at night."

"I've been riding at night a couple times a week for the last month." I let that sink in before I said, "I know, I'm not allowed to, and you can ground me forever tomorrow. Tonight we need to find that mare."

He stared at me. "Why have you been sneaking out to ride at night?"

"I like it," I said simply. "So does Sali." As the sheriff

pulled into our drive I saw what was left of the front gate. The entire gate panel had been broken off its hinges and flung a dozen feet.

I got out and walked over to where Rika had left deep tracks in the sod. They went straight through the gate and across the road into the woods.

Trick joined me. "She barreled right through it."

"I didn't think so." I crouched down and measured the distance between the hoof marks. "She never even slowed down." I saw a different, fainter track crossing the mare's and peered at it. The impressions had been left by a man's shoe. "Someone was running in front of her." I showed Trick how the mare's trail crossed over the footprints.

He went over and retrieved the broken gate, the top rail of which had been smeared with blood. "This is horse blood. Whoever did this had to be the guy who attacked Jupe."

I didn't bother to ask him how he knew the blood wasn't human; I had to get saddled up. "Tell the sheriff."

I ran to the barn, where Sali and the other horses were still milling back and forth. "Just me, guys," I said as I grabbed my bareback pad and led Sali out. She rubbed her nose all over me, sniffing and nickering like an anxious mother. "I'm okay, girl, but Rika isn't." Once I had her bridled and padded, I pulled my hair through the back of my ball cap and mounted her. "Let's go find her."

Trick was standing outside the barn door. "Wait for me to saddle Flash."

I reined in Sali. "That is a terrible idea," I told him.

"He'll buck you off in a heartbeat and you know it. Please, Patrick. I can do this. Just for once, trust me."

"I want you back here in thirty minutes," he said flatly. "Whether you find her or not."

I nodded, and trotted Sali out through the gate and across the road. I stopped there to examine the trail, which wound around to the left. Horses were creatures of habit, and would choose a familiar path over a strange one every time. Rika knew the Ravenovs' old abandoned manor house and the trail that led across their land to Kari's apartment building; if she hadn't caught the jerk who'd attacked Jupe, that might be where I'd find her.

I followed the trail for as long as I could make it out, past the Ravenovs' old manor house and into the trees. Sali seemed to read my mind as she picked up the pace, gliding into her running walk while avoiding the various obstacles along the trail. By the time we reached the place where Connor and I had found Rika, the tracks became confused, as if the mare had been turned around several times. I found tracks going in three different directions, but lost all of them in the dead leaves and undergrowth.

I dismounted and held Sali as I listened to the night. The utter silence told me the Arabian was long gone.

I rode the rest of the way to Kari's apartment building to be sure, and then turned Sali around to head home. I felt sure Rika was somewhere on Jesse's land, but there was no way I could search five hundred acres in the few minutes I had left.

Trick had Flash out and was saddling him as I rode

into the barn. "Don't bother," I said as I dismounted. "She's probably halfway across the county by now."

Trick eyed me. "You're sure?"

I told him about the tracks I'd found in the woods as I took care of Sali and put her away. "We should call animal control, and Dr. Marks, too. They can put the word out about her."

I sat down on a hay bale and rested my head in my hands. "Where is Gray, and why wasn't he here?"

"I don't know." Trick offered me his hand. "Come on inside and get cleaned up."

As we walked to the house I saw the sheriff, still waiting in the drive. "You should invite him in. I can make some coffee."

"Yeah, I think we'll need it. Thanks, Cat." Trick walked out to speak to him.

Once I had the coffee brewing, I went upstairs to shower and change. I glanced at the gift baskets still sitting in my closet; I'd completely forgotten it was Christmas Eve. I carried them down and put them under our mostly dead tree, brushing off the shower of needles that fell on them in the process.

"Cat," Trick called from the kitchen. "Would you come in here?"

I turned on the tree's lights before I went to join my brother and the sheriff, who were standing by the table. "I baked some cookies this morning," I said as I went to retrieve the tin. A rush of cold air came from the back door. "Trick, shut the door, it's letting all the heat out. Sheriff, do you like chocolate chip?"

Neither of them said anything, and I saw why as I came back to the table and saw the words that had been written on it in huge black letters. The tin fell out of my hands.

*BRING THE QUEEN OF CATS TO THE
PARK MIDNIGHT TOMORROW OR THEY
ALL DIE*

At that moment Gray strode into the kitchen carrying a huge decorated box. "We won the Christmas turkey dinner contest at the market," he said as he set it on the counter. He shut the back door. "They called and I had to go over and pick it up." He looked at us. "What? It's a free turkey."

"Miss Youngblood," the sheriff said, his voice almost kind. "You have to tell them now."

I looked at my brothers. "You'd better sit down."

———

It didn't take long for me to destroy all of my brothers' illusions; I talked only about twenty minutes. I began from the night Jesse and I had first met, and how we'd met in secret during the weeks that followed. For the first time I told Trick how my dark boy had saved my life at the zoo, and again at the lake on Halloween night. Yet the more I told him, the darker his expression grew.

I admitted to getting the job in town so Jesse and I could continue to see each other, and how that had led the two of us to discovering what Julian Hargraves had done. I explained the two blood visions I had gotten, and what they had revealed about the old man.

"He's been trying to find me all this time." I took out the piece of Sunny's jacket sleeve from my pocket and placed it on top of the words on the table. "I'm the one he wants. He believes I'm immortal, that I'm this Queen of Cats, and that I'm the only one who can finish his transformation."

No one said anything, and after a few uncomfortable moments the sheriff put his hand on my shoulder. "You did the right thing, young lady. Patrick, I'll put out an alert on your missing horse. Merry Christmas."

"I'd better put this food away." Gray got up and started unloading the box.

Trick took out his keys. "I'm going over to the clinic to check on Jupiter. I'll see you two in the morning." On a grim note, he added, "Merry Christmas."

"That's it?" I shoved my chair back and got to my feet. "That's all you have to say? Merry Christmas? What about 'How could you, Catlyn?' or 'You're grounded for the rest of your life'?" I waited, but my brothers just stood there. "Oh, that's right. I won't remember any of this after you brain-wipe again, will I? So why waste the oxygen?"

"We'll talk tomorrow," Trick said.

I stepped in front of him and pointed to the table. "Before or after the vampire does that?"

"It's not your concern," he snapped.

"He took them because he thought they were me," I shouted. "If it wasn't for me none of this would have happened."

"What do you expect me to do, Catlyn?" Trick said. "Deliver you to the park tomorrow night? Hand you over to another vampire? I feel terrible about those girls, but you're my sister. I'm not trading your life for theirs, so just forget whatever stupid idea—"

Gray closed the fridge with a slam. "Shut up, Patrick." He never used our brother's full name, and we both stared at him. "She's right. We can't stand by and let the vamp kill those girls. We're the only ones who can stop him."

Trick got up and grabbed the front of Gray's shirt. "Our parents sacrificed everything so we could be free of the Van Helsings," he said through his clenched teeth. "I swore to them that I would do the same. So we are not hunting this vampire or any other." He let go of Gray. "We're going to live like normal people."

"Normal." Gray nodded. "Yeah, that's what we are. I dream of the future, you erase people's memories and then, there's Cat." He faced me. "You're the family killer."

"*Gray.*"

He ignored Trick. "You don't do it yourself. You make the cats do it."

I took a step back. "I've never killed anyone." I looked at Trick, who wouldn't meet my gaze. "Patrick?"

He sat down and dropped his keys on the table, and buried his face in his hands.

"Vampires are drawn to us," Gray said. "We don't know why, they just are. That's the reason we've had to keep moving around so much. A few times we stayed too long in one place, and they found us."

"Are you telling me that I've killed vampires?" I demanded. "What, in my sleep?"

"You were awake. You even saved our lives a couple of times." Trick looked up at me. "You don't remember because I made you forget."

"How many times?" When he didn't reply I hit the table with my fist. "How many?"

"Eight," Trick said.

Now I had to sit down. "I've killed eight people?"

"They were vampires, and they were trying to kill us," Trick said. "The first time it happened, the vamp got into the house while Gray and I were sleeping."

"It was the sound of the cats attacking him that woke us up," Gray added. "By the time we got to you it was all over."

"When did this happen?"

Gray ducked his head. "It was when we were living in Wyoming. We thought we were okay there because it was pretty remote."

"I killed a vampire in Wyoming," I said, just to be sure. When he nodded, I said, "I was in the first grade when we lived in Wyoming."

"Yeah." Gray looked uneasy. "You kind of started young."

"I'm a serial killer." I stared blankly at the words the

vampire had written on the table. "I've been a serial killer since I was six years old."

"You never harmed anyone in your life." Trick glared at Gray before he said in a softer voice, "We never went looking for those vampires; they came after us. You saved us, Cat. If not for you, they would have gotten to me and Gray."

I suddenly remembered something I'd once found in Trick's desk. "Those articles about the wild animal attacks you've been saving. It wasn't wild animals, was it? It was me."

"No," Trick said quickly. "Those people were the victims of vampire attacks. I've been tracking vampire activity for years. It's the only way I could avoid moving into an area infested with them."

I only had one question left to ask. "Why did you make me forget all that?"

"You were just a little girl the first time it happened," my brother said. "You didn't understand. You kept asking me why the bad man wanted to hurt us. You cried for days, and then you stopped talking. I knew the shock was too much. So I made you forget, and then you were fine again."

I looked at Gray. "You didn't make him forget."

"Oh, he tried," Gray said. "His ability doesn't work on me."

Trick studied my face. "I can give you back all your memories, Catlyn. You can relive every one of those vampire attacks if you want. But what do you think that will do to your mind? To your soul?"

"You think you've done me some kind of huge favor?" I was shouting again, but I didn't care. "Patrick, you've stolen my life away from me, eight times. Add a few more for all the things you've tried to make me forget since we came here."

"And what did I make you forget?" he demanded. "That you'd fallen in love with a vampire?"

I gritted my teeth. "Jesse is not a vampire."

"He's six pints of human blood away from becoming one." He uttered a bitter sound. "Oh, I know, he only feeds on animal blood, and he's kind, and he's promised he'll never hurt you. But you have no idea how dangerous that boy is. How little it would take for him to lose control, attack a human and turn into one of those monsters."

"You don't know Jesse, or how strong he is." I couldn't shout at him anymore, not with all the cats yowling at the back door. I didn't want to, either. I felt sorry for him and the way he saw everything, just in shades of black and white. "You're not God, Patrick. You don't have the right to decide what's okay for me to remember. You can't choose who I love. You aren't going to control me like this anymore, and if you try, I'll leave."

"You are forgetting something very important now." He leaned forward. "You're not the only one who can kill vampires, Catlyn."

"Cut it out, both of you," Gray said, his voice so stern he sounded like Trick. "We've got twenty-four hours left to find that vampire and those girls. That's what we're going to do. When it's over, then we'll deal with the rest of it."

I gazed at Trick. "Well, big brother? What's it going to be?"

Trick sat back and ran his hand over his face. "All right. We'll start tracking in the morning." He eyed me. "The three of us, together."

Eighteen

Christmas morning brought brittle sunshine and a light frost, which perfectly reflected my mood. I got down to the kitchen before anyone else, and decided to throw together a quick ham and egg scramble. I didn't want to feed my idiot brothers as much as I wanted to choke them, but I couldn't stomach another of Trick's half-done or partly burnt meals.

Trick came in to silently set the table, and as soon as Gray returned from the barn I put the food on the table and sat down with them to eat. None of us spoke a word, which was fine with me.

I finished first, and after rinsing my dishes grabbed my jacket and headed outside.

"Cat, wait," Trick said, halting me in mid-stride. "It's Christmas morning. We have to open gifts."

I took a deep, calming breath. "I left yours under the tree."

"What about yours?" Gray asked carefully.

"Thanks, but I've had enough from both of you." I stalked out.

In the barn I got Sali ready to take a ride in the trailer Trick had borrowed from Dr. Marks. According to my brothers, we could start tracking the vampire from the cemetery; as the family finder, Gray would be able to track him from there. Sali and I would follow Gray and Flash, and once we cornered the vamp I'd summon my cats to hold him at bay while my brothers retrieved the girls. Since Jupe was injured, and none of the other horses had his stamina, Trick would pace us on his Harley.

Trick had also told us how important it was to find the vampire's hideout during daylight hours, when he would be at his weakest. After the sun set, he would be too dangerous to confront, and we'd have to call off the search and go to Plan B.

No one had talked about what Plan B was, but in my version, I went to the park and traded myself for the three girls.

Gray came out to deal with Flash, who hated being put in the trailer. He glanced at me a few times, but I ignored him.

"The silent treatment won't work," he finally said to me. "We'll have to talk to each other while we're tracking. Trick is bringing walkies for all three of us."

"Whatever." I retrieved my saddle from the tack room

and carried it out to his truck. I stopped as soon as I saw the little red convertible parked behind it. On the roof was an enormous white ribbon and an oversize tag that read "Merry Christmas Cat from your brothers."

I blinked a few times, but the car didn't go away. "Tell me I'm hallucinating."

"You're not." Gray took the saddle out of my numb hands. "Trick was going to give it to you on your birthday, but the dealer wouldn't hold it that long."

"He bought me a car." I watched him nod. "With what? His charm and good looks?"

"He sold some of his computer equipment."

I stared at the car again, until everything around it started turning red. "No. I'm not falling for this. You tell him to take it back." I yanked my saddle out of his hands and marched over to the pickup.

Gray wouldn't leave me alone. "I'm not going to tell him that, and neither are you. It would hurt him too much."

"Were you not listening at all last night?" I tossed my saddle over the side of the truck's bed. "Maybe you missed the part where he admitted to moving us every six months to avoid vampires. Or the eight that I killed. Then there's all the years he spent making me forget that."

"It was for your own good," Gray said. "I was there. I saw how you were. Every time it happened, you turned into a zombie. He tried talking to you and explaining what had happened, but you were too little. Making you forget was all he could do to help you."

"How would I know if that's even true? For that matter, how do you?" I gestured at the house. "He could have made you think you were immune to his ability. Maybe you're not. Maybe he just wants you to think that you are."

"Now you're being paranoid."

"At this point, Grayson, I've got a right to be." I looked over his shoulder at the car and shook my head. "This is insane anyway. We can't afford this. We're almost broke."

He shrugged. "He got a good deal on it. Anyway, it's the thought that counts."

"I'll remind you of this when they shut off our power for non-payment," I warned.

"He did it because he loves you, Cat," he said. "He loves us both. Like we were his own kids."

I stiffened. "He's not my father."

"He knows that. Why do you think he's tried so hard to do what Mom and Dad wanted?" He dragged a hand through his hair. "Look, I don't agree with everything he's done, but at least he tried. Imagine what it would be like for us if he'd handed us over to the Van Helsings."

"Maybe they would have taught us how to deal with it better," I snapped. "Did you ever think of that?"

"They couldn't help Mom," he countered. "You've read her letters. She hated what they made her do. Sometimes she sounded like she was afraid of them."

"You're not allowed to use Mom to make me forgive him." But what he'd said loosened the knot in my chest, and the simple outrageousness of the car in the drive did the rest. "How is he expecting me to react to this gift? Scream, cry, jump on the furniture?"

Gray gave me a wry look. "I think he's hoping you won't use it to leave town."

"I won't need to," I said sweetly as I went to the front door of the house. "Jesse has his own car."

Trick was sitting in the chair beside our dead Christmas tree, and staring down at the circle of needles it had shed since the last time I'd swept. "We should get going," he said to Gray as he got up. "We can do the gifts later."

"Mine is blocking Gray's truck." I watched his face, which looked much older than it had last night. "It's the kind of gift every teenage girl wants to find in the driveway on Christmas morning, too. Thank you, Patrick."

He didn't try to hug me as he normally did on Christmas Day, but a flicker of relief passed over his tired features. "You're welcome, little sister."

I gave them their gift baskets, and Gray handed out his packages of T-shirts and home movies. By the time we'd unwrapped everything, it almost felt like Christmas again.

"There is something I need to tell you both before we do this," Trick said. "I've given Sheriff Yamah a copy of my will. If anything happens to me, you can trust him to help."

I was horrified. "Why are you talking about this?"

"We're about to go hunt a vampire, Cat. Even weakened by daylight, they're the deadliest creatures on the planet." He looked at Gray. "In my will I've named you as Cat's guardian until she's eighteen. I expect you to look after her."

"You are not going to die," I told him. "None of us are."

"I have no plans to," he assured me. "Now let's go and get the horses loaded."

———————

Flash gave us so much trouble while we loaded him into the trailer Gray decided to ride in the back with the horses, and handed me his keys. I glanced at Trick, who nodded to me before he took off on his bike.

"If I get pulled over," I grumbled as I started the truck, "everyone is going to jail with me."

I took my time backing out of the drive, which proved to be difficult with the trailer attached, but once we were on the road I felt more confident. With the trailer blocking the rear view I had to rely on the side mirrors, but it was still early, and all the roads remained practically deserted. As we reached town I saw that all the shops were closed and the sidewalks were empty.

Sheriff Yamah was waiting at the cemetery, and while he gave me a slight frown as I climbed out of the truck, he didn't say anything. I left him talking with Trick while I lowered the ramp and helped Gray get Flash out before I led Sali down the ramp. A couple of apple cookies helped settle them down enough for us to saddle them.

Trick walked back to check them both before handing

us the walkies. "Keep them on. If we get separated, let me know where you are." He turned to me. "Gray may zone out while he's tracking. If he does, you lead Flash until his head clears."

I nodded. "How will I know he's zoned out?"

Trick pointed to his shades. "His eyes turn white."

Gray mounted first, and followed the sheriff back to the Hargraves tomb. I waited by the gate with Sali and Trick.

I saw Gray stop Flash in front the tomb, but he just sat there in front of it. "How does he do this finding thing?"

"You said you had a blood vision," Trick said. "Gray has scent vision."

"He tracks the vampire by smell?" When my brother nodded, I whistled. "That stinks. Literally."

"Don't worry," Trick said. "He won't find your boy-friend by mistake."

"That's because Jesse isn't a vampire." I felt like a broken record.

After another minute Gray mounted Flash and rode out to us. His eyes weren't white, but he looked upset.

"There's no scent," he told Trick.

"That's impossible. He had to change here, or he wouldn't have gotten out of the tomb." He turned to me. "You're sure this Julian Hargraves is the vampire."

"It can't be anyone else." I thought for a minute. "He used Jesse's blood. Maybe that makes a difference." My brothers exchanged an odd look. "What?"

"Gray can't track your boyfriend," he admitted. "We've already tried."

"You went hunting for Jesse?" Unbelievable. "Why?"

"It doesn't matter now." Trick sat back on the Harley. "Without a scent trail for Gray to follow, this is pointless."

"What if we use logic instead of Van Helsing tricks?" I got down off Sali. "We know he comes into town to take the girls. He's always on foot, too. Even if he has super strength, the girls don't, and he wouldn't want to be spotted with them. He'd have to take them somewhere within walking distance, say a mile or two at the most."

Sheriff Yamah, who had been listening, shook his head. "We've already searched the empty houses and buildings within a five-mile radius. He's not using those."

I took the piece of pink fabric from my pocket. "Then we have to use me." I saw the way my brothers were looking at me. "Stay out of my way. I'm probably going to hurl afterward."

I handed Sali's reins to Trick and sat down on the curb. When Gray dropped down next to me, I frowned. "I don't need you to hold my hand."

"My visions are stronger when you're near me," he said. "Maybe I can do the same for you."

"Okay, but I'm not kidding about throwing up." I did feel better with him sitting next to me, and when I closed my eyes and gripped the fabric I was able to slip into the vision almost at once.

At first I thought I was back in the tunnels under the bookstore, but these were rougher, and there were no lights to guide me. I felt different, bigger, stronger, as if I had traded my body for another.

I moved with confidence now, stepping over pools of water and ducking under clusters of roots until I reached a crude-looking door and lifted a plank of wood holding it shut.

Inside candles flickered, and I smelled spoiled food and human waste. The filth offended me almost as much as the pale faces peering out from under the pallet in the corner.

A young hand beckoned to one of them. *Come out here, girl.*

She crawled from beneath the pallet, motioning to the others to stay back before she stood and faced me. *You said you were going to let us go.*

I said when I find her, I might. The young hand tossed a sack at her, and a sour chuckle grated as she caught it. *You should be grateful I'm feeding you. I don't have to, you know. You should be feeding me.*

The girl looked angry now. *Let the other girls go. They should be with their families. You can make them forget they were here.*

What about you?

You can keep me until you find the one you want. If you don't find her, then you can kill me.

Such a brave child. I will have to give you to her first.

I retreated, turning only when the girl tried to rush past me. I struck her and knocked her to the ground. As she cried, I reached down and ripped the silly pink jacket she wore from her back.

No. She tried to pull it away from me. *Please. Don't take it away from me.*

Losing it will teach you to behave.

I closed the door on the sounds of the girl weeping. I had tired of her, tired of all of them, and it would be a relief to put them out of their misery.

I walked back through the passage, stopping at the stone stairs that led up to the hatch before I changed direction. I would have to be cautious until the stupid festival the townspeople had planned was over, or I might be seen.

"That would not do," I muttered, swaying as the fabric fell out of my hand. "Not before I have her."

"Cat."

Someone shook me until I opened my eyes and saw Gray's face. "They're underground, locked in a vault," I said. "He used a tunnel to bring them food and check on them. He took Sunny's jacket from her when she tried to run." I swallowed against a surge of bile. "When he left he was worried about being seen by people during Sparklefest. He's somewhere right here in town."

"Look at me." Gray held my hand in his. "It's okay. Breathe through it."

I watched his eyes as I took in the cold air, and felt the nausea slowly recede. When I could speak, I asked, "Does this happen to you?"

"Mine aren't this bad." He glanced at Trick before he lowered his voice. "You said the guy used your boyfriend's blood to change, right?"

"We think he did."

"Then I think he might be like him," he said. "Part vampire. That's why I can't track him."

"Then he won't change completely until he takes a human life," I said. "But he doesn't know that. He doesn't even realize he's turning into a vampire. He thinks he's becoming an immortal, and that I can finish some ancient Egyptian ritual to give him eternal life."

Trick came over to us. "You okay?"

"I just need a minute." As I rested, I told him and the sheriff what I'd seen in the vision. To Yamah, I said, "The tunnels were different than the ones the Ravens had built. They were smaller and more narrow, and rougher stone. I didn't see any lights."

The sheriff looked puzzled. "There aren't any tunnels like that that I know of."

"You have tunnels?" Gray asked.

"It's a long story," I told him. "I don't think these were under a building, not with those roots I saw hanging down from the ceiling. They might be somewhere in the woods, or under a garden."

"Who built the tunnels that you do know exist?" Trick asked Yamah.

"That was all done before I was born," the sheriff said. "One of the Ravens' people used to be a miner before he joined the circus and became a clown. He managed all the construction."

"That was Stanas," I said. "Jesse told me about him." I stood up. "The Jester's Maze. Stanas lived out there for years by himself. He must have built his own tunnels under it."

The sheriff looked skeptical now. "Why would he do that, Miss Youngblood?"

"To hide his treasure," I said, feeling more sure of my theory now. "No one has ever solved the maze, right? Maybe that's because he built part of it underground."

"That's where we should start searching," Trick said.

"Good luck with that," the sheriff said. "That maze covers at least five hundred acres, and most of that is woods."

"We have until midnight," I said. "We have to try."

Nineteen

What had seemed like such a good idea at the cemetery started looking hopeless as soon as we arrived at the entrance to the maze. Jesse had brought me there at night, so I hadn't been able to see just how overgrown and wild the land was. From the gates it looked like a jungle.

"The Ravens closed it to the public a few years back because of folks getting lost out there," Yamah warned as he unlocked the gates. "You should be all right if you keep your horses on the walkways, but don't take the one that veers off toward the lake. I can tell you that's a dead end."

"You tried to solve the maze, Sheriff?" I asked.

"Everyone is young and foolish at some time in their life, Miss Youngblood. I was no exception." He looked out at the horizon. "You've got about ten hours before the sun sets. Once you've found the entrance he's using, assuming there is one, mark it and come back." He unclipped his handheld and offered it to Gray. "Use the emergency channel if you get into trouble."

Trick brought some granola bars and water bottles, and packed them in our saddle bags. "I'd feel better if you'd stay here and let me take Sali out."

"What do you think, Sal?" I bent forward and pretended to listen. "She says you're too heavy to carry around for ten hours."

He gazed up at me. "Whether or not you find this tunnel entrance, I want you two back here before dark."

"We'll be careful."

I let Gray take the lead as we rode into the gardens and followed the path to the walkways. The wood creaked under Flash's hooves, making him skitter for a moment before Gray reined him in.

I looked at both walkways, but neither looked particularly promising. "Which one should we take first?"

"The left."

He sounded so definite I rode up alongside him. "Are you holding out on me?"

"It's the way you solve a maze," he said. "You keep going to the left."

"Have you ever done this?" I asked as we left the gardens and entered the woods.

"I read about mazes in a book."

I ducked my head to avoid a tangle of Spanish moss. "I mean hunting vampires."

He gave me a narrow look. "Why do you want to know?"

I tapped my temple. "I can't remember anything, so I'd like to know what to expect."

He hunched his shoulders. "Trick never let me track them."

I chuckled. "You should never lie. You completely suck at it."

"I tried a few times on my own," he finally admitted. "There's always more than one, and I thought if I took out a nest we could stay somewhere. I found one in California."

I remembered how fast we'd packed up and left that state. "What happened?"

"I found out why Trick didn't want me tracking them alone." His expression grew bleak. "They were living in this cavern in the mountains. They'd fixed it up like the inside of a house, with furniture and carpets and stuff. I found them sleeping in beds, like real people."

My eyes widened. "You went into the cave and *looked* at them?"

"I had to be sure."

"You *are* an idiot." I sighed. "So what did you do? Stake them in their sleep?"

"I didn't have any stakes," he muttered. "What? I'd never killed anyone. I just wanted to keep them from finding us. So I dragged in some brush and set it on fire, but the smoke woke them up."

I winced. "Oh, no."

"I thought they were just mindless monsters. But they're not." He glanced at me. "They had fire extinguishers."

It was almost funny—almost. "Which they used to put out the fire."

"Yeah, right before two of them jumped me." Absently he touched his shoulder. "I ran out of the cave with both of them on my back, which was the only thing that saved me." At my frown, he said, "The sun was still up."

"Did it kill them?"

"Yeah, but before I could get them off me they set my shirt on fire. Burned it right off my back." He shifted in the saddle. "Flash got me home, but I was pretty crispy. Trick had to take me to the hospital."

Suddenly I felt indignant. "Why don't I remember any of this?"

"One of the vamps from the cave tracked me back to our place that night." His voice grew defensive. "I didn't know they could do that, either. Trick never told me anything about them."

I took a deep breath. "I killed that one, too, I suppose?"

He nodded. "We left California the next day, and I promised Trick I'd never try to track them again."

"Until he made you try to track Jesse," I added helpfully. "What was the point of that, anyway?"

"It was when you got into all that trouble for stealing

my truck," Gray said. "At first Trick thought the guy you helped was a vampire, and he made you do it."

I glared at him. "Why would I help a vampire?"

"That's what I said," he told me. "He didn't believe me until I told him there was no scent trail, only a bunch of tracks out by that old place across the road. I also found some stuff inside the house, like you'd been meeting him there in secret for a while. That really drove him crazy."

Jesse and I had met several times at the Ravenovs' abandoned manor house, and he'd always lit candles in the windows. Once he'd spread an old quilt on the floor and treated me to a midnight feast. We'd cleaned up the food before we'd left, but we hadn't taken the quilt with us.

"Oh, my god." I laughed. "I wasn't having sex with him in there, you idiot. We had a picnic. It was totally innocent."

Now he looked uncomfortable. "I don't need any details of what you've done with that guy."

"His name is Jesse, and not that it's any of your business, but we haven't done anything." I saw the relief on his face. "Aside from some hand-holding, hugging and, oh yes, some pretty fantastic kissing."

He cringed a little. "I told you, I don't want to know."

I laughed. "Grim, I love Jesse. As in, forever and always. We may not be doing it right now, but eventually it's going to happen."

"So then you get pregnant like Mom, and have to run away with him and hide and be scared all time?" He sounded disgusted. "After everything we've been through, how could you do that to your own kid?"

"I don't know," I said. "How could you join the football team just to impress Tiffany Beck? Speaking of which, how could you let Trick take that away from you?"

His face reddened, and for a moment I thought he was going to yell at me. Then his shoulders slumped. "She never wanted to be with me. I was just a rebound boyfriend. I knew that the night Boone got shot."

"But you still blame me for it," I pointed out. "That's why you've treated me like trash since Halloween. I broke up your big romance, and ended your football career, and ruined your life." When he started to say something, I held up my hand. "There's just one problem with your grudge. I didn't do any of that. Trick did."

"Yeah, but he did it to protect you," Gray insisted. "Didn't you ever wonder why this happened? Why this guy kept chasing after you? He's almost a vampire, and vampires can't stay away from us, Cat. It's part of being a Van Helsing. We're like irresistible to them."

"So you think the only reason Jesse cares about me is because I'm a vampire magnet." I nodded. "Of course, that makes perfect sense. Except that he's not a vampire, I'm not a Van Helsing, and actually I chased him first."

He gave me a pitying look. "That's the other part of the Van Helsing thing."

"What?"

"We're attracted to them, too. I didn't want to disobey

Trick and go to that cavern in California." His voice dropped to a whisper. "I *had* to go."

———————

We spent the next three hours following the twists and turns of Stanas's maze, but we never found a hatch or an outbuilding or anything that might provide access to an underground tunnel the way the hatches in the shops in town did for the Ravens' tunnels. After hitting several dead ends and having to backtrack, it seemed pretty hopeless.

We did find a small, pretty lake, and stopped there to water and rest the horses. I didn't feel like talking, and Gray seemed fine with that.

I took a granola bar and a bottle of water out of the saddlebag and went to sit under an oak tree. Although the day hadn't warmed up, the sun was bright, and I'd forgotten to put on some sunscreen before I'd left the house. I'd have to borrow Gray's ball cap or I'd be slathering on the sunburn ointment tonight.

The granola bar tasted like ground-up cardboard, but I kept chewing and washed it down with the water. Jesse had told me that no one had ever solved the maze; my vision had been too vague to provide any clues. Gray couldn't pick up any scent trail. We weren't going to find anyone or anything out here. I had to start thinking about Plan B.

I knew my brothers were probably thinking about

staging some kind of ambush in the park, or having me summon my cats to jump the vampire there. He wouldn't be stupid enough to bring his hostages with him, of course. If we did that I'd be safe, but we'd never find the missing girls.

Jesse and I could do it.

If I let the vampire take me, I could use my bond with Jesse to lead him to the underground vault. He could rescue the girls while my cats and I held off the vampire. When they were safely out of there, then I could order my cats to finish it.

Stop dressing it up with pretty words, my sullen conscience said. *You're going to have to kill him. Just like you killed the others. It's the only way to stop him and you know it.*

A wide shadow fell across me, and I looked up at Gray.

"I checked in with the sheriff," he said, hooking the handheld back onto his belt. "You ready?"

I am never going to be ready for this, I thought, but I nodded and got up.

Flash didn't want to stop grazing, so I rode Sali around the lake while we waited for Gray to get him situated. That was when I saw a flash of something moving fast through the trees about a quarter mile away—too big to be a person—and heard the faint, rushing sound of leaves thrashing and branches snapping.

"Grayson." When he looked at me, I pointed in the direction of the movement. "There's something over there."

He peered. "Deer."

"It's too big." Too fast to be a bear, too, I thought, and then I caught a flash of gleaming red. "It can't be."

Sali shuffled under me as her head turned to watch the blurry movement.

"Gray," I yelled. "It's Rika."

"Hang on," he called back.

"No time." I took off after her, jumping the walkway and crossing the clearing between the lake and the tree line. I got within sight of the Arabian's churning flanks and peered at the swell of her belly. From the bulge in her side she hadn't foaled yet, but she was close.

Sali suddenly veered away from a big tangle of dead brush into the trees and skidded to avoid slamming both of us into the blackened trunk of a fallen pine that blocked our path. For a split second I was smothered in wilted, spade-shaped leaves and then something yanked me out of the saddle and threw me to the ground.

I landed on my side, hard, and felt the air whoosh out of my nose and mouth as the impact knocked it out of my lungs. Somehow I remembered to tuck and roll to avoid Sali's hooves as she fought to free herself from the tangle of dead vines that had unseated me. Dirt pelted my face and I turned my face away to protect my eyes.

Sali tore free and skittered away from me, pounding the ground as she headed back to the clearing. I lifted my head to see her running in a wide circle, whinnying so frantically it sounded as if she were screaming.

"Catlyn."

I wanted to yell for my brother, but my lungs weren't cooperating. My head spun as I tried to push myself up and quickly discovered why that wasn't going to work. When I'd rolled the vines we'd ridden into had wrapped around me, and now cocooned my arms and legs.

I'd definitely need Gray's help, so I focused on what I could do, which was catch my breath. When I got enough air in me, I called out, "I'm over here."

A grunting, snuffling sound answered me.

I looked over at the brush Sali had swerved around, and saw a big dark shadow moving in the center of it. Something was in there, something that had spooked her, and now it was coming toward me.

I struggled against the vines, freeing one of my hands and pulling at the tangle around my legs. The brush shivered and then shook as something squat and dark and ugly emerged.

It had small, beady eyes, and huge, pointed tusks. It also didn't like seeing me laying there trussed up like a Christmas turkey.

I stopped moving. "Hey," I said softly. "Are you the one who went to market, or the one who stayed home?"

The wild boar pawed the ground, and the brush behind it rustled as two smaller versions looked out at me before retreating.

"What cute babies." I hadn't just riled a boar in the

wild, I'd riled one who was a mother with young to protect. "I know you're probably not going to buy this, but I would never hurt them."

The boar lowered her head to gouge the ground with her tusks, and then uttered a furious squeal as she charged me.

"Hey." Gray rode between me and the mother boar and threw his water bottle, nailing her on the head. That, and Flash rearing up over her, convinced the boar to turn tail and run the other way.

"Stay down," my brother said before he and Flash chased the boar and her piglets across the clearing and into the trees.

Sali came back to stand guard over me until Gray returned, but by then I knew I hadn't broken anything.

"What's the damage?" he asked as he helped me to my feet.

"My hip's bruised, but it's not bad." I gazed over to the last spot I'd seen Rika, but there was no sign of her now. "What is that blockheaded mare doing all the way out here?"

"I don't know, and I don't care." He helped me mount Sali. "We're heading back."

"I'm okay."

"I'm not. You were ten feet away from being gored." He pulled a piece of vine from my jacket. "And this could have snapped your neck." He threw it down and scanned the clearing. "We're not going to find them out here, not like this. Not before sunset."

My hip throbbed in agreement with him. "All right, we'll head back. At least we found Rika." I looked out at the trees. "Sort of."

Twenty

As soon as Trick saw me riding up to the entrance to the maze he frowned, and of course Gray had to immediately tell him about my fall and the boar.

"I knew this was a bad idea." Trick made me dismount, and began to check my eyes and ears. When I protested, he said, "Hold still. You could have a concussion."

"I didn't hit my head, and it was bad luck," I assured him. "Sali scented the boar in time to avoid running over her and the babies. It could have been a lot worse."

I still had to demonstrate that all my limbs were working before he quit doctoring me, and even then he wasn't happy.

"You're limping," he said. "We should get that hip x-rayed."

I patted it, hiding a wince. "It's sore, not broken."

"You don't have nine lives, Catlyn," he grated. "You only get one."

"Don't yell at me, because I do have some good news." I told him about spotting Rika out in the maze. "From what I saw she hasn't foaled yet, but her side is swollen. She's got to be close." I glanced back at the maze.

"Don't even think about it," Trick said. "Horses have been foaling in the wild for thousands of years. She can handle it."

"It's not that." I wished I had time to go after Rika, but sunset was only a few hours away. "I need to go home and get cleaned up." I took a deep breath before I added, "Then I have to call Raven Island, and talk to Jesse."

"No." My brother took my arm and marched me over to Gray's truck. He put me in the passenger side of the cab, and as soon as the horses were loaded he climbed in behind the wheel and drove us home.

"So what's Plan B?" I asked as we left town and headed for the farm. "Are we going to ambush him in the park when he comes for me? We won't find the girls that way, you know."

"This is over now." Trick didn't look at me. "You're staying home. The sheriff and the Ravens will deal with the vampire."

So we were back to complete and utter denial of the situation. "I'm the one he wants. He's not going to show unless I'm there."

"You're not going anywhere near that town tonight," he told me. "End of discussion."

Once we arrived home Trick told me that he and Gray would handle the horses, and sent me into the house. I went straight for the aspirin and a hot shower, which helped ease some of my soreness, if not my mind.

I heard my brothers come in, and Trick began rattling pots and pans in the kitchen. Of course, he was going to heat up the Christmas dinner Gray had brought home from the market. We were going back into happy family mode. And if I went downstairs, and pretended to do the same, he'd find an opportunity to give me a hug, or take my hand in his, and then nothing would be wrong because I wouldn't remember any of this.

I couldn't let him do that to me. Not now, and not ever again.

I opened the window to my bedroom, and looked down at the ground. Because of my hip I'd have to climb the pine tree halfway instead of jumping as I normally would, but I could get out of the house. But Trick had the keys to Gray's truck, and tired as Sali was, I couldn't ride her all the way back into town.

Sali isn't my only ride anymore.

I looked out at the little red convertible Gray had parked out by the barn earlier that morning. I closed my eyes and willed myself to remember what I'd seen when he'd done that. He'd gotten in, started the engine, drove it across the lawn, and then had parked it. He hadn't locked the doors ... and he hadn't been holding the keys when he'd climbed out.

I came over and sat down on my bed. If I did this, it would probably destroy my family for good. If I didn't, three girls were going to die.

A knock sounded on my door before it opened and Trick looked in on me. "Are you feeling better?"

Why lie? "Not especially."

He came in and closed the door behind him. "I'm sorry I snapped at you earlier. I've made a real mess of things, and I shouldn't have taken out my anger on you."

"I'll survive." A tiny spark of hope glimmered in my heart. "I talked to Gray while we were out riding the maze. He told me about what happened in California, and some other stuff. I think I understand things a little better now."

"I'm glad." He sat down next to me. "I know you're blaming yourself for what's happened, but Cat, none of this is your fault. I realized tonight how selfish I've been, and how much grief I've caused you and Gray because of it. This is one hundred percent on me."

I looked down at my hands. "You were just doing what you thought was right."

"I used to dream about this place." His expression softened. "I wanted it to be perfect for us. So I waited and saved until I was sure we'd be safe here and I could make a go of it. This was supposed to be our reward for all the years of running." He gave me a sideways glance. "But it was always about what I wanted, not what was right for you. I know that now."

This confession was starting to worry me. "Patrick, what are you trying to say?"

"Until now, I've been making all the decisions for this family." He stood up. "I think it's time I learned how to compromise, and let you and your brother have some say in what happens."

My spark of hope flared back up. "Does this start now?"

"It can," he agreed, "as long as you're willing to tell me what you want, and work out a compromise with me."

"I don't want you to make me forget anything, ever again, for the rest of my life," I told him. "That's number one on my wish list."

"Very well. I promise that I won't tamper with your memories anymore." When I grinned, he lifted his hand. "As long as you agree to stop seeing the Raven boy."

His name is Jesse. "That's not fair."

"In my eyes, it's an even exchange," he said. "To get what we want, we both have to give up something that is very important to us."

My heart wanted to flat-out refuse; my common sense told me to lie and agree. Neither would give me what I really needed, so instead I went with my instincts. "Do you need an answer now, or can I have some time to think about it?"

That wasn't what he was expecting me to say, but he hid his surprise quickly. "It can wait until tomorrow morning."

"Thanks." I smiled. "I'll be down in a minute."

I got to the kitchen just as Gray was taking the pre-cooked turkey out of the microwave and Trick was setting the table. The market had provided all the traditional side dishes, from jellied cranberries to green bean casserole, and there was even a little fruitcake decorated with flowers made of candied cherries and slivers of apricot.

"That looks amazing," I told Gray as I got out a big platter for the turkey. "When did you enter the contest for this, Trick?"

"I didn't." He eyed Gray. "I thought you did."

"Wasn't me."

"Well, I didn't enter the contest." I felt uneasy now. "Maybe they mixed up the phone numbers."

"I saw the entry form in the box." Gray went over to where he had left it by the trash and reached inside for the slip of paper. "This is our address and phone number. It says 'The Youngblood Family.'" He handed the slip to me.

"Someone must have entered it for us." I studied the handwriting, which to my relief wasn't Jesse's, but still looked familiar. I glanced at the corkboard by the wall phone, and saw the note about Rika's feed ratio. The handwriting was identical. "I know. It was Mena Marks."

Gray scowled. "Why would she do that?"

"She has this gigantic crush on Trick," I said, shaking my head sadly. "I don't think she realizes he's old enough to be her father."

"Dr. Marks has at least ten years on me," Trick put in. "But I can wait until she's eighteen."

"If you got married, would that make her my stepsister, or my step-guardian?" I wanted to know.

"Stop it." Gray glared at both of us. "This is embarrassing."

I chuckled. "Relax, Grim. All she did was fill out a contest entry form. It was a nice thing to do."

"I'm going to have to thank her, aren't I?" When Trick and I both nodded, he dropped in his chair. "Great."

The dinner was delicious, and we all tried to enjoy it. I teased Trick about the year he had tried (unsuccessfully) to grill our Christmas turkey, which Gray and I renamed the Christmas jerky before we'd microwaved some frozen pizzas. As we laughed and joked about other holiday disasters, the last rays of the sun shimmered away and the window grew dark.

Once we'd finished eating and tidied up, I made popcorn and hot cocoa while my brothers took out their gift basket goodies, and we carried out everything to the living room to watch Gray's Christmas movies.

"I never get tired of watching *A Christmas Story*," I said as the movie began. "Why is that?"

"It's funny," Trick said, and yawned before he ate some popcorn and took a sip of his cocoa. "Nobody ever gets tired of laughing." He leaned back against the sofa pillows as his eyelids drooped.

Stretched out on the floor in front of the television,

Gray pillowed his head on his arms. "They should make all movies funny. Then girls wouldn't cry through them."

I stole one of his cookies, but I left my mug of hot cocoa on the coffee table. "Movies don't make me cry."

He held up one finger. "*Titanic.*"

"Okay, but all those people drowned, and they didn't have to, and that was very sad." I glanced over at Trick, whose head was nodding. "See, he agrees with me."

Gray held up a second finger. "*Steel Magnolias.*"

I scoffed out some air. "That one made *you* cry, Grim."

"Julia Roberts should never die." He tried to hold up a third finger, and frowned at his hand. "There was...another one."

I took the bowl of popcorn out of Trick's lap before it slid over with him. "It was *Gladiator.*"

"Cat." Gray lifted his head and tried to focus on me. "I can't...stay..."

"Awake." I waited until he slumped over, and then got up to tuck a pillow under his head. "I know."

I made sure they were both sound asleep before I left the house. As I'd suspected, the keys were still in the convertible, but I didn't get in it right away. I went into the barn and slipped into Sali's stall. Still tired from the long day's ride, she shuffled over to me.

"Not tonight, girl," I said as I rested my cheek against her strong neck. "I've got to take this ride without you." I couldn't say good-bye to her, not without bawling like a baby, so I gave her a kiss on the nose. "Look after them for me."

I had to hurry out of the barn before I changed my mind, and then I got in my new car. The dashboard wasn't the same as Gray's truck, but once I tested a few buttons and switches I knew where everything was, and started the engine.

Driving to town I had to resist every second thought. I drove past Kari's apartment building, and the temptation to stop and ask her to come with me. I passed one of the sheriff's deputies in his patrol car, and didn't do anything stupid to attract his attention. Once I reached town, I saw people strolling everywhere, admiring the lights, and didn't pull over to join them. I kept going until I reached the little lot next to the park, and eased the convertible into the very last spot left.

The vampire hadn't told me exactly where to wait for him, but the park was small, and I knew he wouldn't want us to be seen. I walked to a bench at the farthest corner, where only a single string of lights curled around the trunk of a coconut palm. There I sat down, and looked at the beauty all around me, and wondered if this would be the first night of my life, or the last.

He came up behind me, as silent as the shadows, and his cool hand touched the top of my head. "You shouldn't be here alone."

"Those were my instructions." I turned around and looked at Jesse. "You shouldn't be here, either."

"I didn't think you would go through with it," he admitted.

Earlier that day, after Trick had offered me his compromise and left me in my room, I'd used my bond with Jesse to wake him from his sleep and tell him what I'd planned to do. Although some of the details troubled him, he'd agreed to help me.

After that I'd gone downstairs, but before I went to the kitchen I'd slipped into Trick's bathroom to take a few of his sleeping pills from his cabinet. I'd kept them in my pocket during Christmas dinner, and then dissolved them into the milk I'd heated to make the hot cocoa.

My brothers never noticed that I didn't drink any of mine.

Deliberately drugging my brothers so I could escape them was probably the most cold-blooded thing I'd ever done. I knew the risk I was taking, and as Trick had said, I didn't have nine lives. But after tonight, nine lives would be changed forever: mine and Jesse's, his parents' and my brothers', and the three missing girls'. I had to believe that what I'd done was worth saving the three of them.

"My brothers are never going to forgive me for this," I told him.

"Perhaps they will." He rested his hand on my shoulder. "They know how much you love them."

"No more than the Johnsons, the Waynes and the

Hamiltons love their daughters." I gazed up at him. "But not as much as I love you."

He bent down, and the kiss he gave me took away a little of the pain. "I'll be watching from the rooftops."

Twenty-One

The temperature dropped steadily, and a chilly breeze chased most of the Christmas-light lovers out of the park, but I barely felt the icy air as I waited on the bench. From the moment I'd decided to use Trick's pills to gain my freedom, something slumbering inside me seemed to awake. It felt hot and wild and almost uncontrollable, but this time I wasn't fighting it, and I wasn't afraid of it. If this was what gave me the ability to kill, then I would use it.

Tonight I had to be a Van Helsing.

The city hall's clock chimed eleven times, and as I got up to stretch my stiff limbs I heard a commotion and turned around. A lady walking her poodle came running toward me, almost tripping as she bent down to pick up the little ball of fur before she darted behind a tree. At that moment she saw me and shrieked, "Watch out."

The horse burst out of the bushes, her legs churning as she came straight at me, and I spun out of the way just in time.

"Rika."

The Arabian reacted to my call by wheeling around and stopping, her sides billowing in and out as she regarded me.

"Ma'am," I said to the lady with the poodle, "could you throw me your dog's leash?"

"For that thing?" I heard the woman say.

"Please. I need to catch this horse." I looked down as the leash landed next to my foot. "Thank you."

I bent down to retrieve the leash, and then whistled. Rika's ears pricked, and she trotted up to me, shivering and blowing, her hide soaked with cold sweat. Just as I reached for her she stepped back and shook her head.

"Come here, girl." When she backed away, I started toward her. "Rika, it's me. Come on, it's okay."

The mare snorted and turned, trotting down to the corner, where she stopped and looked back at me.

"I can't play tonight. Rika, come on." I walked half-way to the corner, stopped, and whistled for her again. "Rika, here."

Again she trotted a short distance away, halted and waited, watching me. I didn't want to leave the park, but if she ran out in front of a car she might kill herself, the foal and whoever was driving. I hurried after her.

She kept playing her version of keep-away, leading me across town until she stopped just at the entrance of the maze.

I looked at the gates, which were standing open, and then at the mare. "Okay, you didn't do that."

She trotted through the entrance and disappeared into the gardens.

I caught up with her in front of the shrine Stanas had made for his lost love. "Are you tired of chasing wild geese yet?"

The Arabian lowered her head, touching her nose to the top of the tiny bower made of shells.

"Yeah, I know, it's pretty," I told her as I came forward slowly. "Why don't we go back to the park and call Dr. Marks and see if he can come and take you back to his clinic, before you drop that foal on its head?"

Rika snorted and began pawing the ground.

I could see the shrine starting to tip to one side. "No, no, stop that, Rika. Pay attention to me, I'm your friend, remember?"

The Arabian turned around, kicked, and shells went everywhere as her hooves destroyed the top of the shrine. I used the moment to grab her halter and clip the poodle's leash to one of the rings. She pulled against it, dragging me off my feet, and I landed on the ground in front of what was left of the shrine.

"Thanks." I lifted my head and held on to the end of the leash as I rubbed my bruised chin with my free hand. Something creaked as I moved, and I looked beneath me.

Under the dirt some streaks of wood showed through, and when I brushed it away I uncovered one corner of a panel of oak.

I felt curving ridges under my fingers, and traced them. They formed the shape of a heart.

Stanas told them that whoever solved his maze and found its heart would discover a great treasure he'd hidden there.

I got up to tie Rika, who was now quiet, to the iron bench near the shrine. When I went back I saw that the shells and flowers all around the base, some of which Rika had pawed away, had been placed on top of the panel. Since the shrine covering the statue of Stanas's girl was already destroyed, I gave the remaining portion a push, and it slid slow back from the rest of the panel.

Not a panel, I thought as I crouched down to examine it. A hatch.

Catlyn, where are you?

I'd completely forgotten about Jesse. *I'm in the Jester's Maze, with Rika. I think I've found where he's keeping the girls.*

I will get James. Wait for us.

Hurry.

I lifted the hatch and saw the same stone steps that had appeared in my blood vision. The sound of crying drifted up to me, tearing at me as I threw aside the hatch and lowered myself over the edge until my feet touched the top step.

Water trickled down the stairs and formed a wide pool at the base, so I braced one hand against the tunnel wall as I descended. Everything was exactly as I'd seen it in the vision, and I followed the passage to the barred wooden door. Inside I could hear the sound of crying and a voice whispering. I lifted the bar and cast it aside before I went in.

Two of the girls sat huddled beside Sunny Johnson, who held the broken handle of a broom as if it were a spear. I could see the clean trails tears had made through the dirt on her thin face, and she held her left arm tucked against her body, but her eyes were dry and wide and angry.

There was no sign of the vampire.

"Don't you come near us," she told me, her voice like a slap. "Or so help me, I'll stake you through the heart."

"I'm not here to hurt you," I told her. "My name is Cat Youngblood. I'm going to get you out of here."

The broom handle lowered. "Did you bring the sheriff? Are my parents here?"

"No, it's just me right now." The sound of metal clinking made me look down at the chains and cuffs the vampire had put on the girls' feet. "Where are the keys?"

"He's got them." The girl reached into her back pocket and took out a bobby pin that had been bent at different angles. "I've been trying with this, but I don't know how to pick a lock."

Neither did I, which left me with only one option. "I've got to go back up and get some help."

"No." She grabbed my sleeve with her fist. "You can't leave us down here. He's coming back."

I glanced down at her arm, which had been badly

bruised from her wrist to her elbow, and hung limp, as if she couldn't use it. "Did he do this to you?"

"Yeah. He thinks he's a vampire." She pushed the hair back from her neck to reveal more bruises. "He keeps trying to bite me to drink my blood, but he doesn't have fangs and he's too weak to do it with his own teeth."

"After tonight," a dry, horrible voice said, "I won't need your blood."

I turned around and for an instant saw a dark-haired young man with dark eyes and a beautiful face. As soon as I blinked, he changed into a wrinkled old man with ashen skin and bleary eyes.

He bowed. "Welcome, my queen. I had almost given up hope." He shuffled forward. "But at last you have come to me."

"I'm not here for you, old man," I told him. "I'm taking these girls back to their families."

"I will give them to you." He reached into his pocket and took out a ring of keys. "As my gift." When I held out my hand, he closed his gnarled fist over the keys. "As soon as you give me what I want."

"I'm not giving you anything, Mr. Hargraves."

"You know my name." His lips stretched into a ghastly smile. "I am sorry it took so long for me to find you, my queen." He coughed, and for a moment I thought he was going to topple over. Then his eyes shifted past me. "But now that you are here, everything will be fine."

I heard Sunny whisper "I'm sorry" a second before

something hit me in the back of the neck, and all the lights went out.

———

A pounding headache brought me back to consciousness, where I found myself in a big, brightly lit room furnished with antiques. Shells had been glued like mosaic tiles to the rough stone walls, and formed a fantasy garden in white. Colorful gems in the center of every flower glittered in the light of the kerosene lamps. As pretty as it was, the air smelled horribly stale, as if the room hadn't been used in years.

I pushed myself up from the sofa on which I lay, and looked around. I saw no doors or windows, and no one else but the man on the other side of the room.

Julian Hargraves stood arranging things on a table set for two. As soon as I moved he glanced back at me. "Ah, you're finally awake. Good. I've been waiting for hours, and we have to complete the ritual before sunrise."

I looked at the old knife, the shallow bowl, and the small Egyptian statue he had on the table. "Mr. Hargraves, I'm not who you think I am."

"I know you're not mortal, Catlyn. You don't have to pretend with me." He walked over to sit in a chair beside the sofa. "I'm sorry that I made the girl hit you, but we needed some privacy for this."

"What did you do with the girls?"

"They're waiting in the chamber for us." He smiled,

displaying a metal band fitted over the front of his teeth. Two white snake's fangs had been fitted to the metal. "When the ritual is complete and you have finished my change, we will both feast on them."

I could try and explain to him that draining me of blood would just kill me and make him into a vampire. Or I could play along until I could find a way out of here. "That's good." I stood up. "Have you finished your prayers?"

He frowned. "Prince Aktep never prayed."

"I know." I thought fast. "That's why the gift of immortality was taken away from him. He forgot to honor the gods and goddess." I made a gesture at the table. "If you want immortality, you have to pray to them first and ask." As his eyes narrowed, I added, "I don't think they'll say no. They've already brought you this far."

"Very well." He got down on his knees in front of me. "You will have to tell me how to do this."

"It's not that difficult. Close your eyes." As soon as he did, I began looking around the room for a way out. "Now, tell the goddess why you think you deserve to live forever."

As he murmured, I scanned the walls. The shells and jewels Stanas had applied covered almost every inch of stone, but at last I spotted an arching pattern of scallop shells that looked like a door.

"I'm finished," Julian said, opening his eyes.

"No, you're not," I said. "You have to show them that you're grateful." I pointed down. "Touch your head to the floor and thank them for their gift."

He leaned over, closing his eyes as he put his forehead against the stone.

I hurried over to the door, and fumbled with the conch shell Stanas had used as the knob. Once I got it to turn I pulled, and shells and jewels began raining down on my head as part of the wall swung out.

"Catlyn." Julian dragged me back, clamping an arm around my waist. "You're a liar."

I fought him as he dragged me over to the table, but he was too strong for me. "I'm not immortal, you crazy old man. If you do this, you'll just turn into a monster."

"I will be a god," he said as he groped for the knife. "And you will be my queen."

"The blood you took from the boathouse was not hers, Julian," I heard Jesse say. "It was mine."

The old man wrenched me around and held me up against him like a shield. "You can't deceive me. She's the queen of your kind. I read about her in the books. The daughter of Bast, the Queen of Cats."

"You're mistaken. She's only a human girl, just like the others." My dark boy circled around the old man. "I am the immortal."

Hargraves shook his head. "You're lying. I know it's her. I found the proof." He shrieked as Jesse seized him, and then his body shifted, becoming young and strong again. He threw Jesse across the chamber, and when he fell Julian leapt on top of him, slashing at his throat with the knife.

I screamed and lunged, but someone caught me from behind, and I struggled against the iron grip. "Let me go."

"Not this time, Cat." Trick turned me around to face him. "Stay there."

My brother strode over to Julian and pulled him off Jesse. Still holding him, he pinned him against the wall, so hard the shells behind him shattered.

At first Julian howled and fought, but he couldn't free himself. Then his struggles slowed and he fell silent, until all he did was stare into my brother's eyes.

I hurried over to Jesse, who had his hand pressed to his throat. His eyes had gone black, but when he took his hand away the gash on his neck was already closing.

My brother leaned close and murmured something to Julian, whose expression blanked. When my brother released him, his body shifted again into that of an old man as he turned and shuffled out of the passage.

Jesse started after him, but my brother held up a hand. "You don't want to do that, boy."

I didn't understand. "You can't just let him go, Patrick."

"He won't be going anywhere." He walked out after the old man.

I remembered that Julian still had the keys to the cuffs and chains on the kidnapped girls, and ran out after my brother. "Trick, wait."

By the time Jesse and I caught up with him he was at the stone stairwell, and Julian was climbing out of the hatch. Sunlight came pouring down as my brother followed the old man, and then I did the same.

The old man stood by the remains of the shrine, the sunlight pouring over him. His wrinkled face shriveled even more, and his clothes began to sag as if he were shrinking inside them.

I thought it was the sunlight. "Why is he just standing there? Why doesn't he run back into the tunnel?"

"He can't do anything but stand there." Trick spared me a glance. "He doesn't remember how to."

A few seconds later Julian Hargraves collapsed, his body little more than a skin-covered skeleton, and he didn't move again.

I forced myself to walk over and take the keys from his jacket pocket, turning my head so I didn't have to look at his face. I went to the edge of the tunnel, and looked down to see Jesse standing in a beam of light.

"Jesse, no."

He looked up at me. The sun didn't make his skin burn or smoke. He looked at his hand, touched it to his heart, and then held it up to me before he disappeared.

I hardly knew what to think as I climbed down the stairs. The sunlight hadn't hurt him. It wasn't possible.

Trick didn't say anything as he followed me back down and helped me free the girls. I watched while he held their hands and spoke quietly to them, but I didn't object or interfere as he erased their memories of what Julian had done to them and what they'd witnessed. In a way, making them forget their ordeal was almost a blessing.

When we left the chamber I glanced toward the room where Julian had intended to kill me.

"He's gone, Cat," Trick said.

Sheriff Yamah stood waiting at the shrine when we led the girls up to the surface, and he and his deputies ushered them away. I looked down at the empty spot on the ground where Julian's body had fallen.

"How did you know where we were?" I asked, and then I saw Gray standing a short distance away. "I don't understand."

"We're only half-human," Trick said. "Drugs don't work very well on us."

So he knew what I'd done. "I'm not going to apologize."

He met my gaze. "I could have sent that boy up here along with Julian. I can go now with Gray, and hunt him down, and make him forget that sunlight will kill him, and this will be over once and for all."

"Then you'll kill me, too, Patrick," I said quietly. "I love Jesse, and I'm not going to live without him."

Twenty-Two

at?"

Sunny Johnson's voice brought me out from behind the book shelves, and I smiled as I went up to unlock the front door and let her in. "Hey, survivor girl." I glanced at the woman standing behind her. "Oh. Hi, Mrs. Johnson."

Sunny's mom held up her hands. "Don't be afraid, Cat. I'm not armed or dangerous."

"You were never any such thing." I was glad she looked so happy, though. "Everything all right?"

"Yes. All right, wonderful, amazing and miraculous." She beamed at her daughter before she added, "Sunny told me that it was you and your brothers who found her and Melissa and Becca. I just wanted to thank you personally. I'm sure the other mothers will, too."

"It's okay." By this time tomorrow none of them would even remember their daughters had been kidnapped, I thought, my heart turning into a lead weight. "We were just in the wrong place at the right time."

Sunny nudged her mother. "Mom, could you give us a sec?"

"Sure, honey." Mrs. Johnson took my hand in hers as she looked into my eyes. "If you ever need anything, Catlyn, anything at all, please make me the first person you ask."

Sunny waited until the door to the shop closed before she rolled her eyes. "She means that, too. You could even need a kidney, and she'd be first in line to donate one of hers."

"She was really worried about you." I glanced past her shoulder at the Junktique. "How's your dad?"

"He let Nicky drive me home from the hospital. I could hardly believe it, but I guess they talked a lot while I was gone." She bit her bottom lip before she said, "Cat, about that boy who came in after the old man made me hit you."

"His name is Jesse, and . . . ." I trailed off as I stared at her. "Sunny, you remember that?"

She nodded. "I know your brother tried to make me forget everything like the other girls, but it didn't stick. I think I know why. One time, when the old man was biting me, I kind of bit him back. I got his blood in my mouth, and I spit it out, but I felt different after that." She gave me a desperate look. "Will I grow fangs now?"

"I think if you were going to," I said honestly, "you'd already have them."

"That's what I thought." She sighed. "I wasn't going to tell anyone, but... well, I can't stop thinking about Jesse. His eyes, I mean. They were all black." She hesitated. "The old man's turned that way whenever he shifted."

"They're not the same," I said carefully. "Julian was insane. Jesse is... almost as normal as we are."

Sunny took in a quick breath. "So he is a vampire?"

"No. Not all the way." I could see her mom looking in the window at us. "He's very fast and strong, and he doesn't age, but he doesn't drink human blood, and he would never hurt anyone." I saw her mother peering in. "I think your mom is getting anxious, and my brother will be here to pick me up any minute."

"She doesn't even want me to go to bathroom by myself," Sunny complained, and then her expression grew serious. "I thought we were gonna die down there. Thank you for giving me my life back."

I hugged her, and then sent her off with her mom before I went back to dusting the shelves. When I finished that final task, I looked around the shop one last time. If books could talk, I'd be in very hot water, but Mrs. Frost would never know I'd done anything here but the job she'd hired me to do. Assuming my brother let her remember that.

Instead of going out the front door and waiting for Trick, I let myself out through the back. From there I walked slowly down the street to the public docks. I didn't look at the boathouse when I stepped over the chain with the CLOSED sign; instead I went to the very end of the pier.

Lost Lake had gotten lost again. A fine white mist hovered, concealing the dark water and stretching out from the banks and growing denser around the distant blur of Raven Island.

I couldn't see the mansion, but lights from its windows glittered along the farthest edge of the mist. I decided the brightest was coming from his room, and focused on it.

No matter what happens here today, some part of me will always love you, I thought.

"You shouldn't be down here by yourself, young lady."

I turned my head as Jim Yamah came to stand beside me. "I'm not going to do anything stupid, Sheriff. I just wanted to say good-bye."

He braced his arms against the railing. "I don't think even Jesse can hear you from here."

"He's not the one I'm saying good-bye to." The sound of Trick's Harley made me glance back at the street, where he was parking it. The panic I didn't want to feel set its teeth in me. "If I punched you, sir, really hard, would you arrest me and put me in jail and not let me have any visitors?"

"No," he admitted. "But I'd probably have you pick up trash for a month. Two if you broke anything." He eyed me. "Keeping secrets is what started this whole mess,

Miss Youngblood. Maybe it's time you and your brothers got better acquainted with the truth."

Jim Yamah gave my shoulder an awkward pat before he left me there. All I heard him say as he passed my brother on the pier was "Evening, Patrick."

"Jim." Trick kept walking steadily toward me.

I wanted to jump in the water. I wasn't a great swimmer, but I could probably make it to one of the boats at the marina. And steal it, and go out to the island, and try to speak to Jesse again ... or maybe I'd get hypothermia in the freezing cold water, lose consciousness and drown. And then all my problems would be solved. I wondered if my brother could hear me thinking that. I hoped so.

By then Trick was standing just behind me. "Cat, what are you doing here? You were supposed to wait at the shop for me."

"I know." My legs felt weak, and I dropped down to perch on the pier's edge, folding my legs under me so my shoes wouldn't get wet. "I can't seem to do anything right."

Trick gripped the railing as he sat down beside me. "Me, either."

"Are you going to take my memories here, or wait until we get home?"

"It doesn't work that way. The memories are still there; I just plant new ones that cover them up." He looked down at the mist swirling around the pylons. "That's why I'm responsible for what happened to Julian Hargraves."

I stared at him. "You're blaming yourself for what that crazy old man did? What about me? What about

Jesse? I was the girl he wanted to kidnap. He used Jesse's blood to change into … whatever he was. You were never a part of this." And because I wanted to hurt him, I added, "I made sure of it."

"I could have stopped it before anything happened," my brother said slowly. "But I didn't know that Julian had witnessed the attack on you and Jesse on Halloween night. Jim told me the old man was a recluse who never left his mansion, so I didn't bother to check on him or give him new memories."

"And the next day everyone thought he was dead."

Trick nodded. "If I'd been more careful, more thorough, none of this would have happened."

If he was looking for sympathy, he'd come to the wrong pier. "Look on the bright side. You'll be the only one who remembers that you screwed up."

"He's not going to tamper with your memories again, Catlyn," Jesse's voice said, as clearly as if he were sitting next to me.

Trick stood and pulled me to my feet at the same time. A loop of rope lassoed the top of one mooring post, and out of the mist a small dark boat floated up beside the pier. After he tied off another line, Jesse stepped up and faced my brother.

Trick looked as if he'd been kicked in the gut. "We made an agreement."

"Another agreement?" I looked from Jesse to Trick. "Patrick, what did you do?"

"He offered me his blood to give my parents," Jesse

said. "Not all of it, of course; just enough to make them resistant to sunlight, as I am now. He asked only one thing in return: that I never try to see you again."

Of course Trick knew how much Jesse loved his mother and father, and what it would mean for the Ravens to be more human. He'd used that desperation against them, and I'd probably never forgive him for it.

I kept my game face on as I watched Jesse. "Then why are you here?"

"They don't need it anymore, do they?" Trick asked, and when Jesse shook his head, he turned to look out at Raven Island. "I didn't think you'd figure it out."

"When Julian attacked me, he took from me enough blood to enable him to finish making the change." Jesse tugged his collar back to reveal the slash on his neck. "When you sent him above ground, the sunlight should have set him on fire. But taking my blood made him more human."

I reached up and touched the scar on my shoulder. "Because you took mine that night, and it changed yours."

"He's still not human," Trick said abruptly.

Jesse nodded. "But neither am I vampire."

"I told your parents the truth," my brother said, a note of warning in his voice. "Our blood is not a cure. You can never change back completely."

"But you neglected to mention that my blood would help them just as much as yours." Jesse studied his face. "You used our ignorance to extract my promise never to see Catlyn again."

My brother didn't look the least bit ashamed. "If you had a fifteen-year-old sister, you'd do the same."

"So we're right back where we started." I faced my brother. "I'd call you a horse's ass, but that would be an insult to horses." I turned to my dark boy. "You are just as bad as him."

"I know," Jesse said. "I am sorry."

My brother folded his arms. "I'm not."

"Both of you say you love me, and then you do all these terrible things to me." I turned to my brother. "I'll be sixteen in a few weeks. That's old enough to go court and ask to be emancipated. I'll have to drop out of school and work full-time while I rent a room somewhere. Then, once I've saved enough of my earnings, I'll leave Lost Lake for good."

Trick moved his shoulders. "If you remember to do all that."

"I don't have to." I took out the letter in my pocket and handed it to him. "I wrote everything that's happened to me in this letter, and I gave a copy of it to someone you don't know. Every week I will check in with that person. If I don't, the letter goes public."

He read the address on the envelope, which was for an Orlando newspaper. "I can give new memories to nosy newspaper reporters as well as reckless sisters."

"Oh, my letter won't be mailed to a newspaper," I told him. "My check-in person will post it on the Internet."

He crumpled the envelope in his fist. "You're bluffing."

I smiled. "Brainwash me and find out."

"Am I mentioned in this letter?" Jesse asked.

I nodded. "You, your parents, Julian Hargraves, everyone and everything."

"You cannot expose us," Jesse said.

"You chose your parents over me, so why shouldn't I choose to do what I want?" Seeing the genuine-looking hurt in his eyes tore at me, but I had to finish this. "There are private islands all over the world, and you have tons of money. Just go buy another one."

"You've made your point," my brother said. "What do you want?"

"From now on? Leave my brain alone, let me and Jesse date like normal kids, and stop trying to run my life." I regarded Jesse. "And you. You will not lie to me, or make deals with my brother behind my back. You will start acting like a boyfriend instead of a bodyguard."

"Is that all?" Trick asked.

"There's one more condition." I gestured at both of them. "This idiot feud between our families is over. Finished. Forever."

Jesse looked at Trick. "I will speak to my parents and tell them they must end the feud or face exposure. Under the circumstances, I'm certain they will agree to your terms."

Trick looked like he was ready to explode. "I should have let the Van Helsings have you."

"Be careful what you wish for," I said in my sweetest voice. "I'm sure even Grandma and Grandpa have Internet access."

"Catlyn." My brother heaved a sigh. "All right. I'll talk to Grayson. But if you're going to date Jesse, then there will be some rules." When I started to tell him what I thought of that, he added, "You want to be treated like a normal teenager, then you have to behave like one." He turned to Jesse. "You have your car around here?" When he nodded, my brother said, "You can take her home. In the mood I'm in, I might shove her off the bike."

Trick walked off, leaving me with Jesse. As soon as I found my jaw and put in back where it was supposed to be, I felt oddly miffed. "I should have gotten all the dating rules up front. Assuming you still want to see me."

"I don't know." Jesse waited until my brother roared off on his Harley before he smiled slowly. "You were most convincing."

"Yes, I was." I threw my arms around his neck as he twirled me around. "We did it. Don't fall in the water. I love you."

Jesse didn't put me back on my feet until he kissed me breathless. Then I was the one who didn't want to let go.

"My very clever Cat," he murmured as he wrapped his arms around me. "You didn't tell me you were going to bring the letter."

"I wouldn't call it a letter exactly." I pulled the crumpled ball out of my pocket and grinned up at him. "This is more like a blank sheet of paper I folded up and sealed in this envelope."

"You took a great risk." He made a chiding sound. "What if he had tried to read it?"

"As soon as I told him what was—or actually wasn't—in it, I knew he wouldn't bother." I started to toss my bluff into the lake, and then thought better of it. "I think I'd better burn the evidence, just to be sure."

We walked from the pier to the lot on one side of the docks, where Jesse kept his car. As he went to open the passenger door for me, Sheriff Yamah's patrol car entered the lot and pulled alongside us. For once he seemed too agitated to notice that I was with Jesse. "Miss Young-blood, is your brother on his way back to the farm?"

"Yes, sir, he is." I frowned. "Is something wrong?"

"Your brother Gray called the station," he said. "One of your mares is having trouble foaling, and Dr. Marks is tied up at another farm." He finally saw Jesse was with me. "Maybe I should take you home."

"It's okay, Sheriff. Patrick asked him to drive me back." To Jesse, I said, "None of us have ever foaled a mare, and Rika's in trouble. Can you help?"

"Of course." He glanced over at Yamah. "If you will escort us, James, I will not have to adhere to the speed limit."

The sheriff nodded. "Let's not make this a habit. Come on."

With his lights flashing, Sheriff Yamah led the way out of town and back to the farm. Once we were in the drive, I saw all the lights in the barn blazing, and every horse we owned except Rika standing watch at the fence around the back pasture.

"I'd offer to help, but I don't know a blessed thing

about horses, and I'd just be in the way," Yamah said to me from his window. "Jesse, watch the time, and don't make your parents worry." He touched the brim of his hat and then backed out of the drive.

"How many mares have you foaled?" I asked my dark boy as we hurried to the barn.

"More than I bothered to count." He stopped me just outside the door. "This will be a messy business, and if the trouble is too great you could lose the mare or the foal."

"I won't freak out." I hoped.

We went into the barn, and as we passed the lights hung by the stalls Jesse began switching them off. "Too much light disturbs the mare," he explained.

Both of my brothers were in the stall with Rika, who lay on her side in the bedding. She was rocking back and forth and making a low, distressing sound, but it wasn't because of Gray or Trick. Since we'd rescued the girls Rika had undergone a dramatic personality change, as if Julian's death had freed her, too. She'd been gentle and calm around my brothers ever since.

Gray, who was kneeling behind her, looked up at us. "What is he doing here?"

"I can help." Jesse crouched down next to Rika, placing his hand on her shoulder and rubbing it in a soothing motion. "How long ago did her water break?"

Gray's mouth tightened before he said, "I'm not sure. Maybe half an hour ago."

Jesse leaned over to where Gray had bound up Rika's

tail in a clean towel wrap. An opaque white bulge protruded from the mare's birth canal. "That is the foal's sac."

I saw two tiny hooves but no nose. "Why isn't she pushing?"

"The foal is in the wrong position." Jesse rolled up his sleeves. "If she stands it will retreat and perhaps shift. Have you tried to get her up?"

"Twice." Trick came into the stall. "She won't budge."

"Then we must help her deliver, or the foal will drown inside her." Jesse moved behind her. "We must do this quickly, on the next contraction. Catlyn, go to her head and reassure her. Patrick, I will need toweling, baling twine and some elastic bands. Gray, you will have to pull the foal."

"All the books say not to pull," my brother argued.

"In a normal delivery, that is correct. But this foal is presenting back feet first," Jesse told him. "In this position the umbilical cord will break inside the womb, which is when the foal begins breathing. There is no air inside her, only fluid." He stood and backed away from Rika.

"Where are you going?" Gray asked as he shuffled around the mare.

"Your horse does not know me," Jesse told him as he moved out of the stall. He gazed at me. "You and your sister can do this."

I stroked Rika's neck. "It's okay, girl." I moved my hand down to the front of her belly, and felt her muscles tighten. "She's starting to strain again."

"Take hold of the foal's legs, in the pastern just above

the hooves," Jesse told Gray. "Pull steadily and firmly, down toward her hocks." He watched as more of the sac emerged. "The foal's shoulders are the widest and most difficult to pass, and sometimes they can catch. She will stop and rest for a moment, but you must maintain your hold so the foal does not slip back inside. When she strains again, you must bring it out completely."

Several tense minutes passed as Rika struggled to push out more of her foal. Just as Jesse had predicted, she stopped to rest halfway through, and then seemed to tense all over.

"Here we go," I said to Gray.

His jaw set as he pulled on the foal, and then wriggled the sac as Rika pushed harder. The foal's shoulders bulged out, and then the rest of the sac spilled onto the bedding in a gush of fluids.

"The sac is still intact," Jesse said. "You must break it, Gray, so the foal can breathe. Poke your fingers through the membrane and pull it away from the face."

Gray exposed the foal's head, and then used a towel to wipe mucus from the little nose and eyes. "It's not breathing."

Jesse smiled. "The umbilical cord is still attached and intact, which is very good. Use a piece of straw to tickle the nose."

"Tickle it?" Gray echoed, even as he picked up a piece of straw.

"An old trick. It always works."

The foal snorted, and then began breathing on its own as it struggled against the sac.

Rika lifted her head and nickered to the foal before she began rolling back into the position to stand.

"Catlyn, move clear of her, she will be uncomfortable for a few more minutes." Jesse turned to Trick and took one of the towels, handing it over the stall to Gray. "Rub down the foal's whole body, it will help stimulate circulation and breathing."

As I moved over to the wall, Rika suddenly stood, shaking herself and turning toward the foal. Gray got a little more spattered as the umbilical cord broke, but he was focused on the foal.

I finally took a look at the little wonder we'd worked so hard to bring into the world. "Do we have a filly or a colt?"

"Filly," Gray said as he opened a small container of prepared Nolvasan solution and dipped the foal's navel stump in it. He glanced at the membranes still hanging around Rika's hind legs. "She hasn't expelled the placenta."

"That will take another hour." To Trick, Jesse said, "Use the baling twine to tie up the membranes so she doesn't step on them. Catlyn, you must wash her udder before the foal tries to nurse."

I took the warm water and soap Jesse handed over to me and carefully washed away the bedding, dirt and fluids from Rika's udder and hindquarters. She mostly ignored me while she nuzzled and licked the little filly.

Gray stayed with the foal as she bonded with her dam and then tried to get up, her long legs awkward and wobbly. As soon as she was steady, she began nuzzling Rika's belly.

"She's hungry," Trick said, smiling.

The filly had no problem latching on, and after nursing for a few minutes settled back down in the straw for a nap. Trick went in to tie up Rika's membranes and help Gray remove the soiled bedding and spread fresh straw, and then we all left the stall to give the new mother and baby some time alone.

Trick and Jesse faced each other, and Gray came to stand beside Trick. I did the same at Jesse's side.

My older brother looked as stern as I'd ever seen him as he stepped forward. "Thank you for your help."

Jesse inclined his head. "I am happy I could be of assistance."

After another moment, my big brother held out his hand, and Jesse shook it.

That was when I knew we were going to be okay.

Epilogue

When Mrs. Frost came back to town, I met her at the bookstore to go over the results of the inventory. I managed to keep a straight face when she complimented me on the excellent job I'd done, although I couldn't help shuddering a little as I showed her the folder with tally sheets for Julian Hargraves's collection.

She picked up on that, too. "I felt rather guilty for giving you this responsibility. I know some of those books must have seemed a little disturbing."

"I think he was looking for answers in the wrong places," I said. After talking with Jesse about the letter Julian had left for Mrs. Frost, we'd decided to destroy it. "He might have had a happier life if he'd collected friends instead of books."

"That's a wise thing for such a young person to say."

Mrs. Frost put the file back with the others on her desk. "Poor Julian, he was so unhappy. Perhaps now he'll rest in peace."

Once we'd gone over everything and I received my last paycheck, Mrs. Frost surprised me with a small wrapped package.

"I know it's too late to serve as a Christmas gift," she said, "but when I saw this I thought immediately of you."

The little box held an enameled pin of a black cat with emerald eyes sitting atop a wee book. On the spine of the book golden script spelled out *9 Lives*.

"It's beautiful." I took it out and slipped it onto my blouse. "Thank you so much."

"My pleasure." She gave me a fond hug before she said, "I hope you'll also consider working for me again. Perhaps when school lets out for the summer?"

I grinned. "That would be awesome."

That weekend Trick took me to the Driver License Bureau, where I passed the written test for my restricted permit with a perfect score. It would be another year before I could test for my regular license, but as long as he or Gray was with me I could drive my new convertible. Then it was back to school, and a whole new schedule of classes, which included some of the girls we'd found in the maze. No one paid any attention to me except Lissa Wayne in 3-D Art, and she only gave me a brief, puzzled glance before she went back to talking to one of her friends sitting next to her.

I thought I'd be sitting alone again during lunch

period, but Sunny Johnson and a tanned, dark-haired boy came over and sat on either side of me.

"Hey. I'm Sunny, and this is my boyfriend, Nick," Sunny said, loud enough for everyone around us to hear. "He's re-enrolled and he has to repeat his sophomore year." Before I could answer she added in a lower voice, "It's okay to talk in front of Nick. He knows everything."

"Sunny." Dread turned me into a statue. "You're not supposed to ... "

"Talk about what happened? I didn't." She took out a spiral-bound notebook and handed it to me. "Special edition of the Lost Ledger. Seek didn't name Jesse, or old man Hargraves, but most of the story's in there. Nick filled in the blanks from stuff my mom and dad told him."

"Great." I shoved the notebook under my tray before the lunch monitor saw it, and then I looked at Sunny's boyfriend. "Are you going to tell anyone?"

"Who would believe me? Besides, I owe you." His expression grew serious. "If not for you and Jesse and your brother, Sunny wouldn't be here. So you don't have to worry about us, girl. We've got your back."

"Exactly." Sunny handed me a black marker and pulled back her sleeve from her cast. "But I do want an autograph."

After I signed my name we sat and talked about teachers and classes and normal stuff. Some of Sunny's friends joined us, and by the time lunch period ended I'd been invited to a 4-H meeting, a trail ride and a barbecue.

After school Gray stood waiting by the truck with Mena, who was talking with him about the foal. From the sound of the conversation she was doing all the talking and he just stood there staring down at her.

"Hey, Cat." She stood on her tiptoes to kiss Gray on the cheek before she winked at me and took off.

"Hey, Mena." I watched her practically skip to her bus. "Uh, when did you two become boyfriend-girlfriend?"

"We didn't." He unlocked my door and trudged around the truck. When we were inside, he stared at the steering wheel as if he wasn't sure what to do with it. "Why does she keep doing that?"

"Talking to you?" I shrugged. "She must like the sound of her own voice."

"No. I mean. Why does she." He blew out some air. "The kissing thing. Why kiss me?"

"Same reason she entered us into the contest for the Christmas dinner." I laughed at the look he gave me. "Come on, Grim. If the girl were any more obvious they could take pictures of it from the International Space Station."

"I couldn't. She's just … and I'm too … I can't." He propped his brow against the steering wheel before he gave me a sideways look. "She'll get over it, right?"

I made a seesaw gesture with my hand.

He sat up and started the engine. "She will. Eventually."

I wasn't fooled. If his cheeks turned any redder they'd stop traffic.

At home Gray went to check on Rika and the foal while I picked up the mail and went in the house. I found Trick in his bedroom, where I handed over the bundle of bills and advertisements.

"I've got some forms for you to sign for my new classes, and tomorrow I need five dollars for my art class supply fee." I glanced at his computer monitor. "How goes the telecommuting thing?"

"I'm building a web site for a freelance musician." He rolled his eyes. "He wants to call it 'Slow Lazy Sax.'"

"Talk him out of it," I advised.

"Hang on," Trick said as I started to head out, and offered me an envelope. "This is addressed to you."

It looked like a card of some kind, but the sender hadn't included their return address. I opened it and took out an elegant card with the words "Happy Birthday" printed in fancy script above two entwined roses on the front. I opened it to read the message inside.

May your sixteenth birthday bring you as much happiness as finding you at last has brought to us. We look forward to meeting you very soon.

Abraham and Maria Van Helsing

———

About the Author

New York Times bestselling author Lynn Viehl has published over forty-seven novels in six genres. On the Internet, she hosts Paperback Writer, a popular publishing industry weblog and writers' free online resource. When she's not writing or reading, Lynn lives a quiet life with her family in the country, where she spends her spare time collecting great books, sewing traditional quilts, painting terrible watercolors, and rescuing lost farm dogs, wayward baby birds, and the occasional runaway horse.